Rose Macaulay

THE
TOWERS OF
TREBIZOND

THE REPRINT SOCIETY LONDON

First published 1956
This edition published by The Reprint Society, Ltd.,
by arrangement with Wm. Collins, Sons & Co., Ltd.
1959

PRINTED IN GREAT BRITAIN
COLLINS CLEAR-TYPE PRESS: LONDON AND GLASGOW

To
Susan Lister

" The sheening of that strange bright city on the hill, barred by its high gates . . ."

" Barred from all, Phrastes ? "

" From all, Eroton, who do not desire to enter it more strongly than they desire all other cities."

" Then it is barred indeed, and most men must let it go."

" Those who have once desired it cannot let it go, for its light flickers always on the roads they tread, to plague them like marsh fires. Even though they flee from it, it may drag them towards it as a magnet drags steel, and, though they may never enter its gates, its light will burn them as with fire, for that is its nature."

" Who then were the builders of this dangerous city ? "

" Gods and men, Eroton; men seeking after gods, and gods who seek after men. Does it not appear to you that such a fabric, part artifact and part deifact, reared out of divine intimations and demands, and out of the mortal longings and imaginings that climb to meet these, must perpetually haunt the minds of men, wielding over them a strange wild power, intermittent indeed, but without end ? So, anyhow, it has always proved."

Dialogues of Mortality

1

"TAKE MY camel, dear," said my aunt Dot, as she climbed down from this animal on her return from High Mass. The camel, a white Arabian Dhalur (single hump) from the famous herd of the Ruola tribe, had been a parting present, its saddle-bags stuffed with low-carat gold and flashy orient gems, from a rich desert tycoon who owned a Levantine hotel near Palmyra. I always thought it to my aunt's credit that, in view of the camel's provenance, she had not named it Zenobia, Longinus, or Aurelian, as lesser women would have done; she had, instead, always called it, in a distant voice, my camel, or the camel. I did not care for the camel, nor the camel for me, but, as I was staying with aunt Dot, I did what she bade me, and dragged the camel by its bridle to the shed which it shared with my little Austin and, till lately, with my aunt's Morris, but this car had been stolen from her by some Anglican bishop from outside the Athenæum annexe while she was dining there one evening with Professor Gilbert Murray and Archbishop David Mathew. On camel and car, Gothic gargoyles looked down, on account of the shed being enclosed by the walls of an eighteenth century folly built out of stones from the restored Perp. and Dec. village church. Of this folly, a few perp. arches remained, and the gargoyle faces of imps and monks. The camel, an unconverted Moslem, seemed to look at them with a sneer. I gave it a mangelwurzel for its luncheon (though it seemed to be still chewing the cud of the one it had for breakfast) and locked it in.

The camel took aunt Dot to church, but not the Austin me. My aunt was a regular church-goer, which I was not. She was a high Anglican, not belonging, therefore, to that great middle

7

section of the Church of England which is said to be the religious backbone (so far as it has one) of our nation. I too am high, even extreme, but somewhat lapsed, which is a sound position, as you belong to the best section of the best branch of the Christian Church, but seldom attend its services.

Perhaps I had better explain why we are so firmly Church, since part of this story stems from our somewhat unusual attitude, or rather from my aunt Dot's. We belong to an old Anglican family, which suffered under the penal laws of Henry VIII, Mary I, and Oliver P. Under Henry VIII we did indeed acquire and domesticate a dissolved abbey in Sussex, but were burned, some of us, for refusing to accept the Six Points; under Mary we were again burned, naturally, for heresy; under Elizabeth we dug ourselves firmly into Anglican life, compelling our Puritan tenants to dance round maypoles and revel at Christmas, and informing the magistrates that Jesuit priests had concealed themselves in the chimney-pieces of our Popish neighbours. Under Charles I we looked with disapprobation on the damned crop-eared Puritans whom Archbishop Laud so rightly stood in the pillory, and, until the great Interregnum, approved the Laudian embellishments of churches and services, the altar crosses, candles and pictures, the improvements in the chapel of St. John's College, Cambridge, under Dr. Beale, and in Christ's under Dr. Cosin (for Cambridge was our university). During the suppression, we privately kept outed vicars as chaplains and attended secret Anglican services, at which we were interrupted each Christmas Day by the military, who, speaking very spitefully of Our Lord's Nativity, dragged us before the Major-Generals. After the Glorious Restoration, we got back our impoverished estates, and, until the Glorious Revolution, there followed palmier days, when we persecuted Papists, conventiclers and Quakers with great impartiality, and, as clerical status rose, began placing our younger sons in fat livings, of which, in 1690, they were deprived as Non-Jurors, and for the next half century or so carried on an independent ecclesiastical

8

existence, very devout, high-flying, schismatic, and eccentrically ordained, directing the devotions and hearing the confessions of pious ladies and gentlemen, and advising them as to the furnishing of their private oratories, conducting services with ritualistic ceremony and schismatic prayer-books, absorbing the teachings of William Law on the sacramental devotional life, and forming part of the stream of High Church piety that has flowed through the centuries down the broad Anglican river, quietly preparing the way for the vociferous Tractarians. These clergymen ancestors of ours were watched with dubious impatience by their relations in the manor houses, who soon discreetly came to terms with the detestable Hanoverians, and did not waste their fortunes and lives chasing after royal pretenders, who were not, after all, at all Anglican.

It is not, therefore, strange that we should have inherited a firm and tenacious adherence to the Church of our country. With it has come down to most of us a great enthusiasm for catching fish. Aunt Dot maintains that this propensity is peculiarly Church of England; she has perhaps made a slight confusion between the words Anglican and angling. To be sure the French fish even more, as I sometimes point out, and, to be sure, the pre-Reformation monks fished greatly. "Mostly in fish-ponds," said aunt Dot. "Very unsporting, and only for food."

However this may be, our family have been much given to this pursuit. Inheriting the fish-ponds of the Sussex abbey which they so warily angled for and hooked in 1539, they took for their crest three pikes couchant, with the motto " Semper pesco " (it was as masters of trawling-fleets that they had acquired their wealth in the fifteenth century), and proceeded to stock the abbey ponds with excellent carp, which they fished for by way of recreation and ate for dinner in the fasting seasons. Those of the family who took Holy Orders, brought up from infancy to this pastime, continued to practise it assiduously in the various pleasant livings which came their way. One of them, rector of East Harting in the late eighteenth century, wrote in his journal (published in 1810) that he prepared most of his sermons while thus engaged; he thought that his vocation as fisher of men was assisted by miming it out on the river banks, and each fish that he landed caused him to exult greatly, as if he had captured a soul. When they nibbled at the bait, he prayed; when they got away, he repented of his own unworthiness that caused his hand to fail, and took it as divine correction. Subsequently he became a bishop, but did not cease to fish.

The occupation had, of course, its snares. At times the thoughts of these clergymen, angling away in their beautiful and tranquil surroundings, would ramble over speculative theological ground, and encounter, like a dragon in the path, some heresy or doubt. This dragon they would sometimes step over without injury, saved perhaps at the moment of encountering it by a gentle tug at the line: at other times they would grapple with it, perhaps defeat and slay it, or perhaps suffer defeat themselves. Or they would not give battle at all, but would let it slide into their souls, an uninvited guest, not to be dislodged. Some of them were thus vanquished by the assaults of manicheeism, others by the innocent theories of Pelagius, others again by that kind of pantheism which is apt to occur in meadows and woods, others by the difficulties of thus thinking of the Trinity, and still more by plain Doubt. Many became increasingly latitudinarian, some almost Deist, and, as the nineteenth century advanced, they began joining the Modern Churchmen's Union.

But, by and large, the more they fished, the Higher they grew. And the more tenaciously and unswervingly Anglican they were, the better they fished. One of the family, my great grandfather, a keen Tractarian and angler, apt to get into trouble over the Eastward Position, caught, on a holiday in Argyllshire, the largest salmon ever captured in the waters of the Add. But presently, led by his piscatorial musings into another tributary of the great Church stream, he renounced his Orders and

10

became a Roman Catholic. During his Lapse, as the family always called it, he caught only inconsiderable fish, including the smallest trout ever not put back, for my great grandfather put nothing back. At last, wearying of so many small fishes, he poached a large-size salmon in a Devonshire stream, was caught, and appeared before a magistrate, who rightly paid no attention to his false plea that he had supposed his catch to be a wild fish. For this crime he spent a week in Bideford jail; during his detention it came to seem to him that successful angling must be, for him, an Anglican pursuit, and, weary now not only of catching such small fishes but of poaching large ones, lying, and doing time, and wearying too of so many difficult matters that he now found himself expected to believe, he ejaculated, as George Tyrrell was later to do, " Church of my baptism! Why did I ever leave you? " returned to his spiritual home, and was presently rewarded by a miraculous draft of fishes in Loch Tay. Which, as my aunt Dot said, just showed. His son, aunt Dot's father, was of a more steadfast mind; he left his curacy to go up the Amazon with his young wife, preaching to Brazilian Indians and fishing for the delicious *trutta Amazonia*; he met death at the jaws of a crocodile; aunt Dot's mother just escaped this dreadful fate, and soon afterwards bore aunt Dot.

My aunt, therefore, had inherited a firm and missionary Anglicanism, with strong prejudices against Roman Catholicism, continental Protestantism, Scotch Presbyterianism, British Dissent, and all American religious bodies except Protestant Episcopalianism; she had also inherited a tendency to hunt fish.

She was now a widow. Comparatively early in her married life she and her husband, a zealous missionary, had, while travelling in the more inhospitable parts of central Africa, been surprised by ferocious savages, equipped with the most horrible weapons. My uncle by marriage had been told by the British Resident Officer at Nwabo that he had better not fall alive, or let aunt Dot so fall, into the hands of this unamiable tribe, who were inclined to cook their captives alive in boiling water, as we do lobsters, to improve their flavour, so my uncle and aunt took poison tablets with them. Feeling for these tablets, my uncle discovered that he had lost them, on account of a hole in his pocket. So he said to aunt Dot, as the frightful savages appeared, " I think I had better shoot you first, then myself." Aunt Dot was definitely against this plan; but there was little time for argument, so my uncle, after commending both their souls and pronouncing an absolution, aimed his gun at her and fired. Fortunately he was not a good shot, and the bullet whizzed through aunt Dot's topee. Lest he should have another shot, aunt Dot, full of presence of mind, fell to the ground as if dead; my uncle then turned his gun on himself, and this time met with more success; he fell, shot through the head. The savages, being by now arrived close to them, were about to carry off the bodies to the pot, but aunt Dot sprang to her feet and told them in their own language, having prudently learned the appropriate phrases beforehand, that she was a goddess, whose flesh was poisonous to those who consumed it, but that she would confer many favours on them if spared. So they conducted her to the hut of their chief, and, as he was away on a hunting expedition, put her in the haarem to await his return. She was small and plump, which was the shape he preferred; though, as they regretfully said, she would also have done very nicely for the pot.

She found the other haarem women rather boring: they seemed, she said, to know little about anything but sweets and love. She showed them the Book of Common Prayer, translated into central African, and said compline every evening aloud in the same tongue, for she had an office book in it, but they did not think much of either. The wives used to go down to the river half a mile away to wash their clothes and their children; aunt Dot went too, and took her fishing rod, and caught several of a small and distasteful fish called kepsi. Once they met a lioness, who stood in the path and stared at them and waved her tail.

12

"The wives all ran away," said aunt Dot. "Nice little women, but they ran away. I stayed and stared back, and presently the creature slid off. Then *I* ran away."

"How did you escape from the haarem?" I would ask her, when she told me this story in my childhood.

"One of the wives, who didn't want me to wait till the chief came back, bribed one of the tribe to take me away into the jungle and kill me. But he was afraid to do this, as I was a goddess, so he showed me a path out of the forest that led to a Baptist missionary settlement. I had never cared much for Baptists, but they were really most kind. You must never forget, Laurie, that dissenters are often excellent Christian people. You must never be narrow minded."

I promised that I never would.

"Though of course," my aunt added, "you must always remember that *we* are *right*."

I promised that I always would.

I now stayed mostly with aunt Dot when I was not in my London flat. Her children are either deceased, or following some profession abroad. I too follow professions, but at some distance behind, and seldom catch up with them. My favourite one is painting water-colour sketches to illustrate travel books, which is a good way to get abroad, a thing I like doing better than anything else, for I agree with those who have said that travel is the chief end of life.

My aunt looked very pleasant. She was at this time in her early sixties, small and plump, with a round, fair, smooth face and shrewd merry blue eyes. She enjoyed life, and got about, sharing my views on the chief end of life, and was a cheerful and romantic adventuress.

2

WHEN I returned from stabling the camel, my aunt asked me, as she often did, to ring up a house agent about a derelict house she had seen in St. John's Wood. He said the rent would be eight hundred, and the lino, the Hoover, and the bowl of gold-fish, which all went with the house, would cost two thousand more. Aunt Dot said, " Rubbish. Offer him a thousand for the lino and the Hoover and say I won't take the fish."

The agent said the fish must be taken, but that the owner might be prepared to discuss one thousand eight hundred for the lot. He added that this was moderate, as household fittings went, and that one of his clients last week had paid a thousand for some kitchen lino and the lounge under-felt only.

" Tell him I'll think about it," said aunt Dot, rather impressed. " He must keep it open a few days."

The agent said someone else was after it, who would probably be prepared to pay the full two thousand.

I did not suppose it would come to anything. Aunt Dot, who was looking for a home for what she called " all those poor young unmarried fathers, ruined by maintenance," always liked to keep several houses on a string, toying with them, but she seldom took them, she would go abroad with the camel just before the agreement was to be signed.

This, indeed, was what we were about to do now. We were off in three weeks on another mission-investigation expedition, this time to Turkey and the Black Sea, to find out how successful an Anglican mission in the neighbourhood of Trebizond seemed likely to be, and how it would be regarded by the local popula-tion. My aunt belonged to an Anglo-Catholic missionary society, which sent investigators abroad to make these reports on this or that hitherto little tilled corner of the world, all of which they saw as a potential field for Anglican endeavour, for they regarded the Anglican Church as the one every one should belong to, whatever the nature of their previous beliefs.

It was remarkable how large a special currency allowance the Treasury, urged by various ecclesiastical interests and by several High Church bishops, allowed to these A.C.M.S. spies, and, as aunt Dot also had very good black market connections everywhere, she did pretty well. She meant also to write a book about the position of women in the Black Sea regions, which she would call *Women of the Euxine to-day*, for the position of women, that sad and well-nigh universal blot on civilizations, was never far from her mind. She often took me with her on such expeditions, as illustrator, courier and general aide, and, she was kind enough to say, as company. The A.C.M.S. would arrange that she should also take a clergyman, because of having to show potential converts what Anglican services were like. This time she was taking the Rev. the Hon. Father Hugh Chantry-Pigg, an ancient bigot who had run a London church several feet higher than St. Mary's Bourne Street and some inches above even St. Magnus the Martyr, and, being now just retired, devoted his life to conducting very High retreats and hunting for relics of saints, which he collected for the private oratory in his Dorset manor house. He had already assembled in his reliquaries many fragments of saintly bone, skin, hair, garments, etc., and hoped to find many more in the tombs, hermitages and monasteries of Armenia and Cilicia. He was also anxious to explore the ancient lava dwellings of Cappadocia, and Mount Ararat, where planks from the ark still, it seems, lie scattered. He hoped also to push on south into Syria and Jordan and the mountains about the Dead Sea, desiring to celebrate Mass in the Greek monastery of Sabas, and search for such scrolls as might still be lying about in caves. He meant to take some of his relics with him and work miracles, which would greatly impress Moslems and others. He believed everything, from the Garden of Eden to the Day of Judgment, and had never let the chill and dull breath of modern rationalist criticism shake his firm fundamentalism. Aunt Dot, too, though far from a fundamentalist, was all for giving converts the whole works; she thought it made it easier for Moslems (who are themselves of a fundamentalist turn of mind), though harder, of course, for Christians. I felt that Father Chantry-Pigg did not really much like either aunt Dot or me, but he was glad of the chance to travel abroad and win souls from the Prophet to the Church and test the power of his relics, so he accepted the invitation without reluctance, the more so because there had last year come to his London parish a band of very enterprising Arab Moslem missionaries from the Dead Sea, who had worked with great zeal and some success among his congregation, and he felt inclined for a return match.

Aunt Dot had a notion that we might even get into Russia, so she had started some time ago working away at Russian visas, but without success, as this was some time before the Great Thaw. All she would be allowed to do about Russia would be to join a sponsored party in celebration of some Russian literary man, or of the various Russians who invented radio, motor cars, and the telephone, or a party of scientists and people who enjoyed such things as hospitals, lavatories, maternity homes, model farms, underground stations, universities, schools and dams, or at least, whether they enjoyed them or not, would have to see them.

" Certainly not," said aunt Dot. " I should want to see the Caucasus, Circassian slaves, Tartars, wild mares, koumiss, churches, clergymen, and women."

Hearing her say this on the telephone to the Russian Consulate, I started dreaming of Caucasian mountains, over which Tartars galloped upside down on long-tailed ponies, shouting horribly, wild mares with their koumiss foaming into green pitchers, sledges and droshkys speeding over the steppes fraught with fur-capped men and Circassian slaves and pursued by wolves, who, every mile or so, were thrown a Circassian slave to delay them, but, never having enough, took up the chase again, till at last they had devoured all the Circassian slaves, the horses, and the fur-capped men. I dreamed too of the Crimea, of crumbling palaces decaying among orchards by the sea, of onion domes, of chanting priests with buns. . . .

Father Chantry-Pigg thought it would be wrong to go to Russia, because of condoning the government, which was persecuting Christians. But aunt Dot said if one started not condoning governments, one would have to give up travel altogether, and even remaining in Britain would be pretty difficult. It was obviously one's duty to try to convert such Russians as had succumbed to Soviet atheism, and particularly Tartars in the Caucasus. She also had large future designs on Arabs and Israelites. But first it was to be the eastern end of the Black Sea, and we were to sail in a ship that took camels and plan our campaign from Istanbul.

"Constantinople," said Father Chantry-Pigg, who did not accept the Turkish conquest.

"Byzantium," said I, not accepting the Roman one.

Aunt Dot, who accepted facts, said, "How many of our friends are in Turkey just now?"

"A lot," I said. "They are all writing their Turkey books. David and Charles are somewhere by the Black Sea, following Xenophon and Jason about. I had a card from Charles from Trebizond. He sounded cross, and he and David have probably parted by now. David wanted to get into Russia. Freya and Derek are somewhere camping in Anatolia. Margaret Beckford was in the Meander valley when last heard of, digging away for Hittites. I don't know where Patrick is, probably somewhere near Smyrna. And I think Steven is in Istanbul, lecturing to the University."

Aunt Dot said she must get down to her Turkey book quickly, or she would be forestalled by all these tiresome people. Writers all seemed to get the same idea at the same time. One year they would all be rushing for Spain, next year to some island off Italy, then it would be the Greek islands, then Dalmatia, then Cyprus and the Levant, and now people were all for Turkey.

"How they get the money for it I can't think. Turkey costs about a pound an hour. I suppose they have Contacts. People are so dishonest in these days. What do you think they are all writing about?"

"The usual things, I suppose. Antiquities and scenery and churches and towns and people, and what Xenophon and the Ten Thousand did near Trebizond and what the Byzantines did, and coarse fishing in the Bosphorus, and excavations everywhere, and merry village scenes."

"I dare say," said aunt Dot, " the B.B.C. has a recording van there. Reporters for the B.B.C. have such an extraordinary effect on the people they meet—wherever they go the natives sing. It seems so strange, they never do it when I am travelling. The B.B.C. oughtn't to let them, it spoils the programme. Just when you are hoping for a description of some nice place, everybody suddenly bursts out singing. Even Displaced Persons do it. And singing sounds much the same everywhere, so I switch off."

We made out a loose itinerary. Father Chantry-Pigg was for going first to Jordan-Jerusalem and staying with the Bishop, to see the Palestine refugees, then crossing the great Divide to visit the Children of Israel. But aunt Dot said no, we must leave Israel to the last, since, owing to the prejudices of Jordanites, Syrians, Lebanese and Egyptians, it was so difficult to get out of except into the sea. Father Chantry-Pigg said he would like also to go into Egypt and visit the Pyramids, but aunt Dot said we couldn't go everywhere in one trip, and anyhow seeing the Pyramids seemed to drive people (other than archæologists) mad like Atlantis and the Lost Tribes, they got pyramiditis, and began to rave in numbers. So we decided to go first to the Black Sea. In Istanbul we should, said aunt Dot, be able to discover who

18

were our most dangerous religious rivals. It seemed that in Turkey there were few, though the American Missions claimed a Turkish Christian community of some two thousand five hundred souls. Father Chantry-Pigg said, with hostile contempt, that the Seventh Day Adventists were the busiest missionaries in Turkey and the Levant, and met, he feared, with only too much success. But none of the principal Anglican missionary societies worked much, it seemed, in Turkey; nor, he believed, was the Italian Mission very active. When Father Chantry-Pigg said " Italian Mission ", a look of particular malevolence slightly distorted his finely arranged features: the same look, only worse, that was apt to disturb and distort the fleshier and more good-humoured Irish countenance of Father Murphy, the priest of St. Brigid's, when the St. Gregory's clergy and choir filed in chanting, incense-swinging, saint-bearing processions out of their church door and round the square which both churches served. Father Chantry-Pigg took the view that it was emissaries from St. Brigid's who had made a habit of defacing his church notices, and sometimes entered his church in order to make disagreeable remarks and scatter spiteful leaflets, though some of this was done from a very Low church in a neighbouring street, and some of the leaflets had " Catholic Commandos " printed on them, and others " Protestant Storm Troopers ", and Father Chantry-Pigg did not know which of these two bands of warriors he disliked most. When he put a notice on his church door containing the words Eucharist, or Mass, or even Priest (particularly if the priest was going to hear confessions), these words would be struck out by ardent representatives of one or another of these guerrilla armies, or perhaps by both, and the Catholic Commandos would write over it " You have no Mass" (or Eucharist, or priests, as the case might be), and, referring to confession, " Why? He has no power to absolve ", and the Storm Troopers would correct Mass to the Lord's Supper, and alter the bit about confession to " The Minister will be in church to give counsel ", and cross out Benediction,

19

so that, after both sets of workers had been busy with the notices, there was not much of them left and they had to be re-written. As Father Chantry-Pigg said, the Commandos belonged to the Catholic underworld and the Storm Troopers to the Protestant, and underworlds everywhere are pretty much like one another in manners, even when they hold differing views. Anyhow these underworlds, he said, were two minds (if minds they could be called) with but a single thought (if thought it could be called) about the section of the Anglican Church to which he belonged, and that thought was one of powerful hostility. Both underworlds were, of course, strongly disapproved of by the higher minded and better mannered of their respective religious parties.

From time to time the Storm Troopers (who were the more destructive of the two) would enter St. Gregory's and overturn the altar candlesticks and extinguish the sanctuary lamp and cover up the crucifix and the reredos, and had once even removed the tabernacle, so that since then the Blessed Sacrament had had to be locked in an aumbry when no one was on guard, and they left a placard saying " This is the Lord's Table, and not for idolatry ", and the Commandos would leave a placard to the same effect, saying " This is not an altar, for you have no Mass and no Sacrament and no priests to offer the Holy Sacrifice."

Usually these raids would be made on different days, so that the two sets of raiders did not as a rule meet, but one evening after Benediction they both came in, while Father Chantry-Pigg was hearing confessions in the south aisle and a curate in the north aisle, and the Commando went to the south aisle and the Storm Trooper to the north, and the Commando asked, " What do you think you are doing, and by what right? " and no doubt the Storm Trooper was putting similar enquiries to the curate. Father Chantry-Pigg got up and said, " Leave this church immediately, or I shall call the police and have you evicted and given in charge for brawling." Meanwhile the curate, who was young and strong, was pushing the Storm

Trooper before him down the north aisle and out through the west door. Having done this, he walked over to the south aisle, and the Commando went away, and Father Chantry-Pigg and the curate went on hearing confessions, but probably by that time neither they nor their penitents had their minds on the job. It was said in the parish that for some time after that evening a good many more penitents turned up, hoping.

Anyhow, these were the sort of relations that Father Chantry-Pigg had with his neighbours of other denominations, so naturally he felt sour about the Italian Mission.

Aunt Dot said, " Never mind about other missionaries. I don't suppose any of them are specifically concerned, as we are, with the position of women. The extraordinary way they are still treated in the remoter parts of Turkey," she went on, warming up, as she always did on this subject. " One supposed that Atatürk had ended all that, but it seems not at all, among the masses. Dr. Halide Tanpinar told me that once you get outside the large westernized towns and into the country, they're still muffled to the eyes, even in the hottest weather, and crouch against a wall if a man passes, and not allowed to eat in restaurants or sit in the squares and cafés and play dice, instead they work in the fields all day having no fun, while the men sit about. And as to *bathing*! The British Consul's wife somewhere told me that even when her husband has Turks to luncheon, she never sits with them, they would be too shocked. And in mosques the women are hidden away in galleries, because it wouldn't do for men and women to pray together. Though I can't see why the men shouldn't sometimes be in the galleries and the women on the floor. But Dr. Halide says their clergy are afraid that if any of the old traditions went, the whole thing would totter. The sooner it totters the better, I say. I know it's a very fine and noble religion, but I'd rather have atheism, it would make an easier life for women. But we'll try and make Anglicans of them. You know how religious women are, they must have a religion, so it had better be a rational one."

21

Father Chantry-Pigg barked, " Rational? " as sharply as if it had been an obscene word. " *That* won't get them far."

With all those relics in his pockets, he could scarcely be expected to think so.

He added, " As for women, they've got to be careful, as St. Paul told them. Wrapping their heads up is a religious tradition that goes very deep."

" An oriental tradition," said aunt Dot.

" Christianity," Father Chantry-Pigg reminded her, " is an oriental religion."

" Anyhow," said aunt Dot, " Christianity doesn't derive from St. Paul. There is nothing in the Gospels about women behaving differently from men, either in church or out of it. Rather the contrary. So what a comfort for these poor women to learn that they needn't."

" Naturally," said Father Chantry-Pigg, rather testily, " I am for bringing Turkish women into the Church. Jews, Turks, infidels and heretics, as we pray on Good Fridays. But their costume is a very minor thing, and should be approached, if at all, with great caution. Those Arab missionaries in London were deeply shocked by our bare-headed and bare-armed women in the streets. They said it led to unbridled temptation among men."

" Men must learn to bridle their temptations," said aunt Dot, always an optimist. " *They* must be converted, too."

" The great stumbling-block to Moslems," said Father Chantry-Pigg, " is the Blessed Trinity. To a people who hear the One God proclaimed so many times a day, and so loudly, the Triune God raises all kinds of difficulties in the mind, as it did in the minds of many of the early Christians. It needs great tact to put it across successfully."

" Not important," said aunt Dot, dismissing the Trinity, her mind being set on the liberation of women.

" Merely the central doctrine of the Christian faith," said Father Chantry-Pigg, sneering, as if he was scoring a point.

Perhaps he was, I didn't know. Anyhow it seemed to me that Turks wouldn't understand the Trinity; they would never be able even to dispute, as Greek Christians used to do, about Who proceeded from Who (obviously one must not say Whom, the matter being so controversial). There were no complications of that sort with Allah, and I thought he was probably their intellectual limit. But I did not like to discourage my elders, so said nothing. It would never do if they were to lose faith in their expedition.

3

ACTUALLY, WE nearly did lose it, because for some reason the ships all said they were not taking camels that spring, and we thought we should have to go without it in a Landrover, because we had to have something to get about in when we got there. Aunt Dot and I would do the driving; we would not let Father Chantry-Pigg drive much, he drove so eccentrically. Aunt Dot was a clever, impetuous driver, taking the sharpest bends with the greatest intrepidity. A brilliant and unorthodox improviser, she usually managed to work her way out of the jams she not infrequently got us into. We had driven in the Jugo-Slav mountains before, and had several mishaps; there are few service garages, and these are always a long way from where one is, but there are a lot of road-menders, brigands, etc., and they can usually take tyres off, patch them, and produce from their pockets spare parts, such as fan-belts, differentials, and those kinds of things, that get so damaged when one travels and are normally so irreplaceable and yet so essential to replace, and of which we never seem to carry about enough replicas; the brigands, no doubt, get theirs from the stolen cars that they keep in caves.

We were feeling rather low about all this, when we heard of a Turkish cargo ship that took camels, as well as other animals (so that we should not feel odd, having the only animal, though we might feel odd that ours was a camel), so we booked passages on it from London to Istanbul.

This ship mainly took cargo round the Mediterranean ports and to such places as Vigo, Antwerp, Rotterdam and London, and so few people could get on to it that, instead of its being odd to be a camel, it was pretty odd to be a human being.

24

Most of the other human beings were Turks doing the round trip, two Cypriots collected from restaurants in Percy Street, W.1, and all set for starting restaurants in Mataxas Square, Nicosia, and two British physicists got up as yachtsmen and all set for the curtain; they left us at the Piraeus in a caique sailed by Albanians got up as Greek fishermen. Aunt Dot thought one of the Turks was a British diplomat, she remembered meeting him at someone's cocktail party in London, but when she spoke to him in English he only jerked back his head and said "Yok," a discouraging word which we got very used to in Turkey.

I spent the nine days' voyage partly sketching my Turkish fellow-passengers, and partly trying to learn Turkish, and after a time I was able to say, "I would like a shoe-horn," and "See how badly you have ironed my coat, you must do it again." Father Chantry-Pigg said this phrase-book was little use, as it had no sentences about the Church being better than Islam, all it said about religion was "Is there an English church here? Who is the preacher? Where is the verger? The seats must be paid for, there is a strong choir, an offertory is taken," and that kind of conversation, which Father Chantry-Pigg had never had with his flock at St. Gregory's.

So he decided to trust to Patristic Greek. He knew also a little Armenian, but aunt Dot told him this language was a mistake with Turks, and only vexed them, as they had long since pronounced *delenda est Armenia* over this so unfortunately fragmented people, and did not care to hear them referred to. She herself could speak enough Turkish to get about on, and practised it on the ship's crew, but she complained that the Turks were not very quick about their own language.

4

ARRIVED AT the Dardanelles on the ninth morning of our voyage, we decided to disembark at Çanakkale and visit Troy. The camel and our baggage were to go on to Istanbul and stay on board till we joined them next day. The captain told us that we couldn't visit Troy, owing to its being in a military zone, but aunt Dot took no notice of military zones, so we disembarked and the ship steamed off for Istanbul and we went and had coffee in the café garden of a dirty little inn above the sea. At the next table sat the British diplomat got up as a Turk who had said " Yok " to aunt Dot, he was with another Briton *en Turque*, whom he had come to meet there, and they were talking Turkish together and drinking coffee and spying. Actually, we saw so many British spies in disguise spying in Turkey that I cannot mention all of them, they kept cropping up wherever we went, like flying saucers and pictures of Atatürk and people writing their Turkey books. One of these, whose name was Charles, and I had known him at Cambridge, walked into this café garden while we were there. We said we thought he was with David somewhere round the Black Sea; he said he had left David and was going down the west coast alone. He wanted to know what we were doing and where, and was falsely polite, till aunt Dot eased his mind by saying we were chiefly doing mission work, though she was going to write about what women did, about which Charles couldn't care less. To vex him, I said I would be writing some landscape and archæology bits into aunt Dot's book, and that we might be doing the west coast later on. However, since Father Chantry-Pigg was with us, he thought we were probably fairly harmless, and cheered up; he said we were not to believe any stories we heard in Istanbul about his having quarrelled with David, as the true story was quite different, but it wouldn't be fair to David to spread it about. Aunt Dot, who was inquisitive, said it wouldn't matter spreading it about Çanakkale, where there was no British colony, but Charles said the affair was not yet over, and he would prefer no gossip, even in Çanakkale, which as a matter of fact was a very gossipy place, owing to the British war cemetery at Gallipoli, and anyhow we would be in Istanbul to-morrow, and no doubt seeing all the Embassy people who weren't in Ankara, and a lot of archæologists, who were the worst of the lot for tittle-tattle, and as malicious as cats.

" Cats aren't," said Father Chantry-Pigg, who had one at home.

Aunt Dot said that camels were; and, resigning herself to having no more tittle-tattle, asked how one got to Troy. Charles said this wasn't worth while; the Turks had let it get all over-grown with grass and thistles and asphodel and no digging had been done there for twenty years, and anyhow it was hard to get a permit, one had to find the Governor of Çanak for it, and he was never at home, and the police were no help at all, but if we really wanted to go, he would come with us to the police station. When he said police station, one of the diplomat spies looked at the other, and they got up and left the garden, so, though he had answered " Yok " about being who aunt Dot said he was, the one who said it must have known English.

Charles then took us to the police station. A fat policeman sat in his garden in his shirt, mopping his forehead and smoking his hubble-bubble. Aunt Dot explained about Troy, and he said we must find the Governor. So he told a minor policeman to telephone the Governor's house, but it seemed that the Governor was across the Hellespont, lunching in Gallipoli. Well, said aunt Dot, we only have this afternoon, and could nothing be arranged? So the head policeman, a good-natured man, took our passports and tried to read them, aunt Dot interpreting, but our having no Turkish visas bothered him. Aunt Dot explained that Turkish visas had been abolished for the British two years ago, but he doubted this. Even if you know Turkish, you can't get the better of the Turkish police, because they can't reason, Charles said. You may tell them that Turkish visas were abolished two years ago, but still they say, "for why have you not got a visa?" Argument does not register with them; they never say "therefore", or "in that case." Father Chantry-Pigg said later on that this made it difficult to discuss theology with Turks, as one had been used to do with Byzantines, who had reasoned all the time, reasoning themselves in and out of all the heresies in the world, and no doubt they could easily have reasoned themselves into the Anglican heresy. Father Chantry-Pigg always spoke as if he had just parted from the Byzantines, and was apt to sigh when he mentioned them, though, as aunt Dot pointed out, he had missed them by five centuries. His crusading ancestor, Sir Jocelyn de Chantry, had found them, but, being of the Latin Church, had dealt with them unkindly. The fact was that Father Chantry-Pigg would not really have liked the Byzantines much had he encountered them, though he would have preferred them to Turks and other Moslems. He was not actually a sympathetic clergyman, and, had he been with his ancestor for the great attack on Constantinople in 1203, he would have been among those who, brandishing the cross above their heads, massacred and pillaged and looted in the name of Latin Christendom, helping to put to flames the great libraries whose loss he now deplored. He was better at condemning than at loving; aunt Dot used to wonder what Christ would have said to him.

The head policeman said he would have to telephone to someone about our visas, so he sent the minor policeman to do this, and after some time, during which we sat and stared at the large picture of Kemal Atatürk on the wall, and he scowled back at us, the minor policeman came back and said that visas for the British had just been abolished. The head policeman said

28

he should have been told before, and told the minor policeman to copy out our passports, which took a long time, especially aunt Dot's, which was in its tenth year and had travel markings from foreign consulates all over the world, from Arabia to Peru. Some trouble was caused by the minor policeman believing that the Arabic inscriptions made on the frontier of Yemen emanated from the Russian Black Sea port of Batumi; the head policeman told aunt Dot that she had been in Russia, and therefore could not travel in Turkey, but she managed to straighten this out after a time. You really need quite a lot of time when dealing with Turkish police, who are pleasant but rather slow.

When tne copying was finished, an application to the Governor for leave to visit Trua was made out and we all signed it, and it was stamped with the head of Atatürk and put away in a drawer with the copies of our passports so now it was safe for us to go to Troy, provided that the minor policeman went with us. So we got into a car which had been following us about and drove off for Troy, aunt Dot and Father Chantry-Pigg and Charles and I and the minor policeman, which felt very strange and improbable.

Troy was about twenty kilometres away, along a dusty road that wound up and down among the foot-hills of Mount Ida, through pine forests and above bays of the Aegean, all very beautiful, and the woods smelt of dust and incense. Charles, to discourage us from writing it up, because of his being a jealous man, said the Troad was pretty commonplace really, and had gone down since everybody used to come here in past centuries and look for Priam's tomb, and have ecstasies in Alexandria Troas. Father Chantry-Pigg, who knew Tennyson, started reciting *Aenone*, about the vale in Ida lovelier than all the valleys of Ionian hills, and when we came down from the hills and saw the little museum and the rocky hill in front of it where Troy had stood, he said that the gorges, opening wide apart, revealed Ilion's columned citadel, and it was true that there were some

29

parts of columns standing and lying about, some of them having been stood on end to look more like a columned citadel. Charles looked pretty distant about Tennyson and Aenone, but he made allowances for Father Chantry-Pigg's generation. We climbed about the citadel, with a guide who darted out of the museum and showed us round, and there was the ghost of a theatre, and what the guide maintained was Priam's palace, with thrones and rooms and walls, but the walls were too little and too late, for they were all of the fifth, sixth, seventh and eighth Troy, and there had been no excavations since 1932, and everything was grown over with grass and thistles and looked very neglected, and Schliemann, though he had been a disorderly man himself, would have hated to see it. Father Chantry-Pigg, who had been a good classic before he took up with Byzantine Greek and monks' Latin, began to recite the Æneid, Book II, lamenting over poor Priam and Troy in flames. " *Haec finis Priami fatorum,*" he said, " *hic exitus illum sorte tulit, Trojam incensam et prolapsa videntem Pergama,*" and so on. However late and little and ill-tended were Troy's remains, it was exciting and beautiful to be there, looking down over the plain to the sea, which must have gone back some way since the Greek ships lay there and the Greeks looked up at the battlements where Helen walked round.

But aunt Dot could only think how Priam and Hecuba would have been vexed to see the state it had all got into, and no one seeming to care any more. She thought the nations ought to go on working at it and dig it all up again, and perhaps do some reconstruction, for she belonged to the reconstruction school, and would have liked to see Troy's walls and towers rising once more against the sky like a Hollywood Troy, and the wooden horse standing beside them, opening mechanically every little while to show that it was full of armed Greeks.

But I thought there were enough cities standing about the world already, and that those which had disappeared had better be let alone, lying under the grass and asphodel and brambles, with the wind sighing over them and in the distance the sea where the Greek ships had lain waiting ten years for *Trojam incensam*, and behind them Mount Ida, from which the unfair and partial gods had watched the whole affair.

Father Chantry-Pigg, of course, remarked, "*jam seges est ubi Troia fuit*," and Charles, who was vexed about our all coming to Troy, said, well, hardly *seges*, just grass and things, and anyhow Troy had probably never stood there at all. Meanwhile the museum guide had scampered on to more rocks and walls, and we all followed him except the policeman, who was *blasé* about Trua, which he no doubt had to visit too often, so that he looked at it in a bored, supercilious kind of way, as if he did not see why he should have had to come, and we did not see why either, because it hardly seemed like a military zone, and we had not met a single soldier on the way. Anyhow, to Turks the Great Siege had been an affair between Greeks and Trojans and the Grecian dame, of which they knew nothing, it was too long pre-Turk and too Greek, and Turks are not brought up, as Europeans are (or were), to the Trojan legend. The Trojan cycle, the Roman de Troie, the Arthurian cycle, the cycle of Charlemagne, the cycle of Roland, the cycle of Christ—these are the European folk-tales which filled the Middle Ages, and still echo down the modern ages, but not for Turks, who have, presumably their own folk-tales, of Mahomet, of Caliphs, Sultans, Seljuks, Mamelukes, Ottomans, and Kemal Atatürk, and these have shaped the minds of the Turkish police, in so far as they have been shaped at all, which is not really much.

Presently Father Chantry-Pigg said we would now drive on to Alexandria Troas, twenty miles south of Troy. It seemed that his father, who had been a dean interested in St. Paul, had visited this place in 1880, in order to follow up St. Paul's doings there, and had said ever since that its ruins were among the most beautiful Roman ruins in the world, largely owing to being half buried in valonia oak woods, and having fine arches that were partly in the sea. This was what was said by most of the eighteenth and nineteenth century visitors, and many travellers (including aunt Dot, who is romantic rather than accurate) think it is a pity that it is no longer believed to be Troy, and the arches Priam's palace, whereas they had actually been a bath.

But what Father Chantry-Pigg wanted to see was the place where St. Paul preached so long that the young man Eutychus sank into sleep and fell down three storeys and was taken up for dead but revived by the apostle, and where Paul met a man from Macedonia who entreated his missionary help, so that he set sail at once and converted Gentiles, and left his cloak behind in Troas. All this would be very interesting to Father Chantry-Pigg, but when he told our driver to drive there the driver said " yok ", he did not know it. The policeman agreed that it was not known; and the fact is that in Turkey very few places except large towns are known to Turkish policemen, and none of them belong to classical antiquity, for which Turks do not care. Charles said the Turkish name of this place was Eski-Stamboul, and he and David had been there. So we tried Eski-Stamboul on the driver, but still he said " yok ", he did not know it, and still the policeman agreed with him, so aunt Dot said he was to drive down the coast until we stopped him. But the policeman, who had only bargained for Troy, and had had it, said it was all a military area and we could not drive about it. Father Chantry-Pigg, who was seventy-three and stubborn, said very well, he would walk it, and would aunt Dot tell the policeman so in Turkish. Aunt Dot said it would be no use telling the policeman that, because walking through a military area would be as much yok as driving through it. Instead, she mentioned money, and then the area became less military, and the policeman seemed more yielding.

" If it's military," said Father Chantry-Pigg, " there should be some soldiers about. We haven't seen any at all."

Aunt Dot said better not argue, the policeman was softening.

He softened, and the driver softened too, and away we drove south through the Troad in the late afternoon sunshine along a rolling road, the Aegean on one side and the range of Mount Ida some way off to our left, and, when the road climbed high enough to see it, the island of Tenedos swam off shore like a humpy whale with a shoal of dolphins round it.

The driver, who knew a little English, pointed to the hills and said, "Wolf up there."

" A wolf? " said aunt Dot, interested in animals.

" Plenty wolf. In winter, come down near Çanak, hunt sheep, kill men."

" Wolves," Father Chantry-Pigg, who knew about hunting, corrected him, " when they hunt men. Wolf when men hunt them."

Being both old-fashioned and very class, Father Chantry-Pigg called these animals wooves and woof, for he was apt to omit the l before consonants, and would no more have uttered it in wolf than he would in half, calf, golf, salve, alms, Ralph, Malvern, talk, walk, stalk, fault, elm, calm, resolve, absolve, soldier, or pulverise.

The driver, not really taking the point about the hunters and the hunted, said again, " Plenty wolf, plenty jackal, plenty pig."

Presently he pointed ahead, towards some rising ground in the distance, and said, " Eski-Stamboul."

" So he knew it all the time," said aunt Dot.

" Troas," said Father Chantry-Pigg, thinking about St. Paul and the man from Macedonia.

As we got nearer, there were ruins all about, and they had been good ruins once, when Dean Chantry-Pigg had been there in 1880, but ever since they had dwindled, as ruins will, being carried away by sultans for their grand buildings and broken in pieces by the locals for their mean ones, and though a lot of very fine bits were left, you could not see what they had been once. Sheep and camels and men strolled about near by, and some women worked, for there was a village, and it was probably full of Circassians who had been planted there last century in the Circassian-planting period, for that is what Circassians are for, you plant them about like trees, and they increase, and very soon they are what the nineteenth century travellers used to call squalid villages, and these lie about the eastern lands in great abundance.

Dr. Pococke had said that, when he was there, Troas was infested by Rogues; that was over two centuries ago, but Rogues go on in the same places for ever, as churches do, it seems to have something to do with the soil they are on. A group of inhabitants stood by the road as we drove up; they were dark and sad, and they may have been Rogues, but I thought they looked more like those obscure, dejected, maladjusted and calamity-prone characters who come into Tenebrae, such as Aleph, Teth, Beth, Calph, Jod, Ghimel, Mem, and the rest, and they sounded as if they were talking in that afflicted strain that those characters talk in, and saying things like " he has brought me into darkness and not into light ", " he has compassed me with gall and labour ", " he has built against me round about, that I may not get out, he has upset my paths ", and " my eyes have failed with weeping, my bowels are disturbed, my liver is poured out ", and so on, till all the lights go out and there is nothing but the dark.

" There are those two spies again," aunt Dot said, and she was right, the two British spies got up as Turks stood among the rest, spying out the military secrets of Troas, so it seemed that Troas was still infested by Rogues.

We passed the aqueduct and went in among the ruins, which spread a long way, and we saw part of the line of the walls, which were several miles round, and there were broken arches and vaults, and some excavations had been lately done in the great bath, and altogether we thought it was much better than Troy, and were not surprised that Constantine had thought of it for his capital before he thought of Byzantium. It was full of valonian oak trees, and the harbour must have been fine before

34

it got so full of sand. Aunt Dot got out her camera, to photo-
graph a large arch, but the policeman soon stopped that, and
all the Tenebrae types, including the two British spies and the
camels, looked on cynically, for this was just what they had
suspected. Meanwhile Father Chantry-Pigg produced a plan of
the place drawn by his father the Dean, with all the ruins marked
" house where Paul preached all night and Eutychus fell down ",
" house of Carpus, where St. Paul left his cloak, books and
parchment ", " place where Paul saw the man of Macedonia in
a dream ", " beach where he sailed for Samothrace ", and so
on, for Dean Chantry-Pigg, besides being most learned, had
also been full of imagination. When later he came into the title
and retired to live in the family place, he began a large book
about St. Paul, but never finished it, owing to death.

Father Chantry-Pigg began exploring about Troas with his
father's old plan, but of course that did not do; one of the spies
went up to the policeman and told him, out of jealousy, and the
policeman went to Father Chantry-Pigg and asked him what
he was doing, and took the plan from him and held it upside
down, trying to make it out, and the spies came and looked
too, to help him. Father Chantry-Pigg called aunt Dot, who
was looking at the excavated bath, and she came up to interpret.
The policeman said the drawing appeared to be of Eski-Stamboul, and the writing was information useful to the enemy (by
the enemy, Turks mean Russia, which had had a try at the Troad
in 1915), and Father Chantry-Pigg would have to return to
the police station at Çanakkale and explain. Aunt Dot said the
drawing had been made long ago, by the priest's father, and
the writing was about a great Christian prophet who had stayed
some years in Eski-Stamboul, which was a holy place to which
Christians came on pilgrimage, like Mecca. But the policeman
looked as if he was remembering the Russian writing on aunt
Dot's passport which she had said was Arabic, and he and the
two British spies and the driver agreed that we should all go
back to Çanakkale at once, so we did. Father Chantry-Pigg was

very much annoyed, as he had not yet identified Carpus's house or the one where the young man fell three storeys while St. Paul preached, but Charles said one can never hope to identify anything while Turks look on. Actually, he and David had done much better at Troas, for they had been taken there by a high-up Turkish friend of David's so had had no trouble, and had been shewn over the ruins by the archæologist who was digging the bath up, and they had gone down to the harbour and the beach, and it had all been delightful, and Charles was putting it into his book, so he was quite pleased that we were going back to Çanakkale now. Father Chantry-Pigg asked him which were the sites of the two houses he had been looking for, but Charles and David and the Turkish high-up and the American archæologist had not known about St. Paul, so Charles could not tell him that, he had not known even that this apostle had ever been to Troas, or anywhere else. People know about quite different things, and this often makes conversation difficult. Charles, for instance, not being Anglican or Roman Catholic, or indeed Christian at all, would not know about the characters in Tenebrae.

So we drove back to Çanakkale. When we got there it was evening. The policeman took Father Chantry-Pigg and aunt Dot to the police station, to complain to the head policeman about the plan and the camera, and Charles and I went to the hotel where we were sleeping, and had drinks in the garden above the Hellespont.

"Will they lock them up?" I asked Charles.

Charles said, dear me no, it was just a Turkish gesture. He and David had been taken to police stations for spying again and again, but never kept more than an hour or two, while the police probed into their past lives and the lives of their parents and other relations, and wrote a report for the police chiefs, then they were given a drink and let out to spy again.

"They'll keep the plan, of course, and the negatives in the camera. They collect plans and photographs and potted autobiographies of tourists; they're kept in the Espionage Department in Ankara, and no harm is done. . . . Now I'd rather like to tell you why I left David. I don't want inaccurate stories to get about, and if you hear any in Istanbul, and you will, because I know David wrote to a man he knew in the Chancery, I should be glad if you would contradict them."

So he began telling me why he had left David, and it was all rather confused, and I was sleepy after the drive and the drink, and the Hellespont slapped at the sea wall of the café garden, and people were playing tric-trac at the tables round us, and dice clattered, and the radio whined away at that Turkish music which goes on and on like crooning, and which Turks love so much that western music is hateful to them and Mozart just a noise to be turned off. I lapsed into sleep, like the young man Eutychus, and would have fallen three storeys had they been there, and I dreamed of Alexandria Troas, and the Tenebrae types lamenting there, Aleph and Calph, Teth and Jod, Ghimel and Mem and Nun, all afflicted, all put out, all sad about what they had been through, the dark places they had come to, the bitterness and the gall, then the last light went out and the dark was all, and through the dark Aleph and Teth and Jod still wailed for Alexandria Troas broken and gone. And I dreamed of sea winds whispering in rustling grass and asphodel among the fallen columns of Ilium and over the grave of Priam's Troy, and of the Trojan plain stretching level to the sea where the Greek ships lay, and where the Greek sailors, bored to death, played with dice, tric-trac, tric-trac, and the waves lipped on the beach and lifted the ships, and music wailed from the pipes of the Dardan goat-herds on the plain. Ten long years it had gone on, and because of those ten years Troy was our ancestor, and the centre of a world that Turks could never know.

" And then David said . . . and I said . . . and he said . . ."

It was like women talking near you on the bus—she said, he said, I said. And it was like the B.B.C. news—Mr. Attlee has

37

said at Blackpool . . . Mr. Dulles said in Washington . . . Mr. Nehru said yesterday in Delhi . . . The Archbishop of York has said . . . The Pope has said . . . said, said, said . . . The peoples of the Free World, they said, must unite to resist the aggressor. The peoples of the Free World, they said, all long for a just peace . . . "Where *is* this free world they all talk so much about?" aunt Dot would interrupt the News to ask. "*I* never went there. It must be quite extraordinary, every one doing just as they please, no laws, no police, no taxation, no compulsory schooling, nothing but a lot of people all resisting aggressors and longing for a just peace. By the way, the camel was taken in charge for obstruction again by that stupid policeman."

The slapping of the Hellespont on the sea wall woke me, and I supposed myself Leander, for a light was twinkling on the Europe shore in Hero's tower.

"It's time to swim across," I said.

Charles said, "Swim across what? So we agreed it was really *no* use going on together, if that was the kind of thing that was liable to happen. So I packed up and went. It seemed the only thing to do. Don't you agree?"

I agreed, and said, "Shall we swim across, as Leander, Mr. Ekenside and I did? If we go in now, we could dine at Sestos, if we make it, and if any Turk can tell us where it is, but they won't know. Or would aunt Dot want to come too, I wonder?"

Aunt Dot was a very fine swimmer, being the right shape and build, and she probably would want to come too.

Charles said, "One has first to find out about the currents. It took Byron and Ekenside miles out of their course, and Leander never made it at all, that last time. Of course the Abydos-Sestos crossing isn't the shortest, actually. People usually now go in half a mile up the coast from Çanak. But anyhow I'm not in form for it to-night, I should drown. You have to be feeling happy and full of hope for the Leander swim."

So we gave up the Leander swim, and then aunt Dot and Father Chantry-Pigg came back from the police station. Father

Chantry-Pigg was very angry about his father's plan of Troas, and aunt Dot was annoyed about her negatives, and a disguised policeman was following them and sat at the table when we dined, and we saw that we had joined the large army of spies who seemed to be going about Turkey.

Next morning we took a motor boat across to the Gallipoli peninsula to see the British war cemeteries, where practically every one has relations. Aunt Dot had a brother there, so she took some red irises for him, and, as we stood by his grave, she began to be angry again, as she had been in 1915 when he was killed, for she had always thought the Gallipoli expedition very stupid, and the most awful waste of her brother's life. However, she left the irises in a jampot, and Father Chantry-Pigg said "*Requiem aeternam dona ei, Domine*", and aunt Dot and I said "*Et lux perpetua luceat ei*", and Father Chantry-Pigg prayed that all the souls in those cemeteries might rest in peace, and then we wandered about the graves, which were kept very beautifully, and I thought how awful it was that all those people should be lying there under the ground of Gallipoli, when they might by now have been elderly men doing well or ill at something, and it seemed too soon for them to be lying dead, in their sixties, though it was all right for Hector and Achilles and Patroclus and all the Greeks and Trojans who lay in the Troad, for they would have been several thousand years old. Death is awful, and one hates to think about it, but I suppose after all those years of it the dead take it for granted.

5

WE WENT back to Çanak, and got on the steamer for Istanbul, and Charles came too, for he was anxious to be back in Istanbul to tell people about himself and David, in case they should be getting false ideas. When he had given them the true ideas about that, he was going to travel about Turkey and write his own Turkey book, which was now to be a separate book from the one he had meant to write with David. For a time he had an idea that he might come with us down the Black Sea. But when we told him about how we were an Anglican mission to Turks, and how aunt Dot meant to convert Turkish women to independence, and about the camel, whom we were to rejoin at Istanbul harbour, he changed his mind, not wanting to be mixed up with things like that, for he knew what would be said of it at the Embassy and in Shell Company and in the University and in the good houses along the Bosphorus, and in the smart Beyoglu hotels, and by the archæologists, and all down the Black Sea. Father Chantry-Pigg was glad Charles was not to accompany us, as he was so very indifferent to religion.

The boat was gay and crowded with Turks, and it went up the straits between the Dardanelles shores, Asia to the right and Europe to the left, past Abydos and Sestos, and past where Xerxes threw his bridge of boats across the Hellespont to conquer Greece, and the Europe shore climbed up like mountains, dotted with white villages and houses, and the Asia shore heaved down to Troy plain, and between them the Hellespont ran green, and widened out presently into the sea of Marmara.

We voyaged all day, and before dark Istanbul could be seen

ahead, and it is true that it must look more splendid than any other city one comes to by sea. Even Father Chantry-Pigg, who did not think that Constantine's city and the Byzantine capital ought to have had all those mosque-domes and minarets built up to its old Byzantine shape, of which he had engravings in a book, even he thought the famous outline climbing above the Bosphorus and the Sea of Marmara, with all its domes and minarets poised against the evening sky, was very stupendous. Aunt Dot, already knowing the place, was delighted to see it again, and was busy making notes of all the things she wanted to do there before leaving it. She had Turkish friends in the University, and knew Turkish lawyers and doctors and archæologists and Imams, for Istanbul is full of intelligent and cultured Turks, but she agreed that the less she said to the Imams about our expedition the better, as they could not be expected to approve of it. Indeed, aunt Dot herself sometimes felt that it was somewhat impertinent to try and convert the holders of such a noble, powerful and bigoted religion as Islam to another faith. But then she remembered the position of Moslem women, and her missionary zeal returned. She knew a clever and highly educated woman doctor in Istanbul, who would be able to tell her all about the woman position in the country at large, how deeply women were still dug in to Moslemism, how likely they were to prefer Christianity when they heard of it, and what their husbands and fathers would think and do if they did.

Father Chantry-Pigg meant to see Byzantine churches (of which he still counted St. Sophia to be one), and also to get in touch with some Greek Orthodox priests, and with the local Anglican priest, who would give him news of the Seventh Day Adventist Mission, for he would not care to talk to a Seventh Day Adventist himself. He hoped to meet the Greek Patriarch, and to have a Byzantine discussion with him on many interesting topics.

Charles meant to leave us as soon as we had landed.

41

I meant to explore Istanbul and do some sketches and improve my Turkish and keep away from the camel.

The quays and wharves were very noisy and bustling. The boat which had brought us from England was still in the harbour, and after some time we found it, and aunt Dot asked the crew where was her camel, and they took her to a kind of camel stables on the quay, where the camel was tied to a post, with a row of other camels. It did not seem to recognise aunt Dot, but went on chewing and looking distant. We left it there, and took a taxi up to our hotel in Beyoglu. It was a nice hotel, and the management were so eager to help us that they begged us to let them cash our travellers' cheques at a much higher rate than we should have got from a bank, and it seemed very kind that they should want to give us more liras for our pounds than the banks liked us to have, and more than we would have been quite willing to accept, but this is one of the mysteries that only financiers can understand, and it goes on almost all over the world, because the love of the English pound and of the American dollar is so great and wide-spread that foreigners actually compete for them, very quietly, in whispers, and as if they wanted no one else to hear, though actually every one knows quite well what the conversation is about. Aunt Dot, who is very experienced, doesn't whisper, but just asks, " How much on the black market to-day ? " and if it isn't enough she says " No thank you, I can do better than that at the so-and so," and puts her cheques away. Father Chantry-Pigg, being so extreme, agrees with Roman Catholics that to cheat governments is all right, because they spend money so badly, and I like to take all I can get, so we do pretty well, though people like Charles do even better. Actually, aunt Dot knows so many people in all parts of the world who will cash ordinary English bankers' cheques for her that she is very seldom in difficulties. " Have good friends, dear," she says, " make to yourself friends of the mammon of unrighteousness, and you'll be all right everywhere."

She spent a lot of our week in Istanbul seeing her friends, Turkish and British, at the University and at Robert College, and women lawyers and doctors, and the British Institute staff, and the British Embassy, and several archæologists, and some Shell Company people, who were, said she, the most hospitable people in the world, only equalled by the Irak Petroleum Company in the Levant; it was important, she always said, to get in with oil, in whatever part of the world you were, just as it was important to get in with port wine when in Portugal. One of her Istanbul friends was Dr. Halide Tanpinar, the woman who had told her so much about the female position in Turkey. This doctor had trained at a London hospital, and had, while in London, joined the Church of England, from being an atheist like most young educated Turks since Kemal Atatürk had shown their parents that Moslemism was out of date. Aunt Dot, who had known her for some years, asked her if she would come with us and help us with our mission tour, sizing up the situation and the possibilities, and telling the women about the Anglican Church in Turkish, and about what a good time Christian women had, wearing hats and talking to men, not having to carry the loads, and being free to go about and have fun like men, and sometimes ride the donkeys instead of walking. Besides, said aunt Dot, she would be able to heal the sick, which was always the greatest help in mission work. So Dr. Halide said she would come, as she felt it was her duty both to Turkish women and to the Church. Fortunately she was not very busy just then with her practice, and had an accommodating neighbour who would take it over, like Dr. Watson, and she would enjoy the expedition very much.

While aunt Dot saw her friends, I saw Istanbul, the mosques and palaces and the Seraglio and the cisterns and the Turkish cemetery and the walls and the Bazaar, and the excavations going on in Justinian's palace, and the archæologists who were digging it all up, and the ruined house that Justinian had on the sea shore, and so on, and one day I went up the Bosphorus and saw the castles and palaces and mosques and old wooden houses and villages on the shores. But in the evenings I wandered about old Stambul, down by the quays and among the narrow streets and cafés and old shops, and watched the ships in the harbour and the people, till it was time to catch a tram back to Beyoglu and dinner in the hotel. Often Father Chantry-Pigg and I dined there alone, while aunt Dot dined with her friends, and she would come in later in the evening, full of the things people had told her all day. I met people I knew, who were staying in Istanbul for a while; these were mostly writing their Turkey books, and had just come up from southern or western or eastern Turkey, and were just off to some other part. One of them was David, from whom Charles had parted, and he told us why, as Charles had, but it was not the same story, and I was sleepy the evening he told us, as I had been when Charles told his, and I got the two stories confused, so I shall never quite know what happened to make them part. David asked if we had seen Charles, and where he was now, and we didn't know, but next day they met by chance in the bar of the Konak hotel, and were very cold and distant, on account of what they each thought had happened when they were in Trebizond, so, in spite of knowing they had better join again, because Charles's descriptions needed David's drawings, and David's drawings needed Charles's descriptions, and because, though Charles knew more archæology (which was not saying much), David knew more Turkish (which was not saying much either)—in spite of all these reasons for joining, their hearts stayed sundered, and Charles went off in a ship to Smyrna, and David in a plane to Iskenderon, and each would write his Turkey book alone. Travelling together is a great test, which has damaged many friendships and even honeymoons, and some people, such as Gray and Horace Walpole, never feel quite the same to one another again, and it is nobody's fault, as one knows if one listens to the stories of both, though it seems to be some people's fault more than others.

44

One evening aunt Dot brought Dr. Halide Tanpinar to dinner. She was handsome, and seemed about thirty-five, and felt extremely strongly about Turkish women who were backward and still obeyed the Prophet after all Kemal Atatürk had said about not doing this but leading a free life in hats, with education. Father Chantry-Pigg asked her if she thought the poorer Turkish women were ready for education and Christianity and hats. Dr. Halide said she was afraid they were not at all ready for these advantages yet, but she thought they might be persuaded. The Church must come first, as, till they stopped believing in the Koran and the Prophet and the Imams, they would feel it very wrong to disobey them. Father Chantry-Pigg would have to work hard at this, though he would find the second half of his name a handicap with Moslems, and this had better be concealed from them. Then Father Chantry-Pigg asked her if she was herself a fully Catholic Anglican, and would be prepared to help to instruct people in the full faith. He wanted to know what churches she had been used to attend when in London. Dr. Halide, who was experimental, said she had tried many, such as All Saints Margaret Street, St. Mary's Grarm Street, St. Stephen's Gloucester Road, St. Augustine's Kilburn, St. Paul's Knightsbridge, St. Magnus the Martyr, St. Thomas's Regent Street, St. John's Holland Road, Grosvenor Chapel, the Annunciation Bryanston Street, St. Michael & All Angels off Portobello Road, All Souls Portland Place. . . . When she got to All Souls Portland Place, Father Chantry-Pigg, who had passed the other churches with approval, as if they would do very well for the Turkish women, looked cold, and as if anything that Dr. Halide might have got from there would be as well kept from the Turkish women. But I thought a Low church like that might suit Moslems better than the High ones, which are so set about with images.

It seemed to me to be a mistake to think, as Father Chantry-Pigg thought, that all Anglican churches ought to have the same type of service, and that type some approximation to what

45

went on in St. Gregory's, for by no means all Anglicans like scenes of that nature. Some Commander (R.N.) in the Church Assembly or some such gathering, once complained that one of the worst scandals in the Church of England was the variety of worship that occurred in its different churches and parishes, and this scandal, said the Commander, kept many people from going to church at all, though one does not quite see why it should have this effect, one would suppose that variety would induce more types of person to go, since there will always be something for this Commander, and something for aunt Dot and me, and something wonderfully extreme for Father Chantry-Pigg, who had made for himself a church so excessively high that churches such as All Saints Margaret Street seemed to him practically Kensitite. So our Church is very wonderful and comprehensive, and no other Church, it is said, is quite like it, and this variety that it has is one of its glories, and not one of its scandals at all, though there are plenty of these, such as new incumbents having to recite things so strange that they do not even want to believe them, like some of the Thirty-Nine Articles, and such as the Church being forbidden to revise its own Prayer Book by a non-Anglican parliament, so that Anglicans have to use a revised order quietly and illegally without further reference to the House of Commons. And when one considers such scandals as these, one sees that variety of worship is nothing but a merit.

Looking more closely into Dr. Halide's full Catholicity, Father Chantry-Pigg said that he assumed that she herself practised, and was prepared to teach, sacramental confession. Dr. Halide said that she would certainly pass on this idea to the Turkish women, but that she herself, though she had made a first confession, had never got round to a second, owing to being too busy.

"I never got time," she said, "to think of what I should say."

I thought how different Dr. Halide was from me, who knew

46

very well what I should say, but was in no position to say it.

Father Chantry-Pigg nodded gravely, and said in a matter like that one should *make* time.

"Yes," Dr. Halide agreed. "We will tell them. But I think they will not hurry. It will be very strange to them."

Aunt Dot said, "Besides, Father, you don't yet know enough Turkish to hear them. Halide can't interpret *there*, you must remember."

Father Chantry-Pigg murmured something about Greek.

"My dear Father," said aunt Dot, "they don't know a word of Greek. Why should they? No, you must work at your Turkish, and give up hopes of meeting any left-over Byzantines who have joined Islam and yearn to be Christians again. By the way, did you see the Patriarch?"

Father Chantry-Pigg said he had, and that they had had a most interesting conversation about the Immaculate Conception and the Assumption, in neither of which the Patriarch believed, but in both of which Father Chantry-Pigg would have believed if they had not been pronounced *de fide* too late to be part of pure Catholic heritage, by the rival branch of the Church, which he liked to thwart. So, whatever he believed in his heart, he followed St. Bernard, St. Thomas Aquinas, and St. Bonaventura, in outwardly rejecting the one doctrine, and the earlier Fathers in not accepting the other, and was not intending to offer either to his Moslem converts as *de fide*, and should not recommend the A.C.M.S. to do so if they started a mission.

He had also had conversations with the chaplain of the Anglican church, and with an American professor at Robert College, and had learned that a mission conducted by some followers of Dr. Billy Graham was busy converting people down the Black Sea, and was having a great success. When he mentioned this Dr. Graham, he looked scornful and disagreeable, as he did about All Souls Portland Place, and as if he did not at all care for that kind of thing, and would be greatly vexed if we were to come across it down the Black Sea.

47

I told him how I had been to Harringay arena one evening with my friend Joe, who was a literary editor, because we had press tickets lent us by John Betjeman, so we drove down, and because of the press tickets, we were shown right to the front of the arena, and sat on chairs just below the platform, where all the thousands of people behind could see us, which was embarrassing, and when we looked up Dr. Graham was above us, holding up his Bible and being eloquent and the whole arena hanging on his words, which were about Immorality, for he was taking the ten commandments, and that night he had got to the seventh, which was the only one, he said, that was about Immorality, and Immorality was worse than all the other sins. He said it happened continually everywhere, in the streets and in the fields and on the beaches, and at the Judgment Day God would say "You thought no one saw you that evening on the beach, but I saw you, I took a picture of you." Joe wanted to go out, but I said we couldn't as we were right in front, so he had to bear it. Later Dr. Graham told every one who wished to decide for Christ to come forward, and slow religious music played, and many hundreds or thousands of people left their seats and came forward and stood under the platform. I thought it would be very nice if Joe decided for Christ, it might improve the literary world, which is full of Immorality and other faults, but he wouldn't. He said why didn't I; but when I decide for Christ (which I sometimes do, but it does not last) it is always in an Anglican church (high), and I didn't think I would care to decide thus in the Harringay arena, so neither of us got up.

I wondered what effect Dr. Graham's disciples would have on Turks, and if they would come forward when he told them, but I thought that if they did they would probably only be deciding for the Prophet, and the missioners would send them back to the mosques they attended, with notes for their Imams.

6

So AFTER a week we left Istanbul, collecting the camel and boarding a Black Sea ship called *Trabzon*, which is the Turkish for Trebizond. It was full of Turks, Americans, Germans, Scandinavians, and a few British, and was very smart and clean and comfortable in the first class. A less smart and clean and comfortable class was very full of Turks; they had large baskets of food, and slept on the deck, and every morning and evening the male Turks had a service, praying together and reading the Koran aloud. No women were seen to pray; if they prayed at all, it was in secret and in whispers. Aunt Dot thought this was hopeful for our mission; women, being the more religious sex everywhere, like public worship, and would be ready converts to a religion which allowed them this. But we all thought it was very admirable in the male Turks to meet for worship so regularly when voyaging; Christian travellers are seldom seen to do this, unless they are pilgrims. But Father Chantry-Pigg set up his portable altar in a corner of the upper deck where it could be seen from the steerage deck and said Mass before it each morning, and aunt Dot and Dr. Halide and I attended, and we were watched by the Turks on the steerage deck and sailors and bar waiters and passengers, among whom were two American girls in bikinis sun bathing, and more Turks watched the American girls than us. The girls thought the altar and the candles and the Mass very cute; one of them had been sometimes to that kind of service in Cambridge, Mass., at a place called the Monastery, which Father Chantry-Pigg said was where the Cowley Fathers in America lived, but the other girl and her parents were not Episcopalian, they belonged

49

to one of those sects that Americans have, and that are difficult for English people to grasp, though probably they got over from Britain in the *Mayflower* originally, and when sects arrive in America they multiply, like rabbits in Australia, so that America has about a hundred to each one in Britain, and this is said to be on account of the encouraging climate, which is different in each of the states, and most encouraging of all in the deep south and in California, where sects breed best. The parents of the girl who belonged to one of these obscure sects lived in California, where they had a lot of money and oil, and their name was Van Damm, and they were now travelling about Turkey, and Mr. Van Damm was interested in oil and in defending the Turks from the Russians by selling them cables and oil drums and metal litter of all kinds to fortify their beaches, for he disliked Russians almost as much as the Turks did, and was not going to have them landing on Turkish beaches if he could help it. Mrs. Van Damm looked very handsome and bland, with blue hair and eyes and Park Avenue clothes, and she was interested in Billy Graham and the mission some of his followers were said to be conducting down the Black Sea, and she looked at the shores through bird glasses to see if they had got there yet.

"We should hear them," she said, "quite a way off shore. They set every one singing. Now you Episcopalians, you don't sing so much. But some of your churches have very fine choirs. You folks should have brought a choir along with you. Listen now; do you hear singing?"

We were lying off the port of Zonguldak, which is full of coal, and above the noises coal makes we could hear singing. Mrs. Van Damm got out her bird glasses, and we all looked through them in turn, and we saw a little van on the shore among the coal, and round it a crowd of Turks stood singing Turkish songs, and Turkish music whined, but it was not missionaries, for on the van was written B.B.C., and it was one of those recording vans, with tapes, that aunt Dot hated so much, and it was collecting a slice of Black Sea life for a Home Service programme.

"Isn't that cute," said Mrs. Van Damm.

"How every one gets about," said aunt Dot. "I wonder who else is rambling about Turkey this spring. Seventh Day Adventists, Billy Grahamites, writers, diggers, photographers, spies, us, and now the B.B.C. We shall all be tumbling over each other. Abroad isn't at all what it was." She looked back at the great open spaces of her youth, when one rode one's camel about deserts frequented only by Arabs, camels, flocks of sheep and Gertrude Bell. "Odd," she said, "how the less money one is allowed to take abroad, the more one goes there. But of course all these people are on jobs, and get as much as they want."

Father Chantry-Pigg said that he had heard in Istanbul that a party of Seventh Day Adventist pilgrims was journeying to Mount Ararat for the second coming of Christ, which was due to occur there this summer on the summit of this mountain. It had been due in this same spot on earlier occasions, and pilgrims from all over Europe had several times travelled there to meet it, but it had been delayed, and now it was really due. If we climbed Mount Ararat, as Father Chantry-Pigg intended to do, we should find the pilgrims waiting as near the top as it was possible to get, collecting pieces of the ark, singing hymns and preparing their souls against the Coming. It seems that life on Ararat has always been immensely strange.

"Not at all an agreeable mountain," said aunt Dot, who had been up it with my uncle Frank in 1920. There had been pilgrims that year too, she said, waiting for the Second Coming; many of them had come from the Caucasus, where strange races and religions had been used to congregate once. There would, of course, be no Caucasian pilgrims now. Those poor Caucasians, said aunt Dot, we must get to them somehow, and she and Father Chantry-Pigg looked secretive and determined, and as if they were planning to crash the curtain. Crashing the curtain is a very popular enterprise, like climbing Everest, but more private; a lot of people try it, and some succeed in getting in, but not all get out again, they are just swallowed up quietly, and no more heard, though sometimes years later they are spewed out, rather the worse for wear. Of course the best plan is to be a scientist or engineer, and become missing, but most people want a less long visit than that, just a dip in and out, such as ambassadors and their staffs get when they are appointed to Moscow; they just have time to collect copy for their Russia books, then out again and write them. I supposed that if aunt Dot and Father Chantry-Pigg were set on crashing the curtain in order to convert Caucasians, I should have to go too, though I did not think Dr. Halide would, but I would rather stay in Turkey, which became more and more pleasant the farther we got down the Euxine sea, the intimidating Black Sea, so-called, said my Turkish guidebook, on account of its storms and high waves, which arise so sudden that many people have perished.

But the days we were on it, it was not black and had no storms or high waves and no one perished. It was dark blue, shading to light green near the coast, and all along the mountains ran, and the forests on them, and every now and then a little port, made by the trading Greeks long ago, and, but for the ports, the coast was what the Argonauts saw when they sailed to fetch the Golden Fleece, and those who are good at Greek history give the year of this as 1275, but no one seems sure, which always vexed me when I was a child, and vexes me still. And, when the weather was clear, a faint shadow loomed on the Euxine's northern side, which was the shadow of the Crimea; when I commented on this to the captain of the ship, he and the first officer gave the Crimea a dirty look. Turks do not believe in peaceful co-existence with Russia, they never have, and Father Chantry-Pigg agrees with them. Fortunately for most of our voyage Russia was out of sight. Aunt Dot looked towards the Crimea through her glasses, and sighed after that menacing shadow, and I sighed too, because of those orchards and palaces and seaside villas that I might never see.

But on the southern shore all was animation, for from each little port boats rowed out to us full of people, full of bundles, full of hampers of food and fruit for the passengers on the steerage deck, or full of animal carcasses, live fowls, donkeys, pigs, sheep and female goats, immense tyres, trucks, metal tools and bundles of planks, to be conveyed by the *Trabzon* to the ports along the shore. They rowed back with landing passengers, but more embarked than disembarked, and the crowds on the decks grew, and were most amiable and cheerful. I would have liked to go on shore at all these ports, but this was not allowed, and I could only sketch them from the deck. I decided that I liked Turks very much.

When we anchored off Inebolu, the B.B.C. recording van chugged past us in a motor launch, on its way to some other port, where it would record more native life. Perhaps we should catch up with it at Trebizond, which is really the social hub of the eastern Euxine, though Samsun is now a more important port. Trebizond, having once been for seven years the last bit of the Byzantine empire, has cachet and legend and class, besides being so near to where Xenophon and the Ten Thousand marched down from the mountains, and went mad from a surfeit of the local honey. Perhaps the Billy Graham missioners would also be there, and perhaps the Seventh Day Adventists, having a rest before they set out for Ararat and the Second Coming, and no doubt a lot of writers scribbling away at their Turkey books. And, of course, a number of British and Russian spies. Life in Trebizond, I thought, would be very sociable, animated and peculiar.

So, really, was life on the *Trabzon*, what with the Van Damms, the ship's officers, the Turkish tourists who strolled on the decks and looked in at the cabin windows at the other tourists dressing, a party of university students from Istanbul, the arrivals of people and animals from every port, the Islamic devotions

53

conducted on the steerage deck, the Christian devotions conducted
on the cabin deck, and the spies who murmured to one another
in corners in various tongues. Aunt Dot made it her job to
converse with Turkish women, on whatever deck they might
be found. The university students made it their job to practise
their English on us and the Van Damms and tell us about
Turkish literature which, it seemed, was in a very thriving and
interesting state. Several of them, both male and female, wrote
poetry, and were inclined to recite it to us in Turkish, with
prose renderings of its meaning in English. They read us
other Turkish poets too, and so did Dr. Halide, and they asked
Father Chantry-Pigg, whom they admired, whether he did not
find them extremely good.

"Obscure," he said, for he found most modern poetry this,
and actually modern poems in Turkish were not much more
obscure to him than modern poems in English. Aunt Dot was
indifferent to verse, she thought prose better.

"Obs-cure?" they enquired. "What means that? You
like?"

"He means he doesn't understand," I explained.

"Ah," said Dr. Halide, who was very patriotic for the New
Turkey. "I will translate."

I told her that would be no use, Father Chantry-Pigg still
wouldn't understand. "He doesn't understand most English
modern poetry, either," I said.

They looked at the priest, whose eyes were now closed in
sleep or prayer, with pity, and without surprise. They knew
that the Church, being backward and reactionary, had been
left behind in the spectacular progress of Atatürk's modern
secular Turkey. Imams, priests, patriarchs, prophets, Turkey
had left them all behind, and doubtless Britain had too, though
not so far behind as Turkey had, Turkey having got further on.

"We study English poetry," they said. "Dylan Thomas,
Spender, MacNeice, Lewis, Eliot, Sitwell, Frost, Charlotte
Mew. It is very like ours, yes?"

" Yes," I said. " Very like."

" It is better, less good, much about the same? "

" Much about the same," I said.

They looked disappointed, for they knew that theirs was better. " English writers," they said, " come to Istanbul and speak at the British Institute on the Poem. Also the Novel. You speak? "

" No," I said.

" You write? "

" Sometimes."

" Excuse. Why then you not speak on the Novel and the Poem? "

" I shouldn't be able to think what to say. I believe it has all been said."

They agreed that it probably had. " Yes. We have heard."

" You understand the Poem of to-day? " they asked, for Turks do not stop asking questions.

I said I understood some of it.

" You like? "

I said I liked some of it.

Perceiving that the topic of the Poem was unlikely to be soon exhausted, aunt Dot changed it to that of the Turkish Woman, and this was one of their subjects too. Turkish speakers, they said, especially women speakers, such as Dr. Halide (who, tiring of all this juvenile babble, which was extremely familiar to her, had strolled off to chat with the First Officer, a handsome man who admired her)—these women speakers travelled abroad and lectured in London, Edinburgh, Paris, New York and Milan on the Woman. For she too, like literature, politics and education, flourished greatly in the New Turkey.

" Lawyers, doctors, teachers, writers, judges, painters, dancers, modistes, beauticians," they said. " And many other important women. Some virgins, some wives. In Turkey to-day, it is no matter. All get about."

"Isn't that nice," aunt Dot agreed. "And these important women, are many of them Moslem or not?"

"Not," they chorused; but added, "Nevertheless, some are," and they seemed to regard with respect the important women who were so behind the times. The youngest of them said, "There is my aunt. *She* is very religious Moslem, and very important woman; she teaches in Robert College."

"And you students? One understands that you have largely left Moslemism behind, it's so bound up with old-fashioned tradition and all that. But what about Christianity? Dr. Halide is a Christian, you know, and you can't call *her* behind the times. It's a most progressive religion actually. Have you ever considered it?"

"Too old. It is over, long past. Dr. Halide caught it in Britain, where it is much about. Here it is the past. The Greek papas—οὐ μην!"

The speaker, a chubby Greek youth in spectacles, threw a scornful glance at two Greek clergymen eating cheese and olives in deck chairs near by, and feeding a goat with the rind and skins. It was apparent that they too had been left behind by the new Turkey.

"My parents, yes," he amplified. "Ourselves, no. It is the same with the mosques. They contain the grandfathers of my friends."

"And up in the galleries, our grandmothers," his friends added. "Our mothers, some. Our aunts, few. Except only the aunt of Mihri. Most aunts, and many mothers, are lawyers, teachers, doctors, modistes . . ."

"Of course, the important women," aunt Dot interrupted. "Now, did you ever hear of the Church of England?"

They looked politely vague. "You too had a church," they supposed. "We have still," aunt Dot rapped out.

At this point Father Chantry-Pigg, who had been dozing in his chair, woke up and took a hand.

" Only," he gently said, " the eternal Church of Christendom. The one holy, Catholic and Apostolic Church. You know of it? "

It seemed to strike a bell.

" The Catholic church, yes. There are many in Istanbul, isn't it? We have seen."

" Only one example of *our* branch of it," Father Chantry-Pigg explained. " The Anglican communion has a church in a small meydan off Istiklal Caddesi."

" We have not seen," they regretted. " It is very fine? "

" No," Father Chantry-Pigg answered, " it is not very fine." He looked sad that it was not very fine, that it was less fine than most of its companion churches of other communions.

" Still," aunt Dot briskly put in, " it is the best Church to belong to, because it has the most truth."

They looked polite, but one could see that they did not think this was saying much.

One of them remembered something.

" It is the Church of Billy Graham? There was a large meeting in Taksim Square. They sang many songs. It is your Church? Yes? "

" No," said Father Chantry-Pigg, sharply. " It is not. Those people are mainly American Baptists."

" Yes, yes. Church of America. America is the great friend of Turkey. That Church too has truth, is it? "

" All Churches have some," aunt Dot told them, before Father Chantry-Pigg could deliver himself on the matter. " But what," she went on, getting back to the Woman, " what about all those women down there "—she waved towards the steerage deck, where at the moment the male Turks were meeting in prayer—" and the women in country villages and small towns all over Turkey, who go about muffling their faces, and mayn't sit down to meals with men, or walk with them, or pray with them, or play games, or sit in the cafés and gardens, or bathe in the sea, but do the hard dull work, and walk by the

57

donkey while their husbands ride—yes, what about the *unim-*
portant women? "

" They are still backwards," the students cheerfully dismissed
their oppressed sisters. " They *look* still backwards. Kemal
Atatürk commanded them to look forwards and wear hats, but
they are very simple women and wear still shawls and rugs and
do as the men say. In time, they will cure. All that, it is not
Turkish, it is from the Greeks before the Conquest. It is
Byzantine."

" Not true," said the Greek young man. " It is Moslem.
The Greeks were not so."

Waving this aside, the Turks spoke of Ankara, the great progressive capital, where women went unveiled and free, as in
Istanbul, where there was a large famous university, as Istanbul,
and many great public buildings. Of course we were going to
Ankara?

Aunt Dot said we were.

Then they told us about Ankara, its government buildings,
the President's house with a swimming-pool, its embassies and
consulates, its great restaurants, its Atatürk museum, its Atatürk
model farm, its new Atatürk mausoleum, where the founding
Father is to lie, its houses of business, its noble streets of shops,
its multitudinous Americans, its racecourse, its Genelik Park, its
colleges and schools and institutes, its railway station, its boule-
vards, its illuminated signs, its hotels. Ankara, in short, was the
New Turkey, born of the Great Revolution that had so stirred
their parents thirty years ago, and it seemed odd that they had
not turned against it. In Britain, the revolution which had
stirred the parents would have been definitely out, reaction
would have set in, and the statues of Atatürk on his horse would
have been mocked. Young Turks seemed to have more piety.

They went on telling us about Ankara, but the only thing
I wanted to see there was the Seljuk citadel in which the old
town lies, and the Roman Temple of Augustus, and the view
from the acropolis, and perhaps the Hittite things in the museum,

though I do not care for Hittites. Modern Ankara was obviously a bore.

Turks, like Russians and Israelites, seem to want you to see the things that show how they have got on since Atatürk, or since the Bolshevik revolution, or since they took over Palestine. But how people have got on is actually only interesting to the country which has got on. What foreign visitors care about are the things that were there before they began to get on. I dare say foreigners in England really only want to see Stonehenge, and Roman walls and villas, and the field under which Silchester lies buried, and Norman castles and churches, and the ruins of medieval abbeys, and don't care a bit about Sheffield and Birmingham, or our model farms and new towns and universities and schools and dams and aerodromes and things. For that matter, we don't care a bit about them ourselves. But foreigners in their own countries (Russians are the worst, but Turks are bad too) like to show off these dreadful objects, and it is hard not to let them see how very vile and common we think them, compared with what was in the country before they got there. We did not like to tell the Turkish students, whom we liked very much, that the most interesting things in Turkey were put there before it was Turkey at all, when Turks were roaming about mountains and plains in the East (which perhaps they should not really have left, but this was another thing we did not like to tell the students, who did not know where they truly belonged, and perhaps actually few of us do). So we voyaged on, and Father Chantry-Pigg looked up the places on the coast in the Anabasis by Xenophon; he had spotted which was Heraclea, and next day we passed, between Zonguldak and Inebolu, the beach where Jason moored the Argo, and we saw the mouths of the Parthenius, the Halys, the Iris, and the Thermodon, and passed the country of the Paphlagonians, who had feasted and danced with Xenophon's soldiers, and then we came to Sinope, where Diogenes had lived, and Father Chantry-Pigg knew about it all, which made the Van Damms and the

Turkish students admire him very much, and we thought it did the Church of England a great deal of good with them, though none of them knew who these people were that he kept mentioning, or when they had done these things or why, for it was all a long time pre-Turkey, and even longer pre-America, and it was not Hittite; still, they saw he was a very learned man. I liked myself to think about Jason and the other Argonauts sailing along this coast, anchoring here and there, tossed about by the high waves, on the way to Colchis and the Golden Fleece.

7

WE WERE due to reach Trebizond on the afternoon of Whit Sunday. That morning Father Chantry-Pigg celebrated Mass as usual at eight o'clock in a quiet corner of the top deck, and aunt Dot and Dr. Halide and the Americans and I attended it, and the Greek priest and several Turks looked on. The Greek priest made his communion, and, as he did not know English, he was not disturbed by the references to Whit Sunday, which of course for him had not yet arrived. The Van Damms rather worried Father Chantry-Pigg when they came forward too, as he did not suppose that they had ever been confirmed, but he let it pass.

Later in the morning, when I was on deck looking through glasses for the first sight of Trebizond, he came and stood by me and said, "How much longer are you going on like this, shutting the door against God?"

This question always disturbed me; I sometimes asked it of myself, but I did not know the answer. Perhaps it would have to be for always, because I was so deeply committed to something else that I could not break away.

"I don't know," I said.

"It's your business to know. There is no question. You must decide at once. Do you mean to drag on for years more in deliberate sin, refusing grace, denying the Holy Spirit? And when it ends, what then? It will end; such things always end. What then? Shall you come back, when it is taken out of your hands and it will cost you nothing? When you will have nothing to offer to God but a burnt out fire and a fag end? Oh, he'll take it, he'll take anything we offer. It is you who will be impoverished for ever by so poor a gift. Offer now what will cost you a great deal, and you'll be enriched beyond anything you can imagine. How do you know how much of life you still have? It may be many years, it may be a few weeks. You may leave this world without grace, go on into the next stage in the chains you won't break now. Do you ever think of that, or have you put yourself beyond caring?"

Not quite, never quite. I had tried, but never quite. From time to time I knew what I had lost. But nearly all the time, God was a bad second, enough to hurt but not to cure, to hide from but not to seek, and I knew that when I died I should hear him saying, "Go away, I never knew you," and that would be the end of it all, the end of everything, and after that I never should know him, though then to know him would be what I should want more than anything, and not to know him would be hell. I sometimes felt this even now, but not often enough to do what would break my life to bits. Now I was vexed that Father Chantry-Pigg had brought it up and flung me into this turmoil. Hearing Mass was bad enough, hearing it and not taking part in it, seeing it and not approaching it, being offered it and shutting the door on it, and in England I seldom went.

I couldn't answer Father Chantry-Pigg, there was nothing I could say except, " I don't know ". He looked at me sternly, and said, " I hope, I pray, that you will know before it is too late. The door won't be open for ever. Refuse it long enough, and you will become incapable of going through it. You will, little by little, stop believing. Even God can't force the soul grown blind and deaf and paralysed to see and hear and move. I beg you, in this Whitsuntide, to obey the Holy Spirit of God. That is all I have to say."

He left me, and I stayed there at the rail, looking at the bitter Black Sea and its steep forested shores by which the Argonauts had sailed and where presently Trebizond would be seen, that corner of a lost empire, defeated and gone under so long ago that now she scarcely knew or remembered lost Byzantium, having grown unworthy of it, blind and deaf and not caring any more, not even believing, and perhaps that was the ultimate hell. Presently I should come to it; already I was on the way. It would be a refuge, that agnosticism into which I was slipping down. But it would always be anglo-agnosticism, and Mass would always torment. Once Anglicanism is in the system, I think one cannot get it out; it has been my family heritage for too many centuries, and nothing else, perhaps, is ultimately possible for us. I was a religious child, when I had time to give it thought; at fourteen or so I became an agnostic, and felt guilty about being confirmed, though I did not like to say so. I was an agnostic through school and university, then, at twenty-three, took up with the Church again; but the Church met its Waterloo a few years later when I took up with adultery; (curious how we always seem to see Waterloo from the French angle and count it a defeat) and this adultery lasted on and on, and I was still in it now, steaming down the Black Sea to Trebizond, and I saw no prospect of its ending except with death— the death of one of three people, and perhaps it would be my own. Unless, one day, the thing should relax its hold and peter out. So really agnosticism (anglo or other) seemed the only refuge, since taking the wings of the morning and fleeing to the uttermost parts of the sea is said to provide no hope, only another confrontation.

8

THE SHORE swept back in higher ridges; cleaving the forests, deep valleys ran down to the sea. The ancient Greek ports, with their red-roofed white houses in front, and always their white mosques and minarets, climbed back to what had been their medieval Byzantine fortifications, but these had largely gone, destroyed by the Turks for modern buildings; the *Trabzon* lay too far out for us to see how much was left of the old Amisus behind the busy port of Samsun, or of the forts that guarded the little harbour of Tirebolu. All the ports were busy, full of ships and trade, and from all of them launches and rowing boats and motor boats and steam tugs came out to the *Trabzon* full of people and things to sell and things to be shipped to Trebizond, and it was all much more animated than it had been in Jason's day, or even a century ago, but not splendid and gay, as it had been when Trebizond was a free Roman city and the gate to Armenia, and later when it was a Greek empire after the Latin conquest of Constantinople, and the Queen of the Euxine and the apple of the eye of all Asia, and trade flowed down the Euxine Sea, but fighting and intriguing and palace revolutions never stopped; or latest of all, when Constantinople fell to the Turks and the Byzantine Empire was for eight years Trebizond, and Trebizond was a legend, and for years after it had fallen English poets wrote of it, and it was a romance, like Troy and Fonterrabia and Venice. As we came in sight of it, having rounded Cape Yeros, Father Chantry-Pigg and aunt Dot told the Turkish students about it, but they had not heard of it, they called it Trabzon, and supposed it had always been a Turkish town, a port on a Turkish sea. Even Dr. Halide did not know much about its Greek past.

When we saw Trebizond lying there in its splendid bay, the sea in front and the hills behind, the cliffs and the ravines which held the ancient citadel, and the white Turkish town lying along the front and climbing up the hill, it was like seeing an old dream change its shape, as dreams do, becoming something else, for this did not seem the capital of the last Byzantine empire, but a picturesque Turkish port and town with a black beach littered with building materials, and small houses and mosques climbing the hill, and ugly buildings along the quay. The citadel, the ruins of the Comnenus palace, would be somewhere on one of the heights, buried in brambled thickets and trees; a great cliff, grown with tangled shrub, divided the city into two parts. Expecting the majestic, brooding ghost of a fallen empire, we saw, in a magnificent stagey setting, an untidy Turkish port. The ghost would be brooding on the woody cliffs and ravines, haunting the citadel and palace, scornfully taking no notice of the town that Trebizond now was, with the last Greeks expelled by the Father of the Turks twenty years back. From cafés and squares loud speakers blared across the water to us the eternal Turkish erotic whine, I dare say no more erotic than the British kind that you get on the Light Programme, but more eternal, for the Light Programme sometimes has a change, though it loves and whines much more than the Home Programme does, and on the Third they scarcely love and whine at all, which is why those whom aunt Dot calls the Masses very seldom turn this programme on. That is to say, the Third does love sometimes, but in a more highbrow operatic kind of way, and it certainly whines sometimes, but not at the same time that it loves, and when it whines it sounds more like nagging than yearning and cuddling. But the Turkish radio seems to love and cuddle and yearn without a break, Turks being an excessively loving people, and if there were English words to their music they would be, " I love only yew, Baby, To me be always trew, Baby, For I love only yew."

The boats came out from Trebizond to take cargo and

passengers back to it, and of the first-class passengers only we and the B.B.C. couple with their recording van, who had joined us at Samsun, were going to stay there. The Van Damms and the students and some other tourists landed to see the place and the shops, but they would return to the *Trabzon* in the evening to go on with their round trip, which would turn and bring them back when they reached Hopa, the last Turkish port before the iron curtain blocked the road to Russia. The boats were filled mostly with steerage passengers who lived in Trebizond or were visiting relations there, and the women carried great bundles and sacks full of things, but the men carried suitcases with sharp, square corners, which helped them very much in the struggle to get on and stay on the boats, for this was very violent and intense. More than one woman got shoved overboard into the sea during the struggle, and had to be dragged out by husbands and acquaintances, but one sank too deep and had to be left, for the boat-hooks could not reach her; all we saw were the apples out of her basket bobbing on the waves. I thought that women would not stand much chance in a shipwreck, and in the struggle for the boats many might fall in the sea and be forgotten, but the children would be saved all right, for Turks love their children, even the girls.

The camel was put on a steam tug that took animals, and it was the one camel, among sheep and calves and donkeys and pigs, and stood looking tall and white and distinguished, showing race, for it was of the tribe of Ruola, and it was very smooth, having just shed its winter coat, and very smart, with white ostrich plumes tossing on its head, for aunt Dot had spruced it up to make a snob impression in Trebizond. So far, this camel had not been of any use on the trip, in spite of being so useful at home in Oxfordshire, but now it would begin to earn its keep, for aunt Dot was going to take it into the interior, and up Mount Ararat, and all that, for conversion purposes. It was a strong camel, and could carry two of us and some luggage, and we might also get a mule. Aunt Dot thought that we would make a much more powerful impression riding about on a white Arabian camel from the famous Ruola herd than if we travelled in a common way by car, which anyhow we had not got. There is something, aunt Dot said, about a white camel that gives prestige, and particularly religious prestige. We put the camel in a nice stables close to the Yessilyurt Oteli, where we had booked rooms.

The B.B.C. were also at the Yessilyurt, in fact there seemed no other hotel, and it was a nice hotel, old and cleanish, and all the rooms opened out of a circular hall on the first floor, and the dining-room was beyond. When I saw it, I felt that I would not mind quite a long stay in Trebizond, and that, hidden in the town and its surroundings, there was something I wanted for myself and could make my own, something exiled and defeated but still alive, known long since but forgotten.

We went out to explore, and the first thing we saw in the street was the B.B.C. van taking records, and round it stood a crowd of Trapezuntines staring, while the B.B.C. couple asked them questions, through an interpreter they took about with them. They seemed to be asking what the favourite games in Trabzon were, and how much football was played, and was it rugger or soccer, but the answer, said the interpreter, was tric-trac, so the second half of the question did not arise. Aunt Dot, as we passed by, asked in Turkish, "What do the girls play?" but did not stop for the answer, as she knew what it would be, and that the girls had to stay at home and work in the house, or else in the fields, and in the evenings, while the men played tric-trac in the cafés, and the boys bicycled or played with balls in the squares, the girls would be toiling away like Circassian slaves. Aunt Dot grew angrier and angrier about the Moslem treatment of women, and could not wait for the A.C.M.S. to get its mission going but Dr. Halide said, "You must not be impatient. One cannot hurry Turks." As we left the B.B.C. van, we heard the interpreter urging the crowd (which increased all the time, Turks being inquisitive about the odd behaviour of foreign visitors, though not much about more impersonal things) to break into song and dance. They did not take any notice, but no doubt they would be bribed presently and would break out, and a nice Home Service programme about Trebizond would emerge.

9

THE REAL Trebizond, about which the Home listeners would
not hear, was in the labyrinth of narrow streets and squares
which climbed up from the sea, and in the ruined Byzantine
citadel, keep and palace on the heights between the two great
wooded ravines that cleft deep valleys down from the table-
topped mountain Boz Tepe to the shore, and in the disused,
wrecked Byzantine churches that brooded, forlorn, lovely,
ravished and apostate ghosts, about the hills and shores of that
lost empire.

I got to know Trebizond, and particularly the ruined citadel
and palace, pretty well before I had done with it. There is all
about it, with maps and plans, in a very large good book on
Armenian travels by H. F. B. Lynch, who was there about
sixty years ago, and a good description of Trebizond to-day,
and all the Byzantine churches, in Patrick Kinross's Turkey
book, and there is a large history of it in German, which is
therefore not easy to read, and some good shorter histories,
and all about the church painting, by Professor Talbot Rice,
and the Empire of Trebizond has a long section in Finlay's
History of Greece, but Finlay disapproved of Trapezuntines, and
says at the end (and this was a bit that Dr. Halide liked and
quoted), " In concluding the history of this Greek state, we
inquire in vain for any benefit that it conferred on the human
race," for the tumultuous agitation of its stream, he said, did not
purify a single drop of the waters of life, which Finlay thought
empires should do, but after all they very seldom have done
anything like that, and he had forgotten all the Byzantine
churches and the Comnenus palace. Still, there is no denying

that Trapezuntines, like most Byzantines, did behave very corruptly and cruelly and wildly very often, and like most empires, they no doubt deserved to go under, but not so deeply under as Trebizond has gone, becoming Trabzon, with a black squalid beach, and full of those who do not know the past, or that it ever was Trebizond and a Greek empire, and women all muffled up and hiding their faces, and the Byzantine churches mostly turned into mosques, or broken up, or used for army stores and things.

Father Chantry-Pigg wanted to see the churches first, but aunt Dot said these would do later, the first thing at Trebizond was to drive up to the citadel and get a view, for this was what aunt Dot always wanted to do first, so we took a taxi from the square and drove up the hill across the western ravine, then climbed up on foot, and got to the walled and gated part, inside which Turkish houses had been built, and it was all covered with wild gardens and fig trees and brambles and thickets and goats and coops of hens, and we climbed up to the keep at the top, and the palace, and there was some confusion as to which ruins were which, but you could see the eight pointed windows of the palace banqueting hall, and through them there was a view of the whole landscape, with the broken citadel walls twisting about among the small gardens and cottages and the jungle of trees and shrubs that sloped down to the western ravine, and beyond was the sea and the western bay of Trebizond. Looking the other way, you saw the mountain Boz Tepe, that used to be Mithras, where the statue of Mithras once stood till destroyed by the martyr St. Eugenios on account of not being Christian, and Eugenios was presently destroyed by Diocletian on account of being Christian, for all was religious prejudice and hate, and Eugenios's church stands on a hill not far from the palace, and it is now a mosque, for Mahomet has defeated Mithras and Eugenios and Diocletian and has made the palace of the Grand-Comnenus a broken ruin in a wild fertile wilderness set with white minarets.

Father Chantry-Pigg read us Cardinal Bessarion's description of how the place had looked when he was there in the fourteenth century, and it had looked much more magnificent then than it did now that the walls were broken and the palace was a ruin with no roof and no painted walls, and grass and shrubs and fig trees hot in the sun sprouting from where had been the marble mosaic floors, and little cottages and sheds clustering against the walls, and goats all about, The mountain side and the sea and the ravines were the same, but the view down across Trabzon, with its minarets and its white houses and red roofs sloping down to the harbour and the quay and the custom-house, had become all-Turkish, the last Greeks gone.

Father Chantry-Pigg said his piece about Turkish apathy and squalor having let this noble palace and citadel go to ruin, as all antiquities in Turkey went to ruin. He had forgotten about St. Sophia, and the ancient Istanbul mosques, and about Dr. Halide being there and being a Turkish patriot. Dr. Halide, who had the lowest opinion of the public and private morals of Byzantines, said that it was understandable that the monuments to such vicious, cruel, violent and murderous profligates and maladministrators as the Byzantine emperors, despots, grand-dukes, nobles, bishops, eunuchs, populace, and above all the Trabzon Comnenus dynasty, of which Anna the historian was the only worthy representative—and indeed in Trabzon history it was notable that the women had been greatly superior to the men—it was understandable, said Dr. Halide, that the Osmanlis, taking over this corrupted and vicious empire, should not care to preserve the edifices reared out of the blood of the citizens and the coffers of vice. The Ottomans, sweeping in with their healthier and more robust strain, armed with the vigour of Islam, had built up a new and nobler régime, too destructive, perhaps, of the past, but that was excusable.

Father Chantry-Pigg and aunt Dot and I scarcely liked to expatiate on the Ottomans and Islam, though aunt Dot did just say that, when it came to bloodthirstiness, murder, torture, violence, and all that, it seemed a pretty near thing between Byzantines and Turks; after all, as she pointed out, both the Comneni and their conquerors were Asiatic, and deeply devoted to cruelty. Look, she said, at the way Mahomet II had massacred or enslaved the Christian Greeks of Trebizond.

Dr. Halide said, look at the religious tolerance of Sulemein the Magnificent in sixteenth century Istanbul.

" So much more tolerant was he than the West," she said, " that no doubt some of your ancestors fled to Istanbul to escape from persecution at home."

I thought this would have been very wise of our ancestors, whatever it was they were being persecuted for, because Istanbul would have been a very beautiful and romantic city to flee to.

But Dr. Halide admitted that neither Islam nor Christianity had exercised a very moderating influence on cruelty down the ages, in fact, both had seemed to heighten it, though she did not think it had been worse in the east than in the west at the same period, when all was shocking, and look at the Crusaders.

Father Chantry-Pigg looked as if he feared that Dr. Halide, faced with all this Christian and Islamic wickedness, might slip into agnosticism again, for her Christianity seemed to him, he had told us, to be a rather brittle veneer. After all, he had pointed out, she had not got behind her, as we had, centuries of Christian, not to say Anglican, ancestors, but a fierce race of nomadic, bloodthirsty and rather stupid followers of the Prophet (Father Chantry-Pigg looked on followers of the Prophet with prejudice and distaste), who had been most uncultured. It would be extremely inconvenient if she should lapse now, just when we needed her assistance in our enquiries and her sympathetic help in preparing the ground. So he changed the subject from Byzantine wickedness to Byzantine architecture, and suggested that we should now visit the church of St. Eugenios, which we could see from the citadel, and he hoped that this and the other ancient Greek churches, so neglected and dilapidated and mosqued, with their paintings daubed with whitewash, would show Dr. Halide the barbarous lack of culture of her ancestors.

We spent several days in Trebizond, seeing it and making expeditions and talking to the inhabitants. Aunt Dot and Dr. Halide called on the mayor, and broached the idea of an Anglican school being started, to teach the children English and Christianity. They asked him if such a school would be welcomed by the Trebizond parents, and he replied " yok ", for the Trabzon people were pretty Moslem and not at all progressive, had excellent schools of their own, and wanted no change. He himself was progressive, too progressive to be Moslem, and too progressive to be Christian, and he liked neither the Imams nor the Greek papas. But the Trabzon poor were backward.

" What would *he* say if he could come back to-day? " he asked, jerking his head in the direction of the nearest statue of Atatürk.

" What indeed? " Dr. Halide echoed. " Look, for example, at those women there."

She pointed to two women in the street outside, throwing their shawls round their faces as they passed a group of men.

The mayor nodded.

" Nevertheless," he said, " it is well for our women to be modest." So Dr. Halide and aunt Dot saw that he was not really at all progressive about women, only about religion, education, intercourse with the west, and things like that, whereas, as aunt Dot told him, the important thing was women, and there was no call for them to be any more modest than men. He nodded and was benign, but any one could see he did not agree, and that women were only important for field work, house work, bearing sons, and for what D. H. Lawrence called that ugly little word, sex, though it always seems odd that D. H. Lawrence should have thought that word either ugly or little.

Anyhow, the mayor was not encouraging about starting an Anglican school in Trabzon.

Next day was Corpus Christi, so Father Chantry-Pigg said Mass at eight at his portable altar in a corner of the public gardens, and a crowd collected and watched, and they thought we were the Greek Church, but they were stolid and tolerant, and did not behave like the Catholic Commandos or the Protestant Storm Troopers at home. After Mass, Father Chantry-Pigg thought it would be nice to have a procession round the gardens, so he walked off with the portable altar, chanting Ave Verum, and aunt Dot and Dr. Halide and I followed behind, chanting too, and a number of Turkish boys and a few men came after to see what was the matter and what we would be at next. Presently Father Chantry-Pigg stopped and preached a short sermon in English, and Dr. Halide put it into Turkish, and the chief thing it said was that this was a great Christian festival and holy day, always kept in the Church of England, and I wondered what Mr. Scott of All Souls Portland Place would say to that, but we shall never know.

What we did know was what the Trabzon Imam was saying to it, for he suddenly appeared near the end of the sermon, and, though he said it in Turkish, he made it quite clear, waving his arms with stern gestures and cries of disapproval, and sometimes breaking off to cuff a boy who was gaping up at us. He tried to jam Father Chantry-Pigg's voice with his own, and what he was saying must have been terrible, for the boys and men began to slink away. Then the Imam saw a dreadful sight, for two women who were passing by with large baskets of washing had paused to look on, and he advanced on them full of the wrath of the Prophet against women, but before he got to them they had fled, covering their whole faces with their shawls. The Imam returned to us, and now he was chanting the Koran, and his arms tossed and his beard and hair tossed and one saw how dominating he must be over his flock. Halide and Xenophon watched him with great contempt, but aunt Dot was interested.

" Other clergymen," she said, " are so odd compared with

ours." I could see she was remembering the whole strange world of clergymen; mullahs, Buddhists, Orthodox, Copts, Romans, Old Catholics, Anglicans, Lutherans, Presbyterians, Rabbis, and of course they all are odd, for they uphold strange creeds and rites, and that is what they are for, but aunt Dot may have been right to think Anglicans the least odd, or perhaps it is only that they are the ones we are most used to. But Father Chantry-Pigg said later that he had behaved very much like that Imam to the Arab missionaries who came to St. Gregory's, and that the Imam was very right to defend his flock against strange doctrine.

After he had stopped preaching, Father Chantry-Pigg spoke polite words to this Imam and asked Halide to tell him that there was no ill-feeling, but Halide said she could not tell him that, as in the Imam there was quite a lot of ill-feeling. What she did tell him was that this was the Church of England, and Christians were bound to show their religion to non-Christians, it was part of their religious rule. But we could see that the Imam was going to make trouble for us with the mayor.

Then we went in to breakfast at the Yessilyurt, and aunt Dot said we had made a good beginning.

In the afternoon aunt Dot and Dr. Halide called on the British consul to consult him about the mission, of which he took a poor view, not thinking it the thing to try to convert the nationals of a country one was visiting to another faith, when they had a perfectly good one of their own. He had heard about the Corpus Christi procession and the sermon, and thought it a pity. Aunt Dot pointed out how missionary work was often done by foreigners in Africa, Asia and so on, and used in the past to be the thing in all countries. We ourselves, she pointed out, had been converted by Roman and Irish missionaries, Rome by Jews and Greeks, Greeks by Jews, North Americans by French and British emigrants, South Americans by Spanish and Portuguese, and now America was sending missions to convert Britain. It was done all the time; in Syria

75

the Crusaders had had a go at it, and to-day there were several missions at work in Turkey, and no one seemed to mind. Had the consul read the Gospels, he would remember that the disciples had been bidden to go into all the world and preach Christianity. The consul still thought it tactless, but said he had no powers to stop it, and if they must do it, they must. Already, he said, British visitors to Trabzon were thought pretty odd, and indeed seemed always to have been so. They had been apt to take what seemed to Turks a rather morbid interest in Armenia; Mr. H. F. B. Lynch, for instance, in the eighteen nineties, who had stayed in the city for a long time making explorations, maps and plans, and taking notes for a large and remarkable book, had then gone on into Armenia and had climbed Ararat. He had shown a good deal of sympathy, still legendary in Trabzon, for the then recently massacred Armenians. Lord Kinross too, who had been in Trabzon lately, had been thought to have too lively an interest in alleged Armenian church architecture. And now here were those B.B.C. people, who had the population following them about wherever they went, eager to see what on earth they would do next, the boys bribed to sing, while the women and girls giggled from a distance. Then there had been the Billy Graham mission, which had passed through the other day, hired a room in the municipal buildings, and held a revival service through an interpreter, telling people that it was quite probable that they would be dead in twenty-four hours so had better turn to Christ before that. The local Imam had not approved of this, holding that, if his flock turned to any one, it should be to Allah.

"You have to be careful," the consul said, "about these religious matters. The Imams take them very seriously, and national pride comes in. Also the men are afraid of having the women upset. I mean, it would never do if the women began turning to Christ. It might put all kinds of revolutionary notions into their heads. You do see that, don't you?"

From what aunt Dot and Dr. Halide told us, this started an

argument that only ended when the Vali called to see the consul on business, and the ladies had to retire, to be entertained by the consul's wife in another room. The consul's wife told them that she admired their courage in bathing. For her part, she did not dare. It was true that our bathing parties collected great crowds on the beach, and that the boys threw apples and tomatoes at aunt Dot, who dived and swam like a porpoise, while the women, wrapping their shawls over their mouths, looked on in shocked stupefaction. The consul's wife warned aunt Dot that female bathing was thought extremely immodest at this end of the Black Sea, and was not a good advertisement for the Christian Church, but aunt Dot was so sold on bathing that she thought it must be a good advertisement for anything. But she liked the consul and his wife very much, they had been most kind and civil to us, and she did not want to make trouble for them, though actually that is what consuls expect and are for. So she agreed that perhaps Trebizond was not a good headquarters for an Anglican mission, and that it might be better to start it in the villages back in the mountains. The consul and his wife were relieved to hear this, as it did not seem to them that an Anglican mission could do a great deal of harm back in the mountains, it would not be like Trabzon and the other Black Sea ports, where there is so much pride and gossip and scandal that consuls are apt to be nervous about what their nationals may do next. Whereas in the mountains behind, life is so strange and ignorant always that nothing new is very strange and it does not matter much, and consuls probably never get to hear of it. So we parted from the consul and his wife the best of friends, and the consul said he hoped that we might catch up with the Seventh Day Adventists making for Ararat and the Second Coming, for they are part of the strange and ignorant life that goes on, and has always gone on, round about there. No one is surprised at the things that happen in that country, such as the ark landing on the top of Ararat and letting loose on it all those creatures, and no one would really be surprised

77

if the Second Coming happened there, and it may have been the only religious belief that the Seventh Day Adventists shared with Father Chantry-Pigg, that is to say, he did not actually believe, as they did, that it was due to appear on Ararat that year, but it would not have taken him by surprise, as it would aunt Dot, Dr. Halide, and me. Dr. Halide, who had picked up modernism somewhere in England (perhaps in some of the churches she had mentioned to us), and had even attended a conference of the Modern Churchmen's Union one summer at Somerville College, Oxford, was a partial-diluvian, which was a heresy that the flood had not covered the whole earth, and this had been held by Bishop Colenso in the nineteenth century, and he had told Africans so, and in a novel by Charlotte Yonge the arithmetic book he wrote was condemned on account of this heresy. So when she told Father Chantry-Pigg that she had this heresy too (for she was still in the stage of the Christian religion when people think that heresies and unbelief matter and are important, whereas aunt Dot and I, in our ancient Anglicanism, take them in our stride, knowing that they cannot unseat us), Father Chantry-Pigg told her that this was not a theory to be mentioned to Turks, to unsettle their minds at the very beginning of the great Bible story; and in any case Turks themselves believed in the great and total Flood, which had been taught them by the Prophet. So what with the Prophet, and what with Father Chantry-Pigg, and what with the Seventh Day Adventists, and what with the Billy Graham missioners, and, of course, aunt Dot and myself, Dr. Halide would not really stand a chance of convincing the Turkish women in the mountains of partial-diluvianism, she would be one against many, even though she spoke Turkish. She thought it would be very nice if the Turkish women could have an enlightened modern Anglicanism, to go with the enlightened modern education, habits and hats that Kemal Atatürk had tried to give them, and of course this was the only kind of Anglicanism that he would have liked for them, if he had known enough about Anglicanism to distinguish between one kind and another. But it seemed that the kind they would be told about would be Father Chantry-Pigg's, which was superstitious and extreme, and I thought this would go much better with the Turkish women, who were superstitious and extreme themselves, and really probably Roman Catholicism or the Greek Church would be more in their line. But Dr. Halide said they would not make good Roman Catholics on account of the chilly attitude of the Prophet towards images. I said that if they could not take images it would be no use their being converted by Father Chantry-Pigg, they had better be Low Church, and Dr. Halide said intelligently, " Ah yes, Mr. Scott should be here from Portland Place." Aunt Dot said, " That would be very odd," and Father Chantry-Pigg looked as if he thought so too.

Next day we drove up the coast to see if Rize or Hopa would be more encouraging than Trebizond towards Anglican missions. We crossed the mouths of the Pyxitis, where Xenophon's Ten Thousand camped, but the ground was pretty marshy and did not seem a good camping-place, and we found no intoxicating honey. People were fishing in boats on the river, and I thought I would come on another day and do this. We drove on to Rize, the next port towards the Russian frontier, and bathed on a charming beach, which was much nicer than the black beach of Trabzon littered with harbour construction. The people of Rize seemed happy, and the women were about more, so aunt Dot decided it might be a promising place for mission headquarters. We met on the shore the young Greek student, Xenophon Paraclydes, who was staying there with his maternal grandfather, a well-off Turk who had a tea-garden. When we told him we were soon off for Armenia, he looked wistful, and said he wished he could come too.

The next port, Hopa, seemed less prosperous and encouraging, and was the nearest port to Russia, and aunt Dot looked towards the frontier with a determined expression, for beyond it was the Caucasus. Knowing that aunt Dot's chief passion was for strange and exciting places, and that Christianity and the Church of England and even the liberation of women came some way after that, I felt that her journeys for the A.C.M.S. were partly an unconscious camouflage for this great ambition she had and this delightful hobby she indulged in.

Dr. Halide, on the other hand, gazed through her field glasses at Russia with an expression of the firmest hostility.

"That great devil," she said. "Crouching there in its cage like a savage brown bear waiting to give the death hug. But just let it try. *We* are ready for it."

Aunt Dot said, "Now, Halide dear, it's not a bit of good getting het up about Russia. There it is, and there it will stay. Not a thing we can do about it, so we must just accept co-existence."

Father Chantry-Pigg said that no doubt St. Michael and his angels should just have accepted co-existence with Satan, instead of hurling him from heaven. Aunt Dot said that Almighty God, anyhow, still accepted co-existence with Satan, and also that she didn't know where we could hurl Soviet Russia to if we tried. Father Chantry-Pigg said this would be another job for St. Michael and the angels, when the time was ripe.

"Even I may live, I hope, to see the old Russia of the saints and ikons set free."

Dr. Halide said, "When I see those Orthodox papas all about Istanbul, I can't wish them back to power, not even in Russia, though it would serve the Russians right. They are over, they are the past, not the future."

Father Chantry-Pigg said that our branch of the Catholic Church was in communion with these papas, and I saw that this did not make Dr. Halide think any more highly of our branch of the Catholic Church. Aunt Dot saw it too, and changed the subject to those British who succeed from time to time in slipping behind the Curtain from London, Harwell and such places, of whom she spoke rather enviously. She had a theory, and, though I don't know how she came by it, it may

80

be true, that the great secret these disappearers tell the Russians is that we have no H bombs, nor anything nearly so enormous and peculiar, as we have no idea how to make them, nor enough money to make them with, nor would we actually care to make them if we had, they being so dangerous, expensive and cruel, and so liable to go off at the wrong times and in the wrong places, and therefore, behind the immense and complicated façade of mystery and secrecy that has been erected, what we are so busy making is dummy bombs filled with water, and ever and anon, indeed all too often, those who are privy to this secret flit, heavily financed, behind the Curtain to give comfort and succour to the Queen's enemies by revealing it. And aunt Dot did not see why she could not reveal it quite as well herself.

That evening, when I was going to bed, I found a note-book full of writing in one of the drawers in my room, under the newspaper lining, and I saw that the writing was Charles's, and it was all about the places he had been to in Turkey with David, and it seemed to be part of his Turkey book, and he must have had my room when he and David were staying in Trebizond. I did not know where he was now, so I put the note-book in my suitcase to send to him later. It looked interesting, and I thought I would have a read in it presently, so as to know what not to put myself, in the part I was writing for aunt Dot's book. Other people's books on the subjects one is writing about oneself are annoying sometimes, because if one has read them one must avoid saying the same things, and if one has not read them and says the same things readers think one has copied, and when one's own book comes first, the books that come after it have either copied from it or not copied from it, and when they have copied they get the credit, as readers have forgotten who wrote it first, and when they have not copied they seem to be despising it and to be saying the opposite. It would be better if only one writer at a time wrote on each subject, but this cannot be, and when the subject is a country it would be unfair, as people rely on writing to get them about abroad and let them take money to spend there. At the present time, a great many writers are interested in seeing Turkey, and on account of this many of them are writing books about it, and this has to be put up with. Aunt Dot's Turkey book which I was illustrating and in which I was putting bits, would not be like any one else's really, as it would be mostly about the misfortunes of Moslem women and how their lot could be improved by a change in their religion, but if the Turkish women seemed too much against being converted she would have to give the book a sad end, and it would not be so encouraging for the Church, though of course the Church must never give up hope. But my bits would be about the scenery and churches and castles and ruins and towns, and these had already been so well done lately that I should have to be very careful. The trouble with countries is that, once people begin travelling in them, and people have always been travelling in Turkey, they are apt to get over-written, as Greece has, and all the better countries in Europe, such as Italy and France and Spain. England has not been over-written, at least not by foreigners, on account of its not being very attractive, what with the weather and the Atlantic Ocean and the English Channel and the North Sea and the industrial towns and not having many antique ruins, but above all the weather, for no one from abroad can stand this for long, and actually we can't stand it for long ourselves, but we have to. For the same reason, the Scandinavian countries are under-written, because no one wants to sit about in the open air in the snow and very likely in the long dark night eating soused and pickled fish and writing about what they see, however beautiful it may be, and so there are only a few books about the Scandinavian countries, and those that there are do not seem to sell very well, because so few travellers want to go there. Russia is always written about by those who manage to get there, and in the sixteenth century a lot of English merchants and sailors did, and Muscovy got written up, because it was strange and barbarous; to-day though still strange and barbarous, it has grown more difficult to get into, but those who make it, such as ambassadors, diplomats, scientists, communists, and spies, all write about it, though the books by the spies and the missing diplomats and scientists have not yet come out, and perhaps never will, or perhaps they will only come out in Sunday newspapers as serials, called " How I crashed the Curtain."

Anyhow, we are now many of us writing about Turkey, and I put Charles's note-book away to keep for him. I saw that there was a long piece about Trebizond in it, and I hoped he had when there different thoughts from mine.

Next morning the consul rang up aunt Dot and said had she heard that Charles Dagenham, who had been stopping with a friend at the Yessilyurt a month or two ago, had just been killed by a shark while swimming off Smyrna. I was very sorry about this, as I had known Charles for years and was fond of him, and it seemed, and indeed was, a dreadful end. Father Chantry-Pigg crossed himself and prayed that poor Charles might rest in peace and have perpetual light shining on him, even though that kind of light had not seemed to shine much on him while he was alive. Father Chantry-Pigg added that this was what came of indiscriminate bathing, and probably the Turks, who knew their own shores, were quite right not to. Aunt Dot said, " Poor boy. He can't have learnt shark technique. That is all one needs." We all agreed that it was terribly sad, and I wondered what David felt about their quarrel now. I did not know what to do with Charles's note-book, but supposed I had better take it back with me to England and give it to his people. To forget this sad end that poor Charles had made, I went fishing in the Pyxitis, where I caught several fish rather like trout, and the Yessilyurt cooked them for our dinner that night. At dinner aunt Dot told me that in two days we were leaving Trebizond for our Armenian travelling. I was sorry to leave Trebizond and stop exploring the town and the citadel and palace ruins and fishing in the Pyxitis; I felt I was settling down, and could have put in a month or two there very happily.

However, I was being taken about Turkey by aunt Dot, to help her, and of course it would be fine to see Armenia and Ararat and do some pictures and get some fishing in some of the rivers and small lakes that I saw marked on the map. Actually aunt Dot would enjoy it too, if I could seduce her away from her missionary work. After all, the best two for missionary work would be Father Chantry-Pigg as a priest and Dr. Halide as a doctor and a Turk.

Our most important and difficult job before starting on our journey was to pack the camel. Being a racing camel, it could not carry seven or eight hundred pounds, as a Bactrian could, but it could manage about five to six hundred. Aunt Dot weighed about a hundred and twenty-six pounds, and Father Chantry-Pigg a hundred and fifty-four, which came to two two hundred and eighty between them; and this left, if they both rode the camel at once, nearly three hundred pounds for luggage and sometimes an extra rider. Thus loaded, it would cheerfully (except for camels never being really cheerful) do some twenty-five miles a day at quite a good speed, and would only want a drink every three or four days. Not that we should be going so far and so fast each day; we would go at a leisurely rate, stopping to talk to people and have drinks in the villages.

The day before we started, Xenophon Paraclydes, the Greek student who had been staying at Rize with his grandfather, turned up at the hotel in a jeep, and asked if he could come with us. It seemed that the jeep was one of his grandfather's and that he had been allowed to borrow it, and it would, as he said, be just the thing for the mountain country. So, he said, would *he* be just the thing, talking Turkish to people and rounding them in to our meetings. Aunt Dot gathered that he greatly approved of the proselytising of Turkish women, which would annoy Turkish men so much, as he had a strong hereditary objection to Moslemism, as well as to the Greek Church, and to Kemal Atatürk, who had expelled the Greeks from Turkey. So he did not like people to be Moslems, and he did not like them to be atheists, as the Atatürk régime had desired, and he did not like them to be Greek Church, and he thought the Church of England would do very well for them.

Father Chantry-Pigg asked him if he was any kind of Christian, and he could not think of any kind he was, but supposed that, if he were to become any kind, it would have to be Anglican, as the Greek papas were so extremely backward, and Roman Catholics were known to be idolatrous, and Seventh Day Adventists insane, and American Baptists talked too much, but he did not think he would do anything like that for the present. Father Chantry-Pigg said that would be all right, so long as he said nothing discouraging about the Faith, as he that was not against us was with us, and he hoped that Xenophon might presently come by the great gift of Faith, and might perhaps be the first convert. Xenophon, with all that long history of ikons in his blood, and, through his mother, of mosquery, did not look as if he thought this was really likely, but he said with great politeness that it would, he was sure, be most enjoyable.

Anyhow here he was with the jeep, which solved all our transport difficulties, and was the very thing for Armenian mountains, and actually Dr. Halide and I and Father Chantry-Pigg much preferred it to the camel, so we agreed that we would take turns riding the camel behind aunt Dot, but that in the villages, where people would see us, it would be Father Chantry-Pigg on the camel, as white Arabian camels give dignity and are a sign of prosperity, and look very religious and fine, whereas jeeps have a scrubby, irreligious look. Father Chantry-Pigg remarked that Job in his better days had six thousand camels, and aunt Dot said she was glad for every reason not to have been Job.

We said goodbye to those we knew in Trebizond, who hoped we should come back, for we had amused them, except the schoolmaster, who did not care for what the mayor had told him about our wanting to start an English school in the town, and except the consul, who had the occupational disease of consuls, which is fear of what their nationals will do next to annoy them.

So we arranged to start at seven next morning. Before I went to bed I finished the letter I had been writing for a week to my second cousin Vere. When one of us is abroad without the other, we both keep a kind of daily journal and post it once a week. Vere does not hold with religion, and thought the mission a foolish, troublesome and exhibitionist way of getting about Turkey, though admittedly it was one way, and you had to hand it to aunt Dot for enterprise.

10

So IN the morning, which, though we meant it to be seven, became eleven, partly on account of difficulties in packing the camel so that things did not slide off it, but mostly because starting at seven tends to become eleven, we set out along the coast road, that wound at first through narrow streets, so that we were followed by a crowd, and the jeep went first with Xenophon driving and Halide sitting beside him, and I sat at the back, looking at the view. The camel paced briskly after the jeep, with aunt Dot sitting astride in blue linen slacks and a topee, in front of the hump and holding the reins, which were scarlet, and Father Chantry-Pigg in khaki riding-breeches and puttees, riding on the top of the hump, with luggage slung on each side, though most of it was in the jeep. I thought we certainly looked sensational, and Vere would not have liked it at all, though it was not really exhibitionist, but the natural drama that was in aunt Dot's character, and this is a useful quality to have, and leads to many conversions. It also leads to the enjoyment of lookers on. The people of Trebizond ran after us and cheered. The children learned a little English at school, and had also mixed with some tough young Britons who had been employed on the harbour works, and had picked up from them uncultured remarks such as bye bye, cheerio, cheery bye, old trout, and so on. So they called these after us, shouting " Bye bye, old trout," as the camel went by with aunt Dot and Father Chantry-Pigg on its back and its ostrich plumes tossing on its head.

Father Chantry-Pigg frowned and said, " These lads need a lesson. Calling a lady names like that. One is ashamed to think that they must have learnt it from our countrymen."

Aunt Dot said, " I think it was you he meant," but Father Chantry-Pigg said he was afraid that old trouts were female.

" They can't all be," aunt Dot, who knew natural history and the facts of fish life, corrected him. But Father Chantry-Pigg still thought he was not an old trout, and that if anyone was this fish it would be aunt Dot. And it is a fact that women get called rude names more than men, because it is not expected that they will hit the people who call them names, so they are called old trouts, old bags, cows, tramps, bitches, whores, and many other things, which no one dares to shout after men, though when they are not there men may safely be called sharks, swine, hogs, snakes, curs, and other animals.

We left the town behind us, and followed the road that wound between the mountain Boz Tepe and the sea, by Eleousa Point and the eastern bay, which was broad and slate blue and full of ships, and tumbled with small shabby waves, and we crossed the Pyxitis and Xenophon's camp, and Xenophon the student said his father had named him that to vex his mother, who wanted to call him Mehmet.

From the Pyxitis I looked back at Trebizond and at the Trapesus rock jutting up between the two great ravines shaggy with woods and crowned with the broken citadel walls that sprawled round the Byzantine palace and the small Turkish houses and gardens that crowded inside them, and below was the sea, and the harbour where the Greek and the Roman ships had sailed in and out and rocked at anchor in the bay, and all the trade from Asia Minor and Persia had flowed in by ship and caravan, bringing to Trebizond the wealth and the pride and the power that made her the Queen of the Euxine, and now the wealth and the pride and the power had ebbed away and Trabzon was like the descendant of some great line who has become of small account, and has a drab name, without glory or romance, but is still picturesque, though the new harbour works that had been planned were a desolate litter on the unclean beach, making it a waste land.

Yet I liked the city, and its people, and I knew that I should come back, to find the glory and the legend, to find Trebizond, the ghost that haunted Trabzon.

Now we were among the rhododendrons and the azaleas which had supplied the madding honey to the Ten Thousand, and the May breezes blew about, sweet with the tangs of lemon trees and fig trees and aromatic shrubs; and pomegranates and cucumbers and tobacco plants and gourds and all the fruits you would expect flourished in the woods we went through, and I thought the Garden of Eden had possibly been situated here. When we stopped for lunch in a wood, I asked Father Chantry-Pigg about this but he said no, that garden had been in Mesopotamia.

I do not think I have mentioned that we were carrying a tent in the jeep, which was a pity, as when evening came we had to put it up, which was a very tedious job, instead of sleeping in the Palace Hotel in the nearest village, or in a wayside *han*, which provided more local colour as well as beds. But aunt Dot was a confirmed camper if the weather was fine, and it was always part of my job to struggle with the tent. We usually found a stream to camp by, and it was also part of my job to find the stream. So the jeep went on ahead and found a stream, and by the time Xenophon and I had got the tent up, the camel arrived at a canter, with aunt Dot and Father Chantry-Pigg on its back and the bags bobbing up and down against its sides.

Xenophon called out, " Here is water," and Father Chantry-Pigg looked encouraging and expectant as he dismounted stiffly from the hump, as if he was hoping that Xenophon's next words would be what the eunuch had said to Philip, " what should hinder me to be baptised ? " But Xenophon's next words were, " There are good meals in the Palas Oteli in that village there," and he pointed at a small group of hovels on a hill-side near by, where it did not look as if there would be good meals, but in Turkey you never know, and anyhow there seemed no other

89

meals at hand, so aunt Dot rode the camel up the hill, and Father Chantry-Pigg and Xenophon went on foot, and Dr. Halide and I stayed behind to look after the tent and jeep till they came back, and that is one of the troubles about tents, they cannot be left alone and locked up, so the natives everywhere will find their way into them, even in Turkey, which is very honest as countries go. There is no saying whether, in most countries, natives or travellers are the more dishonest; gypsies and pedlars and nomads and barrow boys, who move on all the time, are bad, but natives who never move at all, and pick things up from those who do, are bad too, and tents which do not lock are safe with neither.

"Your aunt," Halide said to me when the others had gone off for this meal they had heard about, and we were busy arranging the tent, "will, as well as eating, look about to find out what the women and girls, and perhaps too the men, feel about religion. But I can tell her. My poor countrywomen in these ignorant parts of Turkey are tied to the past, and even if this Church society she works for were to start a mission and schools and a Y.W.C.A. round here, no one would go to them. The men would not let the women go, and the women would not wish it, nor let their children attend the schools. Why should they? We now have village schools all over Turkey to which even the girls go. As to religion and customs, they are tied to their traditions, and they will not change yet. Atatürk did his best, but see them now. Their only chance is to go and live in towns. The religion of other races will not cure them, and what Dot calls 'women's institutes' will not cure them. What are these institutes, do you know them?"

I said there was one in every English village, and women met and talked there and drank tea and made jam and put fruit into bottles.

"Talk, tea, jam, fruit in bottles," said Halide, "we have all those in Turkey too, but they do not emancipate women. Education must do that; education only will give them the

90

intelligence to throw their shawls back from their faces and look men in the face and defy them, wearing hats and playing tric-trac in the cafés while men carry the loads. But the Christian Church they will not accept, it is too far from them, even if they throw off Islam. I have spoken to Moslems about it in Istanbul, I have spoken of it to young medical students, after I returned from London a Christian myself. Some will accept parts of it, they will read the Bible, they will admire Christ, as the Prophet did. But further they will not go. They have said to me, ' The Bible, yes. Jesus Christ, yes. Holy Communion, no.' And the Church of England, isn't it, is built round Holy Communion, what you call the Mass. That is what your Father Chantry-Pigg would tell people; and it won't go well with Moslems, I can assure you. I know what I talk about. Dot is a romantic woman, her feet aren't on the ground. She thinks she is practical, a woman of business, but no, she is a woman of dreams. Mad dreams, dreams of crazy, impossible things. And they aren't all of conversion to the Church, oh no. Nor all of the liberation of women, oh no. Her eyes are on far mountains, always some far peak where she will go. She looks so firm and practical, that nice face, so fair and plump and shrewd, but look in her eyes, you will sometimes catch a strange gleam. Isn't it so? "

" Why, yes. Aunt Dot has always had her dreams. They are what take her about the world. She is an adventuress."

" About the world, yes. Tell me, Laurie, does she love her country? "

" Not that I know of, particularly. Why should she? I mean, she usually prefers to be somewhere else, when she can. Most Britons do, I think. I expect it's the climate. Besides, we are a nomadic people; we like change of scene."

" Still, a man or a woman may love his country, her country, even if they enjoy travelling. We Turks love our country very deeply. We see its faults, but we love it. Don't the English do the same? "

"Some do, I suppose. And lots of us quite like it, for one thing or another."

"Every one should love his country." Halide looked handsome and firm and patriotic, and as if she would fight for Turkey to the death.

I asked, "Why should they? Is it a merit to love where one happens to live, or to have been born? Should one love Birmingham if one was born there? Or Leeds? Or Kent or Surrey?" for I never had been able to see why, except that I suppose it is better to love every place and person. "Or Moscow?" I added, to vex Halide.

"Moscow!" She said it like a curse. "Still, I suppose Russians love it. I cannot reason," she said, "about loving one's country. It is just a thing one does. As one loves one's mother."

"I seldom meet mine. She left my father early for another, and we lost touch. She can't have been the possessive type of mother. My father was a priest, so he didn't divorce her. She is usually abroad somewhere. I rather like coming across her."

"My mother," Halide said, "is a great bore. My father too is a bore."

We mused for a while over parents. Then I went on musing about why it was thought better and higher to love one's country than one's county, or town, or village, or house. Perhaps because it was larger. But then it would be still better to love one's continent, and best of all to love one's planet.

Halide said, "I sometimes wonder if Dot can be trusted."

"Well, actually she can be, I mean she often has been. But perhaps she shouldn't be."

"Always her eyes on the mountains. That disturbs me sometimes."

"Well, if she wants to climb Ararat, she can, so far as I am concerned. I shall stay on the lower slopes myself, and pick up bits of the ark there."

"Ararat!" Halide seemed to wave Ararat and the ark away. "I am not afraid of Ararat."

She brooded darkly for a while, I supposed on some mountains not Ararat, of which she was afraid. Turkey is full of mountains, and most of them are rather alarming. But we did not have time to go on talking, because just then the others came back from the Palas Oteli.

"Was it good food?" I asked. "What did you have?"

"Etli pilav, şiş kebabi, simit, zeytun yagli bakla, blossoms with sugar and yoghourt, and wine of these vineyards, that was not good; the food was small town, but cooked o.k. You will see. You will like the blossoms, they are specialité maison in these hotels around Trabzon." It was Xenophon who answered about the food. Aunt Dot was thinking of other things, and said, "Most vexing. All the women are locked up in their houses. It seems that the Billy Graham missioners were there the other day and held a meeting in the village square, and a lot of the women came forward and decided for Christ, or anyhow for the missioners, and the men were so angry that they all locked up their wives and daughters and only let them out now for their work in the fields, and they mustn't say a word to anybody they meet. So there was no chance of any conversation with them, and if these Graham missionaries are going to queer our pitch all about Armenia, we may as well give it up and go elsewhere."

"We had better get ahead of them," said Father Chantry-Pigg. "I gather their progress is slow, as they delay every day for these long meetings. In the jeep, we could overtake them, and reach Ararat first."

"I am not in the jeep," said aunt Dot. "I am on the camel, and the camel will take a week to get to Ararat. Anyhow, I am not set on Ararat, which is a disagreeable mountain, and will be infested with Seventh Day Adventists waiting for the Coming. For all we know, they will be holding services too. Armenia —perhaps the whole of Anatolia—is obviously over-missioned, and I shall say so in my report. Halide and Laurie, do go and have your dinners."

93

Aunt Dot was depressed and out of humour. She got off the camel, and she and Xenophon unstrapped the sleeping-bags and the rugs and led the camel down to the stream for watering and grooming, and aunt Dot fed it roots and azaleas and aromatic shrubs that were good for its teeth, which were pretty yellow, and cud-wort, in case it lost its cud, and Xenophon peered about the jeep engine and fed it oil and water and cleaned the plugs and all that kind of thing, and Father Chantry-Pigg got out his prayer-books and made ready to say evensong or compline or whatever he was going to say that evening, then had a read in his Sarum breviary.

Halide and I walked along the forest path, between the flowering oleanders and azaleas and the copses of oak and beech and spruce fir, and crossed the stream by a foot-bridge and climbed the hill up to where was the village with the hovels, one of which was the Palace Hotel, and it was a small white house with arcades and a small yard in front with mud and goats and hens, and, as it was now become evening, they had just lit the iron lamp that swung over the door and turned on the lights inside, and the radio wailed and whined without stopping, as western radio stops from time to time, to change the tune for another one which sounds the same. We went into the kitchen behind the eating room, to see the food cooking on the stoves in large cauldrons and pick what we would have, which is a great advantage had by Turkish restaurants over most European ones, for not only can you see and smell the dishes but it does not matter not knowing the Turkish for them, as you just point. Of course this did not matter to Halide, who knew what they all were in Turkish, and which were stews of goat and fat and rice and which were minced mutton and rice rissoles fried in batter and onions and which were tough braised chicken stewed with herbs, and what there was inside the stuffed vine leaves and cabbage leaves. She asked for trout, but the trout were all eaten up, so we ate from a lot of different cauldrons, and Xenophon had been right that it was quite well cooked though rather small town, and that the local wine was not good. We dined in the verandah above the yard, and the radio whined so loud that it was a job to talk through it, so mostly we just ate, though passing some remarks every little while.

Halide said, over her vine leaves stuffed with minced mutton, that it seemed obvious to her that the Anglican Church would not stand a good chance against Moslemism, and that, if any Christian religion did, it would be something simpler and more revivalist, like the Billy Graham mission, which didn't have all those doctrines, but spoke to the feelings and just said Come and surrender, then go back to your own churches and worship there, and do not think but feel. Thus they could exchange the Prophet for Christ without much trouble. I said I supposed they would also have to exchange the Koran for the Gospels, for Halide said that, not being intellectual, they would not much notice the differences between these books. Whereas in the organised Christian churches, such as the Anglican, there are creeds and doctrines and baptisms and confirmations and sacraments and the Trinity, none of which would be approved of by the Prophet, and all of which would fuss the Turks.

"So," said Halide, "I don't think Dot's Anglo-Catholic Mission Society is going to have much good fortune in my country, and she will be wiser not to encourage them to think so. The advancement of Turkish men and women must come from within, it must be a true patriotism, as it has been in the past, when we have progressed so much and so fast. When the masses will also start to advance, it will be as when our ancestors rolled across the Asia hills and plains, nothing could stay them. This will surely be again, when the minds of the Turkish masses roll on like an army and conquer all the realms of culture and high thinking. Then we shall see women taking their places beside men, not only as now in the universities and professions, but in the towns and villages everywhere, they will walk and talk free, spending their money and reading wise books and writing down great thoughts, and when the enemy comes, they

95

will defend their homes like men. All this we shall see, but it must be an all Turkish movement; we shall throw over Islam, as Atatürk bade us, but I think we shall not become Christian, it is not our religion. Sometimes I feel that I should not have done so myself when in London, and that it was to betray my country. And now I love a devout Moslem man, and this makes it difficult. He too is a doctor. He wishes that I throw off the Church of England and that we marry. But I could not be a Moslem wife, and bring up children to all that."

She sighed as she ate her yoghourt. I thought how sad it was, all this progress and patriotism and marching on and conquering the realms of culture, yet love rising up to spoil all and hold one back, and what was the Christian Church and what was Islam against this that submerged the human race and always had? It had submerged Antony and Cleopatra, and Abelard and Heloïse, and Lancelot and Guinevere, and Paolo and Francesca, and Romeo and Juliet, and Charles Parnell and Faust, and Oscar Wilde and me, and Halide and her Moslem man, and countless millions more. It kept me outside the Church, and might drive Halide out of it, it was the great force, and drove like a hurricane, shattering everything in its way, no one had a chance against it, the only thing was to go with it, because it always won. All very odd, I thought, but there it was, and I finished my pilaf and got on to the simit and yoghourt, which went well together, then, after coffee, we walked back to the tent, and the moon was rising over the hills and the tent was in a pool of misty light. Our two lanterns stood on the ground outside it, and we saw the white camel lying on its knees beneath a tree, munching and chewing, and Xenophon lay on his back under the engine of the jeep, and aunt Dot was down in the stream, bathing and splashing, and Father Chantry-Pigg was finding the places in his prayer-book for the evening service. Sweet smells of earth and trees and blossoms filled the air, and the running of the stream sounded and I forgot about love and religion and thought how I would go down early in the morning to the stream and see what fish it had. Then I went down to bathe in it, and met aunt Dot coming up.

Before long the tent was surrounded by a circle of boys from the village. They sat staring at us and talking to each other, and it was like being watched by savages in a jungle, and the moonlight glittered on their eyes. Xenophon and Halide told them to be off, and they would go a little way off, but soon crept back and sat staring and grinning with the moon on their eyes, while we said and sung compline, then blew up our Lilos and lay down on them in the tent. Xenophon went and harangued them; he came back saying they were Turkish bullfrogs and had no shame, and that Greek boys would never behave so. Aunt Dot, who had travelled all over Greece, and was half asleep, opened her eyes to say " Rubbish," rolled her blankets about her, and slept. Halide said that not only Greek boys but the boys of half Europe had manners far worse than Turks, and recalled how it had been said often that the Turk was a gentleman. Xenophon and she then continued the conversation in Turkish, and their contentious murmurings mingled with the running of the stream and the rustling of the trees and the chatter of the ill-bred Turkish boys outside the tent and the distant whine of the radio, and it all slipped into the dark dreams that one has when sleeping in woods.

Also when sleeping in woods one wakes very soon, and I woke when the dawn came through the chinks of the tent on to my face. So I got out of my bag, saw that the others were all rolled up in theirs, and got my fishing-rod out and crept quietly down to the stream, past the camel, which lay on its knees with its eyes shut, chewing its cud, and it opened its eyes as I passed and looked at me spitefully, as it always did, and I went on down through the rhododendrons to the stream and walked a little way up it to a pool and sat down to watch it, till I saw fish moving about. I fished that pool for half an hour, and caught three Anatolian bream, then I moved on to another pool and got two more, which made five, and that would be one each for breakfast. So then I walked downstream again and bathed in a running bit of it that wouldn't disturb the pools, and I lay on the grass edge to dry in the sunrise, and thought this was a good expedition we were having, and I was glad that aunt Dot got these notions that took her about the world, which is the chief end of man. And I thought how Turks too had always got about. Father Chantry-Pigg, who had unfair anti-Turk prejudices, owing to his devotion to Greeks and to the Trinity, said that Turkish hordes had always made where they settled barren deserts only fit for camels, and every few centuries they move on somewhere else and make more howling deserts. (Father Chantry-Pigg pronounced it hooling, and I believe this is right, like Cowley and owl.) But those are the common Turks without money and without culture, and the rich Turks, the Sultans and Pashas and eunuchs and nobles and tycoons, have built palaces and mosques and harems and castles and cities, out of the stones they take from the Greek and Roman cities and temples, and fountains play in their courts and beautiful girls dance for them and beautiful boys serve at their banquets and they have troops of concubines and camels and much culture. And I wondered how soon the Turks would feel it was time to do one of their great treks again, and thought this would perhaps be into Greece, which had once been theirs. Then there might be a minaret again on the Parthenon, which looks very pretty like that in the old pictures, and I thought it might improve the Parthenon, these mixtures of styles being often very pleasant. And perhaps the little Turkish houses would come huddling back up the Acropolis and all round it, looking most charming and really setting the Acropolis off. I thought I would mention this idea to Xenophon.

I lay by the edge of the stream among tall ferns, and the bank was covered with rhododendrons and azaleas, white and pink and yellow and scarlet, growing in great bushes beneath spruce firs and large oaks, and the wood smelt of earth and damp moss and sweet blossoms, which I chewed, and the stream ran brown like a Scotch burn, and I felt that I was in a wood in Perthshire, staying with my grandparents, for the smell was the same, and I and the others used to go out early and fish the burn for trout, and I was very happy there. I thought the Turks would be stupid if they left these parts, even to roll on into Greece and mosque the Parthenon.

As I was thinking about all this Xenophon came scrambling down to the stream to bathe. He got into a pool with my landing-net and spooned up fishes, which he said was less trouble than throwing flies for them. I did not think that aunt Dot or any of our clerical ancestors would have approved of this way of fishing, but the main thing was to have fish for breakfast, and we got lots.

While we climbed up from the stream I asked Xenophon what he thought about the Turks going into Greece and occupying Athens. It was not a new idea to him, for his Turkish fellow students sometimes spoke of it, thinking that Greece should be still theirs and that there should be another war of liberation about it. He said, as the Turks always said about the Russians, " Let them try. We are quite ready for them," and I thought how ready nations always were and how brave. As we passed the camel, I gave it some azalea flowers to chew, and it seemed to like them.

Then we got to the tent, and aunt Dot and Halide were boiling water for coffee on the little Primus, and we threw the fish into a pan. When he smelt them frying, Father Chantry-Pigg came out of the tent, pleased about the fish, because it was a fasting day. He said, " To-day I shall be in the jeep," so it was for me to ride the camel.

We set off presently up the road that climbed up into the hills, but the camel took camel paths and scampered up them at a great pace, roaring, and aunt Dot thought it might be in love, though out of season. When we stopped for lunch, Halide, who has done quite a lot of work among mental cases, looked at the camel closely, and into its eyes, and watched the way its mouth worked while it chewed, and said, " Has it had mental trouble before? For I think that it now has."

Aunt Dot said that she believed that camels usually had a certain degree of this, they were born with it, and without it they would never lead the peculiar lives they did, but her camel had, she thought, not yet been actually round the bend. Father Chantry-Pigg said that Pliny had mentioned that camels were given to going round the bend, and that when they did they were apt to become dangerous, as they also did, said Pliny, when interrupted in making love.

Halide, still observing the camel, said, " It certainly looks odd."

" It looks odd because it *is* odd," said aunt Dot. " Camels are." She thought this settled the matter, but of course it did not, because the point about a camel (as about a human) is, is it odder than other camels, or other humans?

Halide said, " I fear we may have trouble with this animal. It ought to see a psychiatrist, or even an alienist. I am nearly sure, my dear Dot, that it is not quite right in its head."

But aunt Dot only said " No camel is ", and got out her note-book to write a little more of her book *Women of the Euxine*, for the less she saw of these women, the more she had to say about them. They had now become to her shackled, gagged and oppressed slaves, who must be liberated at once. Halide too agreed that they wanted liberating, but she now took the view that this must be done by their countrymen, and that foreigners, coming with a foreign religion, would only annoy the women's countrymen and make the position worse. Particularly, she added, when the mission priest was called Pigg.

So what with the women of the Euxine and what with the mental state of the camel and what with Father Chantry-Pigg's view that Christianity must be a universal cure and my view that it was someone else's turn for the camel, we talked contentiously all through lunch. Father Chantry-Pigg always called our coffee and bread and cheese and fruit luncheon, but aunt

Dot and I thought that for luncheon you need a table, even if you only wander round the table with forks, pronging up what you want, and that eating out of doors on rocks is only lunch. But for Father Chantry-Pigg, who, as I have said before, is old-fashioned and class, any mid-day meal, however and wherever it is eaten, has always been luncheon. He usually said over it the longest Latin grace there is, and the hungrier we all were, the longer it became, and sometimes it was Greek. Perhaps this lunch we had that day was really luncheon, as Xenophon had made for it a fine dessert of azalea blossom done up with yoghourt and sugar and nuts, like what we had at the Palas Oteli, and it was a speciality of these parts.

11

THE DAYS went pleasantly by. We got higher into the mountains, and the scenes were most extravagant and dramatic, and all of us but aunt Dot, who feared nothing and had great experience, were frightened of falling off the narrow roads and paths into deep ravines. Father Chantry-Pigg became so alarmed by the jeep and by Xenophon's driving that he returned to the camel, thinking it more sure-footed, even if not at all right in the head. Every now and then Armenian churches or fortresses would rear themselves up on rocky heights above us, and we would stop to examine them.

I had practically decided that instead of writing bits into aunt Dot's book, I would only do the pictures for it, and I would write a separate Turkey book of my own, and perhaps I would call it *Rambling round Anatolia with rod, line and camel*. I liked thinking about this book, and sometimes I would take notes for it, or even write a few lines. I thought aunt Dot's book *Women of the Euxine* was not really well named, as she was filling it with animals and fish and plants and things which were not actually women of the Euxine at all, but she did not seem to think this mattered. Meanwhile, Xenophon, when he had a moment to spare from seeing to the jeep, was writing poetry in Greek, and Halide was writing an article for the Istanbul University Journal on *Evidences of present-day Culture in the Taurus*, which Xenophon said would be an extremely short article if that was its subject, but would take a long time to write, as hunting for these evidences might take years. Father Chantry-Pigg was writing something very retrospective, about the Armenian Church. So we all had our Turkey books to amuse us when we were not otherwise occupied, but this was not often, and I also did a lot of sketching.

We had conversations in the villages and little towns with people in inns and cafés, and with policemen and small officials who talked to us very affably, but usually when we asked them about going to some place they said " yok ", either because it was up high mountains without roads or because it was in a forbidden zone and too near the frontier, or because Turks like the word yok. So soon we gave up asking these questions, and rambled on saying nothing about it till someone stopped us. The camel could not have been more eager and noisy and swift on its feet, and usually it raced ahead of the jeep, with aunt Dot and Father Chantry-Pigg clinging to its reins. In the towns, such as Artvin, we caused a great deal of interest. But when aunt Dot and Halide talked to any of the local people about Anglican mission schools, it did not seem to go well, for they had lately had the Graham missioners on their motor bicycles, and the imams had forbidden their flocks to have anything to do with these infidel religions, and, when Father Chantry-Pigg said Mass in the square, Artvin men and boys watched us from their tric-trac in the café, but the women and girls were not allowed anywhere near us because women and girls are easily upset and cannot resist temptation as men can. This was the same in the other towns, and when we had spent a night at Ardahan aunt Dot got tired of prospecting for the Church, which she began to think was too good for Turks, and set her mind on a small lake we saw on the map, which seemed only twenty or thirty miles on from Ardahan, in the mountains, and aunt Dot had stayed there once long ago, and had had very good fishing there, so we thought we would stay there for a time and have a rest, and give the camel a chance to relax, before pushing on to visit Ani, the ancient ruined Armenian capital on the frontier, on which Father Chantry-Pigg had set his heart.

It was a tiresome climb up to this lake from Ardahan; the

jeep boiled and the camel roared and only aunt Dot seemed happy. I do not care for going up mountains, and it seems waste to cross over them in a boiling jeep or on foot, and when you come down on the other side be no higher than you were before, and tunnels through them, like the Mont Cenis, would be better. However, when we looked down from the track we saw the little lake shut by rocky mountains, and it was a very good deep green colour because of the pines and the gloomy shadows of the hills, and wild geese were flying over it, and we came down to its western corner, about a mile from a village, and there were some boats drawn up on the shore and a group of fishermen's houses and a khan. The lake was about half a mile long, and had an island, and was well outside the forbidden frontier area.

We put up the tent and hired a boat and rowed out for the evening rise. That is to say, aunt Dot and I did, while the others explored round the shore and walked to the village to see what the food there was like. We got several good trout, and two odd-shaped fishes which must have been a specialité of that lake, as we had never seen them before. Altogether it seemed a nice lake; I thought that next day I would land on the island, where there was a ruined church standing on a rocky ledge above the water.

At supper, which we had at the khan, we ate our fishes, fried by the cook there, and the specialité fish were not bad, and I said I did not mind how long we stayed on this lake, it was much better than driving or riding about Armenia hawking the C. of E. to infidel dogs who thought we were mad and were probably right. Father Chantry-Pigg did not mind how long we stayed there either, as he had observed several ruined Armenian churches about the landscape which he would like to see closer, though the one he most hankered after was St. Saba, some way the wrong side of the Russian frontier. He went off on foot next morning with Xenophon, while I went on the lake again, and Halide and aunt Dot went to the village to see if it had any evidences of present-day Taurus culture for Halide's book, and any women longing to be liberated by the Anglican Church.

Over supper, aunt Dot said there had not seemed to be much of either of these, though there was a village institute and a school with a school-master.

" And the women? " asked Father Chantry-Pigg.

" Cowed," said aunt Dot. " We couldn't get anything interesting out of them. They were afraid to speak out. Of course they're not allowed to speak to strangers at all, really. One keeps remembering what Lynch says about Turkish women in his book—' they appear conscious of some immense and inexpiable sin '."

Father Chantry-Pigg said nothing, but he looked as if he thought the Turkish women, and indeed all women, did well to be conscious of this, for they had committed it in Eden, and had been committing it ever since merely by existing. He did not dare, however, to say this to aunt Dot and Halide, who erroneously believed men to be equally sinful, and even (in Turkey) more.

" By the way," aunt Dot went on, " those two spies are staying at the inn there: you remember, the ones we saw in the Troad. I knew them in a minute."

" What would you think they are doing here? " I said.

" Spying, naturally," said aunt Dot. " They had fishing-rods, and no doubt presently we shall be seeing them on the lake. Perhaps this evening. Laurie, I was told that round that island with the little ruin is very good for fish in the evening. We might have a try."

Father Chantry-Pigg said, " I did too much climbing about to-day. To-morrow I should like to ride the camel to that church beyond the one on the near ridge."

" Very well, I'll come with you. It needs exercise, anyhow. It was very restive in the night; stamping and pawing and crying out; people don't like it."

"It is very mad," Halide repeated, with indifference. "It gets no better."

Aunt Dot and I had a very good evening on the lake, and we caught quite a number of fishes. The two spies turned up, and landed on the island, spying all about it and peering into the little ruined church, where probably messages had been hidden for them, and it was a pity we had not found them first. They crouched behind a wall while they put the documents in their pockets, at least I supposed this was what they were doing, but aunt Dot said that when they reappeared they were chewing something, and that they must be eating the documents up. All this spying was very interesting to us, as we had so often heard of it but had not known that it flourished in Turkey to this extent.

"I wonder how much they are paid," said aunt Dot, "and how often."

"And who by," I said. "Were they collecting it on the island, would you say?"

Aunt Dot thought not, because they would not have eaten it. "Of course they have Contacts, who hand them their pay quietly, in the bars of hotels, so that it looks like ordinary black market business. I believe the pay is excellent." I could see that she was envious of this pay, and would have liked to get some of it, for she sighed.

"We all have our price," she said, "but we don't all get it. If our government had seen fit to employ me to report to them about Turkey, I could have told them quite a lot. Though I can never imagine what it is that countries want to know about each other, or what they flit away by night to tell. I expect none of it is the least use really. But governments get these fancies, and are prepared to pay for them, so why not be in on it? How many spies have we noticed in Turkey?"

"About fifty so far, I should think. But of course there must be hundreds more that we haven't noticed, because they spy

106

more quietly. Istanbul was a hot-bed of them, and Trebizond a nest. And this lake seems a hunting-ground."

"Well," aunt Dot said, "these fish seem to have stopped rising. They rise better in the Caspian, where they are as thick together as sardines in a tin—sturgeon, salmon, herring, most delicious, all pushing up to be caught. Now that *is* a sea. A pity Turkey has no access to it." She sighed, thinking of that Caucasian sea so crowded with fish and the mountains and forests sweeping down to its shores.

" And," she added, " that dear little lake just beyond the frontier, where the road runs through the gap. . . . But we had better go back. I can hear that camel crying out. I suppose it wants its supper. I think it gets tired of all that cud it chews, nasty thing. We'll ride it out early to-morrow, and Father Hugh can see all the churches he wants, and I shall gallop it about to make it quieter. It keeps trying to run away with me now; I have to tug on the reins. If they broke, it would race off like a rocket, heading for its herd in Arabia. I dare say it's homesick and doesn't care for Turkey. I sometimes feel I agree with it."

She was silent for a minute, then said, " How I should like to see the Troglodyte city of Vardzia. And the river Terek, and all that Cossack country Tolstoy wrote about. Not that he wrote enough about it; *The Cossacks* would be a much better book without Maryana and so much love interest. And really that applies to so many novels. But I should like to see all that country, its mountains and forests and villages and Tartars and herds of horses. A pity it's the wrong side of the curtain."

There were a great many things that aunt Dot desired to see, and it was certainly a pity that so many of them were the wrong side of the curtain.

We rowed in and went to bed. All night I heard, between sleeping and waking, the lake water running on the shore, and the pine trees singing on the hills, and the mosquitoes droning and the wild geese squawking and the radio whining from the khan, and the camel grumbling and stamping outside the tent, and I believed that it loved another camel and could not at all get over it, and I felt that I ought to go and tell it how I was in a similar plight and could not get over it either, so that we could comfort each other.

In the morning, quite early, it raced off up a hill to see churches, with aunt Dot and Father Chantry-Pigg clinging to its back, and the fir woods and the oak woods and the rocky mountains received them all.

12

I HAD a very nice day on the lake, fishing and landing on the island, and watching the flying of the geese, and walking round the shore with Halide, while Xenophon pottered about the village and drank in the café with the villagers. The spies were still about, and Halide had a few words with them, as they pretended they only spoke Turkish, but they were very reserved men in any language, and would not say much about fish. Halide and I had a bathe from the island, but the spies did not, and this rather shook my faith in aunt Dot's theory that they were Britons, still, they had to impersonate Turks after all, and though Turks sometimes bathe, they do not do so with British enthusiasm, and anyhow undressing and leaving their clothes about is awkward for spies. It was a beautiful hot day, and when it was evening the fishes dashed up from the deep and leaped for flies. Halide, who was out in the boat with me, said, " How you and Dot love angling. It is your favourite pastime, no ? "

" No."

" What then do you prefer ? "

" I think, love."

" Oh, love. Oh, that goes without saying, that one prefers love the best. I too, even with all the other things that I like to do. But then, love is also sad, and stabs the heart."

" Yes."

" You too find that, poor Laurie. But still you find it great pleasure also."

" Great pleasure, yes."

We both reflected on Love, its pleasure and its pain, while I threw flies over the green lake, and Halide was remembering the Moslem man whom she loved but would not marry because of not wanting to be a Moslem wife, and I was thinking of Vere.

"Dot, now," said Halide presently, "she is older, she is perhaps past this delicious torment and grief. Or is one never past it? One day, Laurie, you and I will know that. But Dot seems to have all her heart in other adventures—seeing the world, spreading the Church, hunting fish, riding that detestable camel about, enquiring into the sad lot of women, and just being alive. By the way, are they not out a long time? I hope they are well and safe. That camel is not to be trusted. Trust no camel, and less this one than most. It could have escapades, it could run wild, it could break its reins and be off who can say where, at a speed to break the neck. It gets dark. Shall we row back?"

We rowed back, and it got darker, and still aunt Dot and Father Chantry-Pigg and the camel tarried. We had supper at the khan, and sat on there smoking and sipping raki and talking, while Turks played tric-trac at little tables beneath the trees. They told us what we knew, that it was unsafe to be out so late on these hills, for the paths were difficult and steep, and the camel might miss its footing or its way. Besides which, they might get too near the frontier zone and have trouble with the guards. Or even—it had been known—so near the frontier itself as to have trouble with the Russian guards on the further side. Halide and Xenophon and the local Turks had animated conversation about all these possibilities, and at last Xenophon said we had better go up the forest path on foot and search. So we all set out through the hot night along the narrow track that wound through the pine woods up the steep ridge that shut the lake to the east. The church they had gone to see was on the ridge beyond, and would be a walk of about four or five miles. It took us two hours to get there, guided by a young man from the khan. Of course there was no sign of them, and nothing to shew that they had passed that way. The little Armenian church stood on the steep hill-side, grown about with trees and shrubs, and branches pushed through the roof, and yellow lilies stood about, smelling very sweet. The moon rose from behind the hill and shone on the further rim of the lake below, but the church was still in shadow, a black haunt of murdered Armenian ghosts.

"What next?" said Halide, sitting down to rest on a broken wall. "What direction after this? It might be anywhere, yes? There is no way to know."

The Turkish young man said it would be better to wait for daylight before looking further. In the morning the police would come from the near villages, and a search could be made. Useless, he said, to go on over these hills and ravines with no direction, and we might find ourselves by mistake in the frontier zone. For his part, he thought they had got themselves arrested by the guards and had been taken off to some village police station, where they were being held.

"It is the Russians," Halide said, and her voice had the tone of doom in which she habitually spoke of these persons. "They are being held by Soviet Russia. Or else they have been shot. Do you know what I think? I think that Dot had it in her mind to cross that frontier. Or else was it the camel, which ran away with them? Or Father Hugh, whose mind roved after churches on the other side? But I think they have crossed it, and are now behind the curtain. If they are alive," she added, and her voice shook with anger and fatigue.

As it seemed no use to stay there or to go on in the dark towards that bourne from whence no traveller returns except under police escort, we stumbled back to the lake, and this time it took us two hours and a half, the shadows and light of the moon deceiving us so that we lost the paths and strayed among deep woods and ravines, and the smell of the woods and ravines was sweet and heavy like honey, and it was so hot as the moon climbed higher that we were soaked in sweat, and wild creatures

III

that we did not know nor want to scuttered about among the bushes, and Xenophon was bitten in the leg by a small jackal.

It was three o'clock when we came to the lake shore, and a tiny cool wind stirred, and the first thing we did was to swim in the lake, because we were so tired with the heat and with climbing up and down, and we lay in that bland dark water and let it slip about us in moon-silvered ripples, washing away the sweat and the scratches and the aching, while the faint light of dawn began to glimmer. Then, after Halide had cauterized and bandaged Xenophon's leg, we got into our sleeping-bags and mosquito nets and lay in the tent while the morning grew, and it was odd not to hear among the night noises the peculiar noises the camel used to make, chewing and snorting and moaning and giving little cries as it dreamt, as if it was answering the wild geese, and I wondered where it was making these noises now.

When day came, we got hold of several policemen from the near villages and they and Halide and I, because Xenophon's leg still hurt him, deployed about the hills on strong little ponies, which was much better than walking. These ponies scrambled first to the ruined church, then down into a ravine, and the policemen shouted and we shouted, in case our party should be lying injured in this ravine, but no one shouted back, and Halide said, "How should they answer from the place where they now are? We should not hear them," and the place was a Russian gaol, or perhaps a Russian hole in the ground with earth shovelled over them, while the camel cavorted about Soviet Armenia with Soviet soldiers on its back, and perhaps cried aloud with love for some new-met mate.

Halide said we must ride on to the frontier, where we might get some news, but the police said yok, that was impossible for civilians without a permit, and the whole party might get shot on sight. For the police, it was possible, and three of them would go and reconnoitre, while the other two rode back with us to find out if any news had come in.

Halide said, " There will be no news."

We rode back, and Halide and the two policemen talked all the way about what had probably happened and about what to do next. Every little while Halide would say in English, " But it will be of no use. Nothing will be of use. They have gone, and they will shortly be digging for salt, if they are let to live. It must go up to high levels. Ambassadors, ministries, heads of states, your archbishops, Sir Winston Churchill, our President, yes, and our army chiefs—they must all write. Our friends must not be permitted quietly to disappear, as if they were scientists or engineers, or young men from the Foreign Office. It is not to be borne."

I agreed that it was not to be borne, unless of course they had disappeared on purpose, because they wanted to see Russia. I remembered aunt Dot's expression when she had mentioned the troglodyte city of Vardzia, and always when she spoke of the Caucasus, the Caspian, and what she called " that little lake on the frontier ", and Father Chantry-Pigg's talk of the Armenian church of St. Saba, and how they were both fanatics when they set their hearts on anything, and were like those who seek a country and will not be deterred. I thought they would get themselves out of Russia in the end, for aunt Dot always got out of the jams she got into, even the harems of African cannibals.

And Halide was wrong when she said there would be no news, for the thing we saw when we rode down the track to the lake shore was a group of Turks, and Xenophon among them, crowding round our camel, which stood with its nose in the air, masticating with that unpleasing sideways motion of the lower jaw which is one of the reasons why we dislike camels. It did not look tired, but indifferent and bored, and its broken scarlet reins dangled from its neck.

" The camel! " cried Halide. " Dot's camel. She has been thrown."

But when we got off our ponies and joined the camel,

Xenophon shewed us an envelope addressed to me which he had found in its saddle-bag, and in it was a letter written in aunt Dot's lively scrawl, " Dear Laurie, we are going in, but not the camel, which would be in the way and attract too much notice. Please do not start a fuss with police, consuls, the A.C.M.S., etc. etc. We shall be all right, and shall see and do a number of things we both want to do. Don't know when we shall be out. Don't wait in Turkey for us, why not take the camel south into Syria, Lebanon and Jordan? If you get to Jerusalem, as we planned, you might tell the Bishop and Stewart Perowne and Katy Antonius that I shan't be coming for the present. Look after the camel, give it plenty of hard roots, they are good for its teeth. I expect it will miss me, I know you don't like it, but be sympathetic sometimes, even if it seems to take no notice. It is very reserved and backward, and I think has its own troubles and ambitions and seems to live in the past and I think it broods sometimes on Sex and is a bit frustrated, so treat it gently. Better not let it run after other camels as it goes about, it is very excitable. Well, my love for now, I shall be seeing you before very long, no doubt."

The letter was signed in full, " Your affectionate aunt, Dorothea ffoulkes-Corbett", and the name, written out like that, seemed a valiant and gentlewomanly flourish, a gesture of dignified valediction before departure into the unknown, an emblem of the adventurous pride and resolution which was the firm background of aunt Dot's brisk eccentricity and *joie de vivre*.

I passed the note to Halide; she read it with a face of doom, then folded it tightly and returned it to me.

" I guessed it," she said, in a low, urgent voice in my ear. " Dorothea has gone through the curtain to Spy. It was a project that I thought she was playing with. But who can be paying her? Not your government; not mine. She is being paid by Soviet Russia, and she is reporting to it on Turkey. Father Pigg too. Oh they have sunk to the lowest vileness, they are betraying Turkey to the enemy for gain, in order that they may see the Caucasus and the Russian part of that miserable Armenia with its churches and troglodyte dwellings and those dirty Cossacks and Tartars, and fish for female sturgeon in the Caspian and go on that little lake beyond the frontier gap, and eat caviare and drink koumiss from wild mares. Oh yes, I know well what Dorothea hankered after and would sell her soul to get. But she cannot have got it, they will be captured and taken to Moscow to tell what they know about Britain and Turkey."

"It's not very interesting, what they know about Britain and Turkey."

"Interesting! They will spin romances, they will tell fine tales that those brutes will like to hear, they will broadcast them to the people. *That* is what Dorothea and Father Pigg will have to do, not at all rambling about the Caucasus and fishing for caviare in the Caspian and in that silly little lake. Yes, that is what Dorothea, who was my friend, has sunk to. Well and good, I leave the Church of England, perhaps I marry a Moslem. No, that is impossible, I cannot be a Moslem wife. From now on, I am a Turkish free-thinker. And so much for your Mass and Vespers and Compline and Matins and Evensong and incense and beautiful Prayer Book and missals, that were to convert Turks but do not keep people from betrayal."

"Well," I said, "how could they? No Church has ever succeeded in doing that, I suppose. But it does seem a pity. Though we don't know that they mean to betray anything, actually. Perhaps they only mean to see a little of the country."

"Without visas, without leave, without Russian money, my poor Laurie? They would be noticed and discovered immediately, they would be arrested, shot, taken to Siberia to dig for salt. All that salt—what can it be wanted for? To eat with caviare? To preserve herrings? No, to make bombs. Or, because Dorothea and Father Pigg are not so young, they might put them in gaol and keep them there."

"Well, it would be better they should tell stories about Britain than that. Aunt Dot thinks we haven't made any atomic bombs, and that Russians ought to be told so, to discourage them from making them too. Then we would like to tell them how well off we are, and how progressive our social arrangements are, and all that."

"She would not be let out of gaol to say that," said Halide bitterly. "No, they will have to say what will please. . . . But do not let us talk about it. We will not speak of it to any one here; we must let them think it a kidnapping. You must not show that letter, Laurie; you must destroy it."

I too thought it a letter better not shewn to Turks, and when Xenophon asked what was in it, I said, "nothing in particular, just private messages about the camel."

Xenophon said, "But why messages? Did they then know they would not be coming back to us?"

I said you could never be sure, when near a frontier, on which side you would be, and for how long, and anyhow aunt Dot sounded all right.

"They had money with them?" Xenophon asked. "They had some luggage, clothes, maps? They will surely be made prisoners. The British consul at Trebizond, he will do something?"

"I expect so," I said. "We must tell him. Unless they come back before long. But we won't get up a great fuss, Xen. There's nothing much, anyhow, that the police here can do, as they seem to have left Turkey for a time. You and Halide had better tell them that."

"We had better leave here to-morrow," Halide said. "In any case I must get back to Istanbul soon."

"And I to Rize," said Xenophon. "My grandfather will be missing his jeep."

Halide spoke to the police, and they had no objection at all to giving up the search. The disappearance of these two foreign tourists would become yet one more incident in the files at the local police stations. Tourists come and tourists go; Turkish police remain, and do not take much notice, and any one venturing near the Russian frontier is out of bounds and no one is responsible for him. Either these tourists would return, spewed out of Russia, or Russia would retain them; the Turkish police regarded the alternatives with bored, lethargic eyes.

I took charge of the camel, and tethered it to its tree and unharnessed it and fed it, and mended the broken rein. It seemed tired, and I wondered how far it had wandered since yesterday. When I went into the tent, Halide was looking among aunt Dot's things.

" She has taken her canvas bag," she said. " And of course she will have her wallet, for that she always kept on her. She had planned to go, oh yes, she had planned it. What did she keep in her wallet? Her travellers' cheques, no doubt, and her passport. And of course Father Pigg had his. You have yours, Laurie? "

" I have some travellers' cheques, yes."

But it was aunt Dot who paid the bills, it was her expedition and her money; I had not brought much. It seemed likely that I should have to get hold of some more. Perhaps I could touch some consul somewhere. Or perhaps not. Many people think that this is partly what consuls are for. Consuls do not always agree with this. Time would show. But it is certain that they do not always care much for the nationals under their protection. I thought that Halide would be warmer-hearted.

She and I looked at aunt Dot's things, to see what she had taken with her. Her miscellaneous collection of medicine bottles was here; it was a largish collection, because she did not know what most of them were, or for what complaints, on account of chemists not caring to say more on the labels than " The Pills ", " The Tablets ", " The Mixture ", and other non-committal titles, so aunt Dot took a great many of these anonymous bottles about with her on her travels and ate and

117

drank them at random when she ailed. She always said this anonymity was owing to chemists not being able to read the handwriting of the doctors who wrote the prescriptions, or understand the abbreviations of the Latin words used, so that they did not know whether they were making up the things prescribed or another set of things altogether, and thought it better that the labels should be non-committal. I once asked a doctor why he did not write better, and also in English, and put the words in full. He said that the patient might in that case understand it, which would not do. Chemists too think that this would not do, and that if a patient knew what he was taking it might even prove fatal, because of nerves, and the name of the remedy might make him guess what illness he had, which would prove still more fatal. For the same reason, nurses who take temperatures will not ever tell the patient what the thermometer says, because that too might end in death, so that people who like to know how they are getting on have to hide their private thermometers somewhere about them and take their own temperatures. Anyhow, aunt Dot had left her array of bottles and pill-boxes in her medicine bag, and I thought I would take them along with me and eat and drink some of them when I felt weak, and one would counteract another, so they would do no harm.

Aunt Dot had taken, we thought, a change of clothes, her sleeping-bag and pillow, her toilet things, and a map. "Father Pigg too," Halide said. "His shaving things are not here." Since her revulsion from the Anglican Church, she no longer called this priest Father Hugh, as we did, and the tone in which she said "Father Pigg" was full of Moslem distaste for the word.

"He was in it too," she said, with her melancholy rancour. "They planned it together, this wicked expedition. I think too that he has taken that little altar and candles, and those relics of his. Perhaps he will convert the Soviet Union to the Church of England, and make those barbarian Tartars who raid our frontiers pray to the saints." She said this not with hope, but with anti-Anglican irony.

"You never know," I said, "do you."

We packed up everything, our own things, aunt Dot's, and Father Chantry-Pigg's, and Xenophon got the jeep ready, and we arranged to leave early next morning by the road we had come by, I riding the camel and the others in the jeep. Xenophon was rather gloomy, now that the expedition was so nearly over and he had to return to his grandfather at Rize, who, he now admitted, had not given him leave to take the jeep and might make himself unpleasant about it. Whenever Xenophon displeased his Turkish grandfather, the old gentleman said it was his Greek blood, and that his daughter Mijirli had so much vexed Allah when she had married into Greek scum that he had visited her with this deplorable offspring.

13

WE SET off next morning for the Black Sea. I rode the camel, and the jeep had to keep down almost to its pace, which, when it ran, was about 25 m.p.h. over the rough mountain tracks, though in the flat, such as a desert, that kind of racing camel can do about 40. I liked much better riding in front of the hump, as I now could do, and saw for the first time why aunt Dot enjoyed riding this animal.

It was melancholy to turn our backs on the mountain lake, and on the mountains and lakes beyond it, and on all the Armenian places we had hoped to see, such as Kars and Ani and Ararat (on whose lower slopes even now Seventh Day Adventists awaited the Second Coming, their transports and their hymn-singing recorded by the B.B.C. for a Home Service programme), and the splendours and islands and fishing and Armenian churches of Lake Van. But we had not the money for the expedition, and anyhow the heart and zest had gone out of it, and all the time I was wondering what was happening now to aunt Dot, and when we should get any news, and I wanted to get to Trebizond and the consul, and we had melancholy meals by the road and gloomy nights in the tent, grumbling at one another and at the camel, and Halide brooded over the betrayal of Turkey by aunt Dot, and her own breach with the Anglican Church, and the dichotomy between Love and the Islam oppressions of women, and Xenophon brooded over what his grandfather would do to him at Rize about the jeep.

On the third day we got to the point in the mountains where it is proper for travellers sighting the Black Sea to cry "Thalassa" (or if they prefer it "Thalatta") like Xenophon's army, but we were too dispirited to do this, and anyhow Halide, who despised this Greek army, would not have copied its ways, either in crying Thalassa or in making herself sick and mad with honey from the local rhododendrons, which she was now sure that the camel had done, if not aunt Dot and Father Chantry-Pigg too. So we descended the mountain quietly, except for the camel, which began to roar when it smelt the Euxine rhododendrons, and galloped on ahead of the jeep.

Our road did not come down to the sea at Trabzon, it took us to Hopa, the port eighty miles up the coast and the nearest to the frontier. At Hopa Halide would board the steamer *Trabzon*, which would be starting next day from there on its return journey to Istanbul. Xenophon would drive the jeep to Rize, the next port, and I would ride the camel down the coast to Trabzon. So at Hopa we parted.

Halide said, " Directly I get to Istanbul, I shall speak to the British Embassy and to our own Intelligence Service and Police. Everything that can be done to rescue them, even should they not wish to be rescued, shall be done. Be assured of that, my dear Laurie. But it is no use to hope too greatly. It may be many years before we see our friends again."

Whenever Halide talked like this, in her discouraging Turkish fashion, I felt very unhappy, and saw a vast twilight wilderness full of chained prisoners digging away for salt, or shackled in deep dungeons incommunicado, or kept in Moscow offices where they pour out glib streams of news about Britain to men with lumpish Slav faces who write it all down in note-books to show to the Kremlin. Then I see the lumpish men conducting aunt Dot about the most horrid buildings—hospitals and prisons and schools and institutions and factories and maternity homes and collective farms, and these are the very things that she has always sworn she will never look at, but where are the wild mares and wild Cossacks on the wild mountains, and where the frosty Caucasus and the lakes brimming with female sturgeon that she crashed the curtain to see? It must be something like

Hades, or Purgatory, for round her wander all those vanished Britons of whom we hear no more on this earth, their pale faces brooding on physics and nuclear, or on the doctrines of Karl Marx, so that they remember Britain as a dim dream which they do not wish to recall, and they too are Tenebrae types, dejected and cast out and brought into darkness and compassed with gall and labour, except for a few who are rewarded and prosperous and fattened up with boiled chestnuts like Circassian slaves and living in large suites with wine and dice and dancing girls because their value and their services to the Soviet Union are so very great. But aunt Dot and Father Chantry-Pigg would not care for any of these types, and in the mornings they are aroused by songs sung by University students about the efficiency of collective farms, and then it is like a Butlin Camp.

And all the time perhaps instead of all this they are shot and dead.

I thought it would be easier to think of them as pampered friends of the Soviet Union, allowed to go about (though watched by policemen), and talk with Russian clergymen about intercommunion, when Halide was no longer with me, because she looked so much on the dark side, so I was relieved when she boarded the *Trabzon* next morning and when the *Trabzon* at last felt full enough of cargo and people to steam away for Istanbul, Xenophon had already driven off to Rize, and I saddled the camel and took the coast road at noon, and as it was about eighty miles I thought I would sleep at Rize and make Trebizond the next evening.

The road to Rize was very pretty, with the sea on the right, green and warm and full of fishing boats and barges, and the mountainy shore climbing up steeply on the left, all grown with fir forests and ravines (which should have been rivers but they were mostly now dry) sweeping down to the shore, and tobacco fields and tea gardens smelling of tobacco and tea, and roses and oleanders smelling sweetly of flowers and honey in the woods. We ambled along, sometimes walking at three or four miles an hour, sometimes trotting, sometimes cantering at about twenty-five. I was very comfortable up there, and thought that when we were in England again I would ride the camel more often than before. Then I thought that presently, if I obeyed aunt Dot's behest that I should go south to Lebanon and Syria and Jordan, it would be on the camel that I would go, and it would be cheaper than if I had my car, for camels cost much less than cars in food and drink, and need practically no running repairs. So I thought a new kind of life (cheaper, and more getting about) was before me, and that when aunt Dot came back and rode her own camel again, I would get hold of another camel, which would also be a white racing Arabian, and we would journey together all about the east. For there is no doubt at all that one rider is enough on a camel, and that when there are two the one behind is not really comfortable. I thought aunt Dot would be pleased when I told her I was going to get another camel. I kept thinking of things I would tell her, and the only thing I would not think was that perhaps I should not be telling her anything again at all, or not for a very long time, so I got all kinds of things ready in my mind for her.

When we were nearly into Rize we heard a great jingling of bells ahead, round a bend in the road, and a roaring, and when we came round the bend there was a camel caravan, six big brown Bactrians with two humps, loaded up with baggage, and their riders dressed in shirts and baggy blue breeches and leather chaps like Kurds from the mountains, and they were unloading the packs and herding the camels on to a little grassy beach where a river came down to the sea down a deep ravine, and the river for once had water, and spread into a pool between rocky banks before it got to the beach, and the camels were up to their knees in it drinking. Between drinks they threw up their heads and gave solemn roars, as Matthew Arnold heard the waves doing on Dover beach, when they gave melancholy long withdrawing roars which sounded to him like the ebbing of the Christian faith. Then the camels would dip their heads again to the river and drink and drink, storing up enough to last them four days, and their bells jingle-jangled like goat-bells on the Alps, and the drivers shouted and sang and pulled at their reins, and presently pushed them right under the water and made them kneel, and threw the water over them with pails to wash them.

When my camel saw the others, it began to whinny and paw and get excited, just as aunt Dot had said it was not to do, and the Bactrians which saw it got excited too, mine being female and they most of them male, and mine also being Arabian, and white, and more class and breed, so I was afraid that love might occur. The drivers seemed afraid of this too, for they shouted and signed to me to ride on quickly, and they held on firmly to their camels' bridles, and ducked them in the water to blind them and prevent them thinking of love. I put mine at a trot through the river where it ran into the sea, and it splashed up the little waves with its feet and cried aloud with eagerness, but I beat it with my switch and told it to hurry on, and the drivers shouted at us in a discouraging way, and I made it canter on into Rize, with the sunset in our faces and on the smooth green bay that bloomed like a large pink oleander, and round the bay were the tea-gardens and the rich fruit orchards that climbed the wooded hills, and the white houses of Rize clustered round the harbour.

I stopped at a café in the town for coffee, but I did not call on Xenophon, who would be in trouble at his grandfather's tea farm, and I was in trouble too and did not feel like conversation, so after I had drunk my coffee and eaten a melon and some figs and a lot of hazel nuts, I found a stable for the camel and a room for myself near it and had a bathe in the warm evening sea, then dined in the garden in the square and went to bed. I would have liked to stay longer in Rize, which was very charming, but I knew it was Trebizond that I must stay in and wait there for news of aunt Dot, and I knew as well that Trebizond held something for me, and it was there that I might try to sort out my own problems too, in the derelict forlorn grandeur of that fallen Greek empire with its ghosts, and its rich sweet fruits, especially figs, and its sea full of the most exotic fish, which I had heard a lot about and would like to catch. I would stay at the Yessilyurt hotel, and go and see the consul, who would do whatever consuls do about their vanished nationals, and his wife, who was very kind and had liked aunt Dot and would cheer me up, and when my travellers' cheques came to an end, I supposed the consul might lend me some money to go on with. And I should find waiting for me at the Post Office some letters from Vere.

All these things Trebizond held for me, and I left Rize very early next morning to get there, and when at noon I came to Xenophon's Camp and the Pyxitis, with its mouths spreading about into the sea, and the great mass of Boz Tepe ahead, and Eleousa Point, and the harbour bay at its foot where the fishing boats lay in deep purple water for the noon rest, and west of the harbour the white-walled, red-roofed town and the wood-grown height beyond it between the two deep ravines, where the ancient citadel stood in ruin, with houses and gardens climbing up among its broken walls, I felt as if I had come not home, not at all home, but to a place which had some strange hidden meaning, which I must try to dig up. I felt this about the whole Black Sea, but most at Trebizand. A nineteenth century traveller said the only thing the Black Sea was good for was fish, and particularly the kalkan balouk, a sort of turbot with black prickles on his back, which was most delicious. But I do not much care for that kind of turbot myself, and anyhow he was quite lost and unimportant in this long strange, frightening, and romantic drama for which the Black Sea and its high forested shores seemed to me to be the stage. Some tremendous ancient drama long since played, by Argonauts, by Jason and Medea, by the Greeks, by the Ten Thousand, by imperial Rome, by the Goths, by an army of Christian martyrs, by Justinian and Belisarius, by the Byzantines, by the Comneni, by the Latins, by the romantic last Greek emperors commanding the last Greek corner of the Euxine, and ultimately by the Turks who slew the empire; and still the stage was set, and drama brooded darkly in the wings. The deep ravine, shaggy with woodland, the high ruined palace and keep, the broad shining of the sea beyond the curve of the littered shore, the magnificent forested mountains that ranged to right and left behind, this was all Greek; but the shore itself was all Turkish, and the narrow-streeted climbing jumbled town, with here and there a minaret, here and there a Byzantine church that was now a mosque or store-house.

So again I rode through the narrow streets to the central part of the town where the Yessilyurt stood, among small streets that sold grain and vegetables and tools and pots and hardware, but its front faced on a square and the public garden, and not far off down steep streets were the harbour and quays. The manager of the Yessilyurt sat smoking outside his front door, and seemed pleased to see me. He knew practically no English, but my phrase book had "What room have you to let?" and he had a room, and I think he was asking after my companions, but I found no phrase which said, "They have left me, they have gone to Russia," so I put up one finger and said, "One room only," and the porter helped me to take my luggage off the camel and carried it up the stairs to the large central room out of which all the bedrooms opened, and I had the room I had been in before. Then I went back to the camel and took it to the stables where it had lodged and gave it mash and root and things, and said, "Lie down. Go to sleep," and it knelt down and chewed, and I thought that later I would give it something from a bottle that aunt Dot had among her medicines which was only labelled "The Mixture" by the chemist, but aunt Dot had written on it "Camel sedative. Dose according to need." I thought that either she had never given the camel any of this stuff, or that the stuff was no good. However, I decided to give it a dose later, in case it made it stamp and kick and roar less in the night, as this annoys the people near it a good deal.

I wondered if, when I rang up the consul later, he would perhaps ask me to dinner, so that we could discuss what to do next. But when I rang, and asked for him, the answer was yok, he had gone away three days ago for Istanbul and London on leave, and the vice consul was doing his work. The kavass put me through to the vice consul, who was a Cypriot Turk, but of course could talk some English, and I said I would come to the Consulate and see him.

When I saw him I remembered that we had met him with the consul once. He lived down by the quay, and was concerned mostly with ships and cargoes and lading-bills and the commercial troubles of British merchants and sea captains, for there are a great many of these. I saw that he would not be at all up to getting aunt Dot out of Russia or finding out what had happened to her or where she was. He was hardly up to making a call to Istanbul, for they never seemed to get through, whereas the calls of the consul quite often did this. I saw that he did not think it important that two Britons had disappeared to Russia; he said that it often occurred.

"They perhaps go too near the frontier, and then the Russians shoot. Or some Soviet guards perhaps cross the frontier and take them prisoners."

"Or," I said, "they went across on purpose, to see things."

The vice consul said this would not be possible, the Arpa Çay, which was the frontier there, was a steep-banked river ravine, and was guarded all along.

"And what things would they wish to see?" he added.

I said, "The scenery, I think. Mountains, lakes, rivers, all that." Seeing that the vice consul thought this notion absurd, I added, "And perhaps military secrets, to report to the British and Turkish Governments."

That interested him more, and seemed more likely; with

spying he was at home. I had enlisted his sympathy; his round face smiled.

"Ah. You think they spy for us, your friends. In that case, we must wish them luck. But there is nothing we can do to help them. Perhaps your ambassador can make enquiry. But if they spy, they are outside help, they must help themselves. I am sorry."

They don't spy, I thought, at least I don't think they spy, except on the fish in the lakes and rivers. But our ambassador will make enquiry; Halide will see to that. Perhaps we should report to the newspapers; perhaps the press attaché will see to that. For my part I shall wait in Trebizond, because that is where they will come back to.

I left the Consulate. I regretted the consul and his wife; this vice consul was no use. I dined alone in the Yessilyurt restaurant, and a kind young Turk whom we had met before came and talked to me. I could see that he did not think we should see aunt Dot and Father Chantry-Pigg again, for Turks take this view of those who vanish into Russia. But he said he would come down with me to the quay to-morrow and get some fishermen to let me go out in their boat with them and try for kalkan baligi. But I would rather try for khamsi baligi, which is still more liked, and I had read that great quarrels had always occurred in the market place when this popular fish arrived. Hadrian, who always did so much good to towns, and particularly to Trebizond, had a brass model of it put on a column outside the city gate, and this brass fish was a talisman that attracted the similar fish in the sea to throw themselves on the shore, thus saving the fishermen trouble, and this went on till the birth of that spoil-sport Prophet, which immediately, it seems, checked talismans and magic, so unlike Christianity the religion he started was; though what was he doing stopping magic in Trebizond, a Christian Byzantine city? Actually from all accounts a very great deal of magic flourished all through the Middle Ages in Trebizond, which was a great city for enchanters and magicians. But these khamsi baligi did cease to come up on the shore for themselves, though the sea still abounded with them during the fifty days of the season of southerly winds, and I suppose it still does. Evliya Efendi, writing in the seventeenth century, says that when the boats full of them arrive in harbour, the fish-dealers sound a horn and people stop whatever they are doing, even praying, and run after the fish like madmen. And one cannot be surprised, for it is a shining, white fish which does not smell fishy, does not set up a fever, cures sore mouths, and is an aphrodisiac of extra-ordinary potency, and this is a thing Turks value. It is used in cooking many dishes, to which it gives a peculiar flavour, and it is a dish of friendship and love. So I hoped that I should catch some, as it was now the season for them.

After dinner I went and saw the camel, and gave it a dose of its sedative, then I sat in the gardens and read the letters I had collected from the Post Office, which were from Vere, who was one of a party sailing about the Aegean in the yacht of a press lord, and they might be touching next at Smyrna. Reading Vere's letters, and writing a reply to them, filled me with adultery again, our love being so great, and Vere so amusing and so much my companion, and I wanted very much to be on the Press lord's yacht, though yachts always make me sea-sick. I wrote to Vere till long after dark, telling about every-thing, while at the other tables men played tric-trac, and the radio in the trees among the electric lights crooned away like cats on the tiles, and the lights twinkled out from the fishing boats in the bay.

Then I went up to the Yessilyurt smoking-room, which was one of the rooms that opened out from the round central hall on the first floor, and Turkish men of trade sat about drinking water or raki or coffee and reading commercial papers and smoking. The hotel resounded with the shouts of men of commerce trying to telephone to Samsun, which was a thing I remembered that they tried to do most of the day and night, and whenever one of our party had tried to telephone to the Consulate or to Istanbul, we had been stopped by a call from Samsun coming through for someone. I wondered how they had done business between Trebizond and Samsun in the nineteenth century, when the Yessilyurt was the Hôtel d'Italie and then the Hôtel des Voyageurs, and nothing was changed in it except that now there was a telephone which did not work very well, and a chain to pull which did not always work very well either. But it was a nice hotel, and I liked the management and the porter and the restaurant and the old lady who did the rooms, and I felt at home here. I do not know when it was built.

I studied my Turkish phrase book, and learned a few of the most useful ones by heart. One was about how I did not understand Turkish well, which I copied into my note-book and carried about with me; I also copied Is there anyone here who speaks English, can you tell me the way if you please, thank you, what does this cost, it is too much money, and some enquiries about meals. I crossed out some phrases I had copied before, such as when does the bus, train or other conveyance start, because henceforth I should always be starting on the camel. I had already mastered, "Where can I put my camel?" When I had done some Turkish, I read Charles's manuscript about Trebizond, which was very good and detailed, and I decided to take it with me as I went about the town looking at things, as it would help me to identify them and was very intellectual and full of information. Charles also quoted things from the books of old travellers such as Bessarion in the fifteenth century, and Evliya Efendi in the seventeenth, and various nineteenth century tourists, so that one got many views of Trebizond, how it had looked at different times, and he had put in bits from H. F. B. Lynch, and descriptions of church paintings from Professor David Talbot Rice, and a lot more, besides what he had invented himself, so that altogether it was a very interesting manuscript. I supposed that what I had was probably a rough draft, and

that there was another copy, which would get published somewhere, and I thought I would keep this one so long as I stayed
in Trebizond, as it was such a good write-up of the town and
neighbourhood. He quoted from Evliya Efendi about the
delicious wines and fruits, fine-flavoured grapes, cherries red as
woman's lips, apples called Sinope, figs called something else,
which are the sweetest in the world, purple oranges, pomegranates and olives, and as for flowers, there is a ruby-coloured
pink peculiar to this place, each blossom like a red rose and
perfumes the brain with the sweetest scent. I would look out
for this pink, as well as for all that fruit, and the delicate fishes
that abounded.

Another feature of Trebizond life which interested me seemed
to be Charles's own discovery. It had been generally noticed in
the Middle Ages that this famous but remote Byzantine city had
been much addicted to magic and full of notorious wizards,
enchanters and alchemists, who practised their arts for the
benefit of those who paid for their services. It had, of course,
been a Byzantine art and industry; the arrival of the down-to-
earth, matter-of-fact Ottomans, who were neither clever nor
imaginative, and thought wizardry wrong, had driven it underground, to be practised privately and lucratively by the Greeks
who remained in the city after the Turkish massacres. Like the
fairies, the enchanters were of the old profession. The expulsion
of the remaining Greeks by Atatürk had, you might suppose,
dealt the obsolescent craft its *coup-de-grâce*; but this was not, it
seemed, the case, it still survived in corners, among pseudo-
Turkish Greeks who turned an honest lira by selling fair winds
to fishing-boats and charming the desired fishes into the nets,
making up love potions (which no doubt they merely labelled
" The Mixture "), making marriages fruitful, restoring youthful
beauty to women and youthful potency to men, bestowing on
unborn infants the gift of maleness (money refunded if the charm
failed to work, unless the enchanter could prove that the mother
had not obeyed instructions faithfully), blessing business enter-

prises so that they resulted in wealth, and inflicting all kinds of malicious damages on enemies by means of wax images and so on.

Charles and David had been introduced to some of these enchanters, who plied their craft unostentatiously in back streets or in walled gardens up in the citadel, concealed from the eyes of scornful and disapproving Moslems. Here they wove their spells, made brews and stews out of herbs and fruits and fishes which should bring love or death, fortune or grief, success or disaster, to their consumers, and in quiet corners of the beach they sold winds and blessed the nets and cast spells on the fish in the sea. Charles had noted some of their names and addresses on his manuscript, though I supposed not for publication, and I thought I would seek them out and buy myself some luck, and a nice potion for the camel. Altogether, it did not appear that in Trebizond, so long as you did not call it Trabzon, you could have a dull moment.

I went to bed, and fell asleep to the shouts of those who had got through to Samsun but could not attract the attention of their correspondents there, and this seemed not surprising, as it was so late at night that the Samsun men of affairs would have left their offices, in which they did not seem anyhow to spend much time.

14

NEXT MORNING while I was having breakfast, the Imam came into the restaurant, the one who had followed us about on Corpus Christi when we had the procession and service in the square, and had started a counter-offensive. It seems that he had heard of my return, and came round to warn me. So he warned me through my Turkish friend who sometimes explained to the management what I was trying to say, and who was called Odobasiogli and he had an office on the quay. He told me that the Imam was saying that I must hold no services in Trabzon, or he would call the police. I said I would hold no services, since I was not, as he could see, a priest. Then he said I was not to make speeches to the people, and I promised I would not. He looked at me suspiciously, remembering aunt Dot and Father Chantry-Pigg, and asked where they were, and I said to Odobasiogli that I wished I knew. The Imam looked as if he knew quite well that they were up to no good somewhere, but so long as it was not in Trabzon, he could do nothing about it, so he went away after he had drunk two cups of coffee, which relieved me, as I was a good deal frightened of this Imam, a very dignified and formidable clergyman.

After breakfast I went out and rode the camel up the hill and across the ravine to the palace and citadel, and I had a good plan of the citadel which Charles had copied from Lynch. The porter said things to me in Turkish as I went out, but I said my phrase about not understanding Turkish. Many Turks can't understand that any one really does not know Turkish; they think that if they say it often enough and loud enough it will register. They did this whenever I said this phrase; it seemed to start them off asking what seemed to be questions, but I only said my piece again, and after a time they gave it up. Sometimes they said " Yorum, yorum, yorum? " as if they were asking something, but I did not know what this word meant, and I thought they were mimicking what they thought I had said. This was all that happened about it for a few days, then one day when I said my piece to the porter he nodded, and went to the telephone and rang someone up, and presently a man came downstairs and bowed to me as I stood in the hall and said something to me in Turkish. I had better explain here that there was a misunderstanding which was my fault, for I discovered some time afterwards that I had copied the phrase in the book which was just below the one which meant " I do not understand Turkish," and the one I had copied and learnt and had been saying to every one for days meant " Please to phone at once to Mr. Yorum," though this seems a silly phrase to print in a book for the use of people who do not know Mr. Yorum at all and never would want to telephone to him. But one day this Mr. Yorum turned up at the Yessilyurt to stay, and the porter saw then what I wanted him to do, and he rang Mr. Yorum in his room and asked him to come down. But I did not know then about my mistake, and when Mr. Yorum spoke to me I said again that I did not understand Turkish, and he bowed and pointed to himself. I thought he must be offering to interpret for me, but when I tried English on him he shook his head and said, " Yok, yok," and I could see he knew none. So I looked up the Turkish for " What can I have the pleasure of doing for you? " and said it, but of course I did not understand his answer, and that is the worst of foreign languages, you understand what you say in them yourself, because you have looked it up before saying it, but very seldom what the foreigners say to you, because you have not looked up that at all. So I looked through the book till I found " Who are you, sir? " and he said in reply, " Yorum, Yorum, Yorum." I saw there was some confusion somewhere, but there is always so much confusion in Turkey that I let it go, and ordered drinks for both of us, and we drank them, then he went away, quite pleased that I had telephoned to him to come and have a drink. The hotel people began to be more pleased with me too, so I thought Mr. Yorum must be quite an important man. Several more times on other days I told them I didn't understand Turkish, and each time they rang Mr. Yorum and he came, and sometimes I paid for the drinks and sometimes he did. He and the hotel staff must have thought I had taken a great fancy to him, or else that I was working up to some deal I wanted to do with him. The fourth time he came I had a bright idea that I would give him one of the Mowbray manuals that aunt Dot had left behind her in a haversack, because I thought she would wish me to continue her Anglican work on the natives, and also each manual which I got rid of would lighten the haversack, which bumped against the camel's side when it ran. So I went and got this manual, which was called " Why I belong to the Church of England", and was slightly translated into Turkish by Halide, and I gave it to Mr. Yorum, who thanked me and looked at it with surprise, and it must have dawned on him that I was a missionary and was trying to convert him and that this was why I kept sending for him.

After that he must have told the hotel staff not to ring him for me again, for when I said please to telephone him at once they shrugged and threw out their hands and looked at me despisingly. Soon after this I looked at my phrase book and saw what I had been saying all this time. It seemed an extraordinary thing to say, let alone to be necessary in phrase books, but no one had seemed surprised, and the fact is that no one is much surprised at anything in Turkey. I wasn't myself. They didn't even seem much surprised by the Anglican Church, as most people abroad are, though when I saw it beside Islam and the Greek Church, I didn't myself think it looked nearly so odd, or was, in fact, as Churches go, really odd at all. I mean, with religion you get on a different plane, and everything is most odd. It only goes to show that human beings are odd, because they have always been, on the whole, so religious.

My days settled down into a kind of rhythm. In the mornings I would often go fishing, either in a boat with fishermen casting nets, while I fished with a rod and line, or I would ride the camel down the shore to the Pyxitis or some other river, and fish there for whatever there was. Sometimes there were some nice salmon. In the sea I got several kalkans, and sometimes a khamsi, for it was the khamsi season. I would give them to the hotel cook to cook them in any way he liked for my supper. After I had fished in the morning I would lunch on sandwiches and raki, and spend the afternoon exploring, and sketching, often up in the citadel. There was much less left of this and of the Byzantine palace than there had been at the end of the last century, when Lynch was there and drew the plan that Charles had copied. The outer walls then seem to have been almost complete, and set with massive towers; houses were built inside and against them, but now they were jumbled ruins whose stones had been used to build a labyrinth of cottages and small houses in a wilderness of gardens, so that the plan was lost and overgrown in roofs and trees and shrubs. But one could make out, with the plan, how it had been, and where the different fortresses and gates had stood, and there was the palace banqueting hall, roofless now, and grown with long grass and fig trees, and eight pointed windows with slim dividing columns. It was in the banqueting hall that I spent most time, painting, and looking out through the Byzantine windows at the mountains behind, and down the steep ravine to the sea in front, and imagining the painted walls and the marble floors and the gold-starred roof, and the Comnenus emperors sitting on their golden thrones, and the Byzantine courtiers and clergymen talking to one another, intriguing, arranging murders, discussing the Trinity, in which they took such immense interest, talking to the barbarians who were threatening the Empire and later, after Constantinople had fallen, and Trebizond was the Empire, debating how to hold it, how much tribute could be paid to the Turks, how best to form an anti-Turkish union, whose eyes should be put out, what envoys should be sent to Rome. All the centuries of lively Byzantine chatter, they had left whispering echoes in that place where the hot sun beat down on the fig trees and the small wind and small animals stirred in the long grass. The Byzantines had been active in mind and tongue, not lethargic like the Turks; they had had no dull moments, they had babbled and built and painted and quarrelled and murdered and tortured and prayed and formed heresies and doctrines and creeds and sacramentaries, they had argued and disputed and made factions and rebellions and palace revolutions, and to and fro their feet seemed to pass among the grasses that had been marble floors, and the last Greek empire brooded like a ghost in that forlorn fag end of time to which I too had come, lost and looking for I did not know what, while my camel munched the leaves of the carob tree outside the ruined wall.

Churches had once stood all about this place; St. Eugenios, on a hill below the palace, and the Cathedral of the Gold-headed Virgin, now both mosques, could be seen from the windows; once, it was said, there had been a thousand churches in Trebizond. Most were destroyed, many were now mosques, many used for dwellings or store-houses. Charles had a list of a lot of them, and what state they were now in, and I could see that he had got it from Lynch and from David Talbot Rice and Patrick Kinross, and I thought he ought to have acknowledged these books, but perhaps he had meant to when his own book should be printed, or perhaps he had hoped that people would think he had found it all out for himself from observation and from older writers, who reflect more credit than new ones do, but now that poor Charles was in purgatory, no doubt he was learning to be more truthful. Anyhow, his manuscript was very helpful to me as I went about Trebizond.

Sometimes when I was sketching the citadel and palace, someone or other would come out from one of the cottages or gardens and speak to me. He would point to the ruins and say "Turkceji," looking proud and pleased. But I would shake my head and say, "Yok. Ellenceji," but I did not know exactly what was the Turkish for Greek, because my phrase book had left it out, like Armenia, though it had put in nearly all the other countries, even Rusya. I suppose this was on account of Kemal Atatürk having turned out the Greeks from Turkey, so that they did not need to be spoken about any more, and the Greek buildings that were everywhere about, both ancient Greek and Byzantine Greek, and the Roman ones too, which were all so useful to the Turks for taking stones from for new buildings, had always seemed to them to be Turkish, because they were in Turkey. When the Turks went on repeating that the Comnenus palace and the citadel were Turkceji, I got annoyed, and as they would not accept "Ellenceji," I said "Inglizce," because I thought we had as much claim to have built the palace and citadel as Turks had. They looked at me suspiciously when I said this, as if they thought I was saying that the English were planning to capture and occupy Trabzon, and I wished we could do this, except that we spoil anywhere we occupy, like Cyprus and Gibraltar, with barracks and dull villas and pre-fabs. Actually, if we took Trebizond, we should probably clear away the Turkish houses and gardens and alleys from the citadel and cut away the trees and shrubs and leave it all stark and bare like a historical monument, and we should build a large harbour and fill it with cargo ships, and a few battleships, and there would be a golf club and a yacht club and a bathing beach and several smart hotels and a casino and a cinema and a dance hall and a new brothel, and several policemen, and a hospital, and a colony of villas, and soldiers and sailors would crowd about the streets and call it Trab, and large steamers would ply every day to and from Istanbul bringing tourists, and the place would prosper once more, not as it used to in its great days when the trade from Persia and Arabia flowed into it by sea and caravan, and gold and jewels glittered like the sun and moon and stars

138

within the palace, for no place any more can prosper like that, but it would be prosperous, it would have trade, it would have communications, inventions, luxury, it would have great warehouses on the quays and a great coming and going. The Greek enchanters would dive further underground, Christian churches would spring up, Anglican, Roman Catholic, Dissenting, where the British colony would pray, and there would be a Y.M.C.A. and a Y.W.C.A., where billiards and boxing would be played, and English women would drive about the streets and sit and drink coffee and tea in the gardens, and Turkish women would become like the women of Istanbul and Ankara and Izmir, walking the streets with naked faces unashamed. And that would be the end of the Trebizond of legend and romance, and of the Byzantine empire fallen under the heavy feet of Turks but still a lovely, haunting, corrupt and assassinating ghost, whispering of intrigue and palace revolutions and heresies in the brambled banqueting hall among the prowling cats beneath the eight Byzantine windows.

Seeing me thinking out this fine plan for British occupation, the Turks who had said " Turkceji " shrugged their shoulders at so wild a folly and went back into their little gardens to drink coffee while their wives dug for vegetables. But presently a small elderly man crept out of a lean-to which was propped against a ruined wall and almost hidden by a very large fig tree, and climbed some broken steps up the banqueting hall, and, looking cautiously about him for Turks, whispered to me, " *Ellenes, Ellenes.*" I said " *Panu,*" nodding and smiling to show him how completely I accepted his view. He repeated it, however, saying, " *Ellenes. Ou Barbaros,*" and I echoed " *Ou Barbaros,*" with such conviction that he would realise how utterly I was with him in rejecting the barbarian ascription, whether Turkish or English. I was pleased that the Greeks left in Trebizond still called their conquerors the barbarians, together with foreigners from the north such as myself. We exchanged a little conversation in his decadent and my rudimentary Greek. I asked

him if he was a *pharmakeus*, and I really meant sorcerer, but it
would also do for chemist, so that there need be no offence. He
nodded and looked crafty, and as if he hoped for a deal, such as
selling me a love potion or a fair breeze, so I saw he was an
enchanter in his spare time, and told him we might meet again.
Then, lest we should get involved in expensive sorcery, I went
away and unhitched the camel and rode down across the ravine
to Hagia Sophia, which stands a mile to the west, looking down
at the sea shore from its hill. It is the nicest of the Byzantine
churches; it was turned into a mosque, but is now decayed and
redundant, like so many mosques, for after all what can they
want with all those mosques that stand about everywhere, so
they use them instead for oddments and tools and ladders and
buckets, and the floors are covered with planks lying across
pools of mud, and the whitewash is peeling off the Byzantine
frescos in slabs, and the inside of Hagia Sophia is a mess. I mean,
it was, when I was in Trebizond, but it may now be cleaned
up. The frescos were once very glorious and beautiful, and there
are some good carvings. But the really beautiful thing about
Hagia Sophia now is the outside, which is cruciform and
clustered with tiled gables and apses, and the south façade has
rounded arched windows and moulding and carving, and a long
frieze running right across under the windows, with carved
flowers and trees and even figures not too much mutilated to
see what they are, and the Comnesus eagle spreads its wings on
the keystone of the great arch. And above the frieze there runs
an inscription which says,

Ελέησον με, σῶσόν με ἀπὸ τῶν ἁμαρτιῶν μου, ὦ ἄξιε Κύριε ἀντίλαβοῦ
μου

Hagia Sophia stands alone above the sea, derelict and deserted,
with a tall bell tower standing near it, and I found it usually
shut, except at the times when they were doing something inside
it with the ladders and buckets and planks. I did not mind,
because it was the outside, and particularly the south front, that
I liked to look at and to paint. I would try and make out the

figures on the frieze, and could do this most easily when sitting on the camel, and there were various Genesis creatures, such as Adam and Eve and the serpent, very toughly carved among trees and fruit and animals. It took me some time to make out the Greek inscription, which was about saving me from my sins, and I hesitated to say this prayer, as I did not really want to be saved from my sins, not for the time being, it would make things too difficult and too sad. I was getting into a stage when I was not quite sure what sin was, I was in a kind of fog, drifting about without clues, and this is liable to happen when you go on and on doing something, it makes a confused sort of twilight in which everything is blurred, and the next thing you know you might be stealing or anything, because right and wrong have become things you do not look at, you are afraid to, and it seems better to live in a blur. Then come the times when you wake suddenly up, and the fog breaks, and right and wrong loom through it, sharp and clear like peaks of rock, and you are on the wrong peak and know that, unless you can manage to leave it now, you may be marooned there for life and ever after. Then, as you don't leave it, the mist swirls round again, and hides the other peak, and you turn your back on it and try to forget it and succeed.

Another thing you learn about sin, it is not one deed more than another, though the Church may call some of them mortal and others not, but even the worst ones are only the result of one choice after another and part of a chain, not things by themselves, and adultery, say, is chained with stealing sweets when you are a child, or taking another child's toys, or the largest piece of cake, or letting someone else be thought to have broken something you have broken yourself, or breaking promises and telling secrets, it is all one thing and you are tied up with that chain till you break it, and the Church calls it not being in a state of grace, which means that you can get no help, so it is a vicious circle, and the odds are that you never get free. And, while I am on sin, I have often thought that it is a most strange thing that this important part of human life, the struggle that almost every one has about good and evil, cannot now be talked of without embarrassment, unless of course one is in church. It goes on just the same as it always has, for as T. S. Eliot points out,

> The world turns and the world changes,
> But one thing does not change.
> In all of my years, one thing does not change.
> However you disguise it, this thing does not change,
> The perpetual struggle of good and evil.

But now you cannot talk about it when it is your own struggle, you cannot say to your friends that you would like to be good, they would think you were going Buchmanite, or Grahamite, or something else that you would not at all care to be thought. Once people used to talk about being good and being bad, they wrote about it in letters to their friends, and conversed about it freely; the Greeks did this, and the Romans, and then, after life took a Christian turn, people did it more than ever, and all through the Middle Ages they did it, and through the Renaissance, and drama was full of it, and heaven and hell seemed for ever round the corner, with people struggling on the borderlines and never knowing which way it was going to turn out, and in which of these two states they would be spending their immortality, and this led to a lot of conversation about it all, and it was extremely interesting and exciting. And they went on talking about their conflicts all through the seventeenth and eighteenth and nineteenth centuries and James Boswell, who of course was even more interested in his own character and behaviour than most people are, wrote to his friends, " My great object is to attain a proper conduct in life. How sad will it be if I turn out no better than I am! " and the baronet he wrote this to did not probably think it peculiar, and Dr. Johnson thought it very right and proper, though some people like Horace Walpole naturally found Boswell a strange being, and when he had to meet him Horace " made as dry answers as an unbribed oracle." But they went on like this through most of the nineteenth century, even when they were not evangelicals or tractarians or anything like that, and nineteenth century novels are full of such interesting conversations, and the Victorian agnostics wrote to one another about it continually, it was one of their favourite topics, for the weaker they got on religion the stronger they got on morals, which used to be the case more then than now.

I am not sure when all this died out, but it has now become very dead. I do not remember that when I was at Cambridge we talked much about such things, they were thought rather CICCU, and shunned, though we talked about everything else, such as religion, love, people, psycho-analysis, books, art, places, cooking, cars, food, sex, and all that. And still we talk about all these other things, but not about being good or bad. You can say you would like to be a good writer, or painter, or architect, or swimmer, or carpenter, or cook, or actor, or climber, or talker, or even, I suppose, a good husband or wife, but not that you would like to be a good person, which is a desire you can only mention to a clergyman, whose shop it is, and who must not object or make dry answers like an unbribed oracle, but must listen and try to assist you in your vain ambition.

Having spent a little time looking at Hagia Sophia again, and making a drawing of the tiled apses, I rode down to the shore, and along it to the quays, where I liked to watch the cargoes being unloaded from the ships. I used to spend a lot of time doing this. I always hoped to see a ship come in loaded with beautiful Circassian slaves, who would then be sold on the quays, though I knew that I could never afford one of these. But I waited in vain, and presently I rode along the shore road to the western ravine, which is very deep and woody and cool, and I rode up it by the stream that runs through it among bracken and oleanders and moss and toadstools, where the camel and I like to sit and rest on hot afternoons. We came out through the town looking for the mosques and churches and bazaars which were on Charles's plan but not usually to be found, owing to Charles's plan being partly drawn from an older one in another book, still, some were there, and some had left bits, now parts of houses or shops, and it was an interesting search. I called at the Post Office for letters, and there were many for aunt Dot and a few for Father Chantry-Pigg, and two for me, one from Vere and one from Halide. I opened Halide's first, to see if she had any news. She also sent some London newspapers which she had bought in Istanbul. She had called at the British Embassy and told them about the disappearance of our friends.

"I did not say," she wrote, "that it seemed to have been voluntary. No, I told them that it was probably a kidnapping, one of those cases of dragging people over the frontier into Soviet territory and then seizing them and holding them captive. There have been many such cases. The Embassy does not know what they do with their captives. Perhaps they make them work, or make them talk, who knows?" I thought, it would be very easy to make aunt Dot talk, any one could do that at any time. Perhaps she was now sitting talking gaily away, fed with vodka and caviare and paid with roubles, giving the news from the west, from Turkey, from London, from everywhere. I hoped so. I always think that countries should share their news and gossip in a neighbourly way, and not practise apartheid and secrecy, for that is not the way to be friends. Father Chantry-Pigg, with his strong anti-Soviet prejudices, might not be so conversational as aunt Dot, indeed, he never was, still, he could tell them something about the Anglican Church, though what they would really want to know was how our football teams were shaping this year, and what were the prospects of Arsenal being annihilated by the Dynamos, and, though neither of the two would really know much about this, no doubt they could think up some views.

"So," Halide went on, "the Embassy are making enquiries,

144

and are telling the Soviet Embassy that they take a grave view. Of course the Press has got hold of it, you will see that it is in these papers that I send. If any reporters try to ask you questions, as they do already to me, say nothing of Dot's letter, the disappearance must appear to be altogether involuntary, or else they will simply join the great army of those who have Chosen the Curtain, and their government will do no more for them, and, however greatly I grieve over their action, I could not wish for this."

I opened the papers. There were four Sunday ones and the *Church Times*. Of the Sunday ones, two were meant for the upper and upper middle classes, one for the lower middle, and one for the barely literate. One of the upper class papers had a paragraph on an inner page, recording the disappearance a few days ago of two British travellers in Turkey, Mrs. ffoulkes-Corbett and the Rev. the Hon. Hugh Chantry-Pigg, the well-known and lately retired vicar of St. Gregory's Church, Westminster, who had been exploring the ground for an Anglican mission to Turkey. It seemed that they had gone into the prohibited frontier zone near Cildir in Turkish Armenia, and had vanished, though their camel, a white Arabian, had returned to the small lake where they had been camping with friends. My name was mentioned, also Halide's. The *Church Times* had rather more, on account of the Anglo-Catholic Mission Society, and Father Chantry-Pigg being such a well-known priest. The two popular papers had a great deal more, and particularly the quite illiterate one, which had a splash on its front page saying,

" TWO MORE BRITISH BEHIND CURTAIN
 CLERGYMAN AND WIDOW VANISH
 WAS IT PREMEDITATED, OR SOVIET FRONTIER
    GRAB?
 TURKISH WOMAN DOCTOR SAYS NO CLUE
 GRAVE VIEW OF EMBASSY
 WIDOW KNEW MACLEANS "

145

Beneath these headlines there were two columns of personal gossip about both of them, but particularly about Father Chantry-Pigg, clergymen being even more News than widows. Owing to their advancing years, there was not much to be made out of the Romance angle, but there was quite a lot about St. Gregory's and its ways, picked up from the congregation, from the new vicar and the curates, and from the People's Churchwarden, who was very proud of St. Gregory's and its extreme tradition and reputation, which, he boasted, outdid all the other extreme London churches.

" Pretty close to Catholicism, I suppose? " the reporter had asked him.

" We are a completely Catholic church," the People's Warden had told him, and this reply had, it seemed, so fogged the poor reporter's mind that he had written no more about St. Gregory's, but left his readers to make what they could of it, while he turned to the widow's white camel and her acquaintance with the Maclean family. I too was mentioned, as waiting for news beside the Black Sea, in company with my aunt's camel, to which I was devoted.

Having read all this, I turned back to the upper class papers, read the book reviews, and then saw a full-page article signed David Langley, and it was called " The Lure of Trebizond ". So I read it, and saw that it was exactly the same as part of Charles's manuscript that I had; it was about two thousand words long, and would be followed by others on Sundays to come. There was a piece above it about David, and how he and Charles had been travelling in Turkey together, but unfortunately Mr. Dagenham had been killed by a shark, and these articles by Mr. Langley were instalments of a book he was writing, which would be published next year.

As the manuscript I had was all in Charles's handwriting, and full of Charles's corrections and insertions, I saw that there was no excuse for David's perfidy. I wondered if I would tell him that I knew about it, when we met next. Also, if I should send

Charles's manuscript to his family, as I had meant to do. I decided that I would probably do both these things, to avenge poor Charles. Perhaps I should meet David somewhere in Turkey, and tell him I had this manuscript. If I wanted to blackmail him, for money to get about Turkey, it would seem a very good way, and, as I mentioned above, I was becoming pretty hazy about right and wrong, so I might come to that in the end.

I was not sure whether I was surprised at David or not. I did not know him well enough to be sure. But I thought that what he was doing was definitely worse than adultery, and that he was not in a state of grace any more than I was. Only, as David was not a Christian, being in a state of grace did not arise, as this dilemma only worries Christians, though non-Christians too know about right and wrong, and do both, as Christians do, but perhaps few of them notice it so much. I wondered if David despised his own perfidious conduct, and how much. And if ever he would feel that he must own to it. Perhaps when I met him I would know. Meanwhile, poor Charles was deprived of the credit of his book, but I did not suppose that this was bothering Charles much now, unless it was part of his purgatory to know how mean David had been. However, I remembered that he had really known this before, and it was the sort of thing he had been telling me about when I was half asleep in the Çanakkale café garden by the Hellespont. It seemed that David had a mean character, even meaner than most characters. One thing I thought was that most of David's friends would be surprised when they read his articles, because they were much better written, and written more in Charles's style, than most of what David wrote, and I wondered if people would guess. And I thought, live and let live, and that it wasn't my business to say anything, and that David would probably be exposed in the end anyhow, like most of the people who have committed literary frauds. Though it may be that the ones who have been exposed are the only ones we know about, and perhaps a great deal of what we read was really written by someone else who has died and left his manuscripts in drawers, and this is a very interesting thought.

So when I had finished reading these newspapers and Halide's letters, I put the camel away and read Vere's, which was about Greek islands and the yacht of the Press lord, and how this yacht was presently going to the Dodecanese islands and Rhodes and then along the Antalya coast to Alexandretta, and could I not manage to be in Alexandretta in about three weeks and wait for it? I did not see how I could, because of money, which was running out; in fact by now I was getting pretty short, and had only twenty pounds left in travellers' cheques, and there was no one in Trebizond to borrow from, the vice consul seeming quite selfish. I could not afford to go to Istanbul, nor, really, to go on staying at the Yessilyurt, though it was pretty cheap as Turkish hotels go. I explained this to my Turkish friend Odobasiogli, and asked him if he knew of any cheap room where I could lodge for a few days, and he told me of one, which was above a blacksmith's forge, so I took it and moved in. I thought I would spend the rest of that week there, in case any news of aunt Dot came through, and then ride south for Alexandretta, which would take a long time, and I would have to raise some money for it.

I began to live very cheaply, not eating at the Yessilyurt restaurant any more, but in low cafés, and sometimes I fried the fish I caught on the little cooker I had. I grew pretty hungry sometimes, and was vexed that I could not afford some of the good Turkish food I read about in my phrase book, except when sometimes Odobasiogli asked me to dine with him at the Yessilyurt, but he was partly away at Samsun on business. The hero of my phrase book, a very greedy man, would order, one after the other, young marrows stuffed with minced mutton and herbs, rice rissoles fried in egg batter, aubergine and chopped meat fried separately and braised together in own gravy, rice cooked with raisins, pine kernels and chopped liver, pieces of mutton fat roasted on spit, layers of pastry placed between layers of onions and pine kernel and baked in butter, vine leaves stuffed with minced meat and cooked in butter, chicken breast cooked to a pulp with milk and sugar, and other delicacies, any of which would have made a rich meal for me. But while he hogged away at it, washing it down with exotic wines (and I hoped it made him sick), I had to do with bread, cheese, soup, yoghourt, and an occasional egg. I wondered if I could get myself bought as a slave; I supposed they would have at least fed me, to keep up my strength. The camel did better, because it was used to roots and it got roots.

Meanwhile, I was going through aunt Dot's, and even Father Chantry-Pigg's, things. Rightly or wrongly, and I knew it was wrongly, but I had to get to Alexandretta and see Vere, I was going to sell a lot of them. This would not only bring me money, but would lessen the things I had to carry about with me, which worried both me and the camel. I decided to get rid of the tent, which was a heavy encumbrance, and most of the cooking utensils, as I only needed a small cooker. Then I put aside for sale aunt Dot's little travelling clock, her Lilo mattress and sleeping-bag, her painting things, two pairs of pyjamas, some day clothes, a bottle of hair tonic, a good many bottles called "The Mixture", which I thought the chemist would buy, a spare wrist watch, a Thermos, eight Anglican missals and six copies of *Why I am an Anglican*, which I thought I would try on the Imam, so that he should know what he was up against, and a straw hat with a Liberty scarf, which I knew Atatürk would have wished me to sell to one of the veiled women.

Father Chantry-Pigg had left his camera behind, which was probably a good thing for him as well as for me. I took out the used films, and decided that some shop would give me a good price for it. He also had his Lilo, some shirts, a clock, a fountain pen, a dog-collar, and some of his relics and little pictures. I knew a small crypto-Greek shop which sold such religious accessories under the counter. It seemed to me better that they should be used here, in this ancient home of Byzantine Christianity, than taken travelling among infidels. It seemed rather much to sell his personal belongings, but this is what happens when you have to get across Turkey to see your lover. When I had sold all these things, and some of my own, I ought to have enough to get to Alexandretta, and I should ride much lighter than before.

At the end of the week I was ready to leave. I gave the Post Office some addresses for sending on letters, first to Kayseri, then to Iskenderon, which are the names the Turks have given to Caesaraea Mazaca and to Alexandretta, and which Father Chantry-Pigg would never use. I went up on my last evening to the citadel, and told the Greek sorcerer that I was going south. He told me that I would come back one day. I supposed that I would. Then I offered him for sale a collection of aunt Dot's anonymous bottles and pill boxes. He looked at the labels, smelt them, and enquired what they were. I said I did not know, but that they were very good for all kinds of diseases and pains. He asked what I wanted for them. I suggested five liras for the lot, which was practically, I said, giving them away. He suggested five kurus instead. I laughed heartily, and began to put the bottles back in my rucksack. He said eight kurus, and I laughed still more heartily, and showed him a bottle which was labelled " The Elixir" as a change from The Mixture. It was, I said, the Elixir of Life; there could be no talk of kurus for it. At that, his eyes grew thoughtful. He retired into his lean-to and I supposed he was sulking, but he came out again carrying a bottle full of a green liquid, which he held up against the sunset sky and ejaculated, " Ah! " in a tone of adulation, and it was obvious that he was showing me something very special. For my bottles and pills, he said, he would give me eight kurus plus this, which I assumed from his exalted manner to be a magic potion of some power. I did not want to bargain or argue any more, only to get rid of my bottles for whatever

I could get, so I handed him my lot, and he gave me eight kurus and his green potion. To show me how good it was, he fetched two small wine glasses from his shed and poured some of it into each, so that we could drink together. From his talk and gestures, I perceived that it was not merely wine he was giving me, but a drink that would do something very marvellous for me. What, he asked, did I desire? To reach Alexandretta, I said. And I added that it would be very nice too to be emperor of Trebizond, as Don Quixotte and others had been used to wish that they were. At that that he waved his wand and stood looking like an elderly Comus as he offered me the charming-cup, and I thought it might transform me into the inglorious likeness of a beast, or chain up my nerves in alabaster and make me a statue, or root-bound as Daphne was that fled Apollo. Or it might be like an oblivion pill, or like another pill that was going about London just then which made people remember their infancies and their lives in the womb. Or it might be good for the Turkey sickness, which our ancestors who travelled in Turkey used to get, and of which I had had touches myself. Or of course it might be a love potion, and I did not really need that, rather the contrary, but it is very popular among Turks, who do not really need it either, and the enchanter might suppose that any one would be glad of it.

Anyhow, I lifted my glass to him and drank the potion in three swallows, and it was very strong and sweet, and then I sat down under the fig tree to think about it, for I felt rather dizzy, and I shut my eyes. The evening was very warm and still, and smelt sweetly of shrubs and flowers and woods, and a long way down I heard the sea sighing on the shore and someone singing in a boat. I was sitting in the banqueting hall, under the row of pointed windows, and the floor was white marble with golden mosaics, and the roof was painted with golden stars, and the four high walls were glorious with bright frescos of emperors and saints and Christ, all the Comneni looking down on their golden-bearded representative sitting on his jewelled throne.

Courtiers stood about the door; ecclesiastics with long Byzantine faces sat together, disputing with hieratic gestures about the aphthartocathartic heresy, in which Justinian had died, and which, it seemed, often rose again to disturb the Church. Marble pillars supported the starry roof; marble porticoes were seen dwindling in graceful perspective into the golden-fruited orchard and balsam-sweet woods; slim-railed balconies supported on delicate columns ran round outside the windows. Through open doors one saw other frescoed rooms, the chapel, the library, the audience hall, and beyond them a great range of towered walls swept down to the ravine. Through the windows I saw the circle of the Circassian mountains, indigo and brown and peach-pink in the sunset, and down their slopes a caravan of camels wound with their packs from the east. On the other side a fleet of cargo ships lay in the bay. On divans in the banqueting hall tall princesses reclined, and slaves knelt before them with palm-frond ferns. In one corner of the hall a young man sat playing chess with an ape, which brooded over its moves like a man, and chattered its teeth in anger when it lost a piece. A group of sorcerers and jugglers and astrologers and alchemists were doing cozening tricks to entertain some of the ladies and courtiers, and one of them looked like my Greek sorcerer.

Suddenly a palace revolution, that occupational disease of Byzantine imperial families, blew up. I saw it blow; it swept through the palace and into the banqueting hall; all was noise, bustle and confusion. Two young princes were dragged in in chains; the executioner put their eyes out while they shrieked and the ladies held their palm ferns before their faces.

"Remove them," said the emperor, with a wave of his hand. "And bring on the dancing girls."

The palace revolution was quelled. The dancing girls, who looked like Circassian slaves, danced and sang, till the emperor yawned and said it was time to go to the hippodrome. He was carried out on a golden litter, sitting very upright and calm, and the priests walked beside him chanting. The courtiers and the sorcerers and the dancers followed after, chattering in a queer Greek, and I supposed it was the Greek of Trebizond in the fourteenth century.

The chatter died away to murmurs, and became the voices of the sorcerer and his wife and the mutter of the long grass in the evening breeze.

The sorcerer asked me if I had had pleasant dreaming, and I said I had.

" You like it? " he asked, lifting up the green bottle.

I said I did, and took it from him and put it in my bag. We shook hands and parted, and it was thus that I said goodbye to the glories of Byzantium and the ancient empire of Trebizond.

15

FOR THE first part of my journey south I rode westward along
the shore, because the road running inland for Kayseri seemed
to start from the port of Giresun, about eighty miles west of
Trebizond, and I thought it would be nice to keep by the sea
as long as possible. Giresun was supposed to be the ancient
Cerasus, where the cherries came from, and the boys were
fattened on boiled chestnuts, and Xenophon's army had made it
from Trebizond in three days, or so Xenophon said, so I supposed the camel could make it in two, if it kept up a good pace.
But a geologist in a book I had, who was called Hamilton, and
had set out from Trebizond on a baggage horse in 1836, said
that the Ten Thousand, at the pace armies go and over moun-
tainous country, could not possibly have done it in less than
about ten days, so he had to move the site of Cerasus much
nearer to Trebizond, and would have it that Giresun had not
been Cerasus at all. But what with this rearranging the sites
of ancient cities, and what with the slowness of his baggage
horse, and the amount of his baggage, none of which he had
sold in Trebizond, and the number of heavy stones that geologists
have to pick up and travel about with (for he made a large
collection of rocks and minerals as he went along, and this
makes for delay), and what with turning aside to see mines on
the way, this Hamilton must have been a slow traveller, which
was probably why he thought Xenophon's army would take
ten days to Giresun. He himself was told that he would meet
with many difficulties, owing to the impracticable state of the
roads and the ignorance of the natives. But, as the camel found
very few roads impracticable, and as the ignorance of the natives

never seemed to slow me down much, since I seldom tried to plumb it, and as I never collected rocks or minerals or turned aside to see mines, for there is nothing I can more easily pass without turning aside, and as I do not even do much about rearranging the sites of ancient cities, though I feel that this would be a charming pastime if one had time, I thought we could make Giresun in about two days and a half.

I did not know where I should spend the two nights. Hamilton had got a Tartar with him, who got his rooms in a comfortable konak whenever he wished to stop. At Platana, just out of Trebizond, he got a konak in a café on the beach, which must have been very nice, and at Giresun, when at last he reached it, he established himself in some empty rooms above a café, and it did not sound as if he had asked any one if he might, but this comes of travelling with a Tartar. However, I was very happy to be riding along the Pontine shore, where, if the Argo had gone by three thousand odd years later than it did, I should have seen it sailing along, keeping well in to shore, though nervous of the natives, who then were not only ignorant but fierce. The road climbed up and down hills and ravines, among forests and myrtle and cistus, and rocky promontories jutted out into the sea, and the camel trotted along at about ten m.p.h., or cantered at about fifteen when we got a nice level stretch. I was delighted to be on so quick a racing camel, not on a baggage horse. We did forty miles the first day, and spent the night in a little port just round Cape Yeros. There did not seem to be any konaks or khans or beach cafés with rooms, but this saved money, and my nineteenth century Murray seemed to think most khans were very poor and dirty. But then Murray used to think all but quite a few places for sleeping in abroad were poor and dirty; he says this of the Yessilyurt (when it was the Hôtel des Voyageurs, which I think it must have been), and it is not poor and dirty now and perhaps it never was, but British standards in the last century were very high, and, feeling dirt as much as they did, it was very brave of them to get about so often and so far, really oftener and farther than anybody else, though they suffered more too. Anyhow, I slept on the bank of a stream that ran into a little cove by Cape Yeros, in my sleeping-bag among myrtle bushes. It was fine and warm; Hamilton complained that the climate of Trebizond was "backward", and liable to sudden changes, owing to the cold winds and fog from the Russian side of the Pontus, but he thought most things in Asia Minor pretty backward. He soon got tired of jogging along on his backward baggage horse, and at Tirebolu he got into a flat-bottomed Argo-like boat for Samsun, which he thought would be quicker, geologists always being in a hurry to get to important places and read the important papers they have written about stones.

I got to Giresun late at night on the second day, the camel having got into one of its excited, galloping moods, perhaps it had been eating azalea pontica the night before. So early on the third morning we took the road that ran inland to Sivas. I was sorry to leave the Black Seaside. I would like to have ridden all along it slowly and seen all the little ports; but there was no time for that now. It was a long way to Iskenderon, and I was thinking of ways to get more money for the journey. It occurred to me that I might offer lifts to people walking on the roads. I knew enough Turkish phrases by now to be able to make it clear to them that these rides would not be free; I thought I would charge so many kurus per mile, according to how many kurus the people looked as if they had; whatever I charged, it would be much less than they would have had to pay for a much shorter camel ride at the Zoo. I did not expect to have much luck with the women, there was probably something in the Koran against accepting lifts from strangers on camels, but men Turks, owing to thinking there is something in the Koran about how they must not tire themselves, and quite likely there is, the Koran being most odd, are usually ready to be carried by anything that will carry them. So I supposed that I should get enough out of them to pay for some of the food I wanted to eat and drink during the fortnight or so I expected it to take to get to Iskenderon.

It had become August, and extremely hot. I adopted the Turkish fashion of riding with an umbrella over my head when convenient. But the road from Giresun climbed up into forests quite soon after leaving the town, and a nice stream ran beside it, and the pines and oaks and chestnuts and cherry trees met across it, and the great rhododendron bushes made a deep, pleasant gloom, and we lurched up the mossy track, which was part of the old caravan road from Erzerum, very comfortably. Seeing ahead a man walking, with a woman walking fifty feet behind him carrying the baggage, I rode up as far as the man and asked him how far he was going. He said to the next village, which was two kilometres away up the hill. I asked if he would like a ride, for five kurus. Perhaps his wife too, I suggested. At that he jerked back his head and said, " Yok ", and smiled contemptuously at the notion of his wife having a ride. But he himself could do with one; he said they had walked from Giresun, after a trip by sea from Samsun, and he seemed to be saying that he was tired. He fished out four kurus and held them out. I said five, and after a little argument on his part, which I did not know the Turkish to answer, but still repeated five, he agreed and gave them to me, and I made the camel kneel down and he climbed on to its hump. I pointed to the luggage which his wife was carrying; she had stopped some way behind us, covering her face. I said " Esayim ? " which means luggage. He said " yok " to that; I would have taken it for nothing, but he said yok, because that was what his wife was for. I thought of aunt Dot, and knew that she would have asked the wife to ride and refused the man, which would have been no use, so she would have told him what she thought of him and ridden on without either of them and without the kurus. But you have to accept Turks and the Moslem religion as what they are, and it is useless as well as rude to come to a country and quarrel with the habits of the population; Turks might as well come to England and object to women going first through doors, and in fact there seems no good reason for this, since the only reason for doing things for women should be that they are less strong and less good at doing them for themselves, and this applies to standing, and walking long distances, and carrying loads, and changing wheels, but not to going through doors, and the right way to behave at doors is for whoever is nearest the door to go through it first, as it really could not matter less.

Anyhow, this male Turk mounted the camel's hump, and we trotted two kilometres to this obscure village where he lived, and he asked me to put him down at a café so that he could have a rest and take some refreshment after his tiring journey. I said, " Oh, what a hot day it is," for this was in the Turkish phrase book, and I often used it, and I hoped he might offer me some coffee, for Turks are usually very kind and polite to strangers, but he did not, so I rode on along the road, and it grew still hotter as the sun got higher, and I put up my umbrella, as for a little way there were no woods. Very soon I began feeling dizzy and strange, and when I came to I was still on the camel but in a coma, and this was the Turkey sickness, or possibly it was partly the camel sickness, and one made the other worse. I had had attacks of it before. So, when the road went through woods again, I got off and lay down on a mossy patch by the stream in the shade of trees, and I thought I would rest there through the heat till it was evening, and ride through the night instead.

I wished I had kept a few of aunt Dot's bottles and pills, in case any of them were good for the Turkey sickness, but the only bottle I had was the green potion I had got from the Greek sorcerer in Trebizond. So I took a small flaskful of this, and lay down on the moss and shut my eyes and relaxed, and possibly I passed out, for it seemed to me that I had landed at Cerasus from the Argo and had wandered up from the coast into these woods that climbed the mountain sides, and had eaten myself full of ripe cherries and of azalea honey, so that I lay in a swoon, pretending to be dead, because the barbarous Pontic natives, the Mossynoici, were all about, and I saw the boys they kept, fattened up on boiled chestnuts and tattooed all over with bright flowers, just as Xenophon had said eight hundred years later, and I saw that the Mossynoici did not change at all, for they were still having loving intercourse with women in public as they lay about the woods, and I thought, this would never do if it was Hyde Park. I wondered which of the Argo heroes I was, but I could not remember, and I did not know if I was a hero or one of their mistresses, for they must have brought some of these, since the mistresses of heroes used to go everywhere about the world with them, and were in every army and every ship, and we do not really hear enough of their doings, as they are taken for granted in histories. They went on the Crusades, and with the Greek armies to besiege Troy, and when during the ten years they grew too much older they sailed back to Greece and some younger ones came out; and they marched with Xenophon's Ten Thousand and must have got drunk on the Trebizond honey, and they marched all about France with our army during the Hundred Years War, and with Wellington's army about the Peninsula, where the Spanish and Portuguese soldiers liked them very much, and with the Royalist troops during our own Civil Wars, where Cromwell did not like them at all so he had them massacred, and some of them came over to Britain with the Romans and the Saxons and the Jutes and the Vikings and the Normans, but not enough, so that British women were largely used to supplement them, which is why we are such a mixed race. Yes, I thought, women have been everywhere with armies, making themselves useful, because soldiers need love, but now the women who go with armies are not encouraged to be so useful to them, they are called Ats and Wrens and Waafs and Wracs and are kept behind the battle lines and are only a small consolation to the troops, though soldiers still need love. But the Argonauts lay about the Pontic shores with their women and ate ripe cherries and chestnuts and rested in the deep woods beside streams, tired with the Turkey sickness and with all that sailing up the Pontus through choppy seas that lurched like a camel, and though Jason longed to reach Colchis and the golden fleece as I longed to reach the Alexandretta gulf, which would be calm and blue and hot and full of ships and in one of them would be my dear love, Jason had rested, as I was resting through the noon heat, bitten by mosquitoes, in a deep wood beside a stream, and let time drift by him.

So I lay in a dream through the hot hours, and when I came to there was more coolness, and I saw that it was six o'clock, and though I felt languid I felt no fever any more. The camel was on its knees near by, ruminating as usual. I got on it, it lurched to its feet, and off we went. At the next village I stopped for some coffee and raki and yoghourt, which in Turkey sickness is a great support, then rode on through a lot of the night, up and down over hills and through woods, and the camel, who was rested and frisky and perhaps drunk again, heard a horse trotting behind us, and as, like most camels, it hated horses extremely, it gave a loud roar and put on a great spurt of speed and ran and ran for kilometres.

So the night wore on, in alternate riding and resting. At midnight I lay down in my sleeping-bag and mosquito net and slept for four hours, then on again till seven, when we stopped for breakfast at a roadside café and rode again till the sun was high and hot, when I lay by till evening. This became my routine, and the days and nights went by, and I got them rather mixed up, still having some fever and feeling pretty dazed, and this was partly the potion, which made the world melt away into a hazy dream, and the far past became mixed with the present, so that I got confused about when and who I was and what I was doing. In fact, my whole journey was confused, and remembering it is odd, because I could not tell how many days it lasted, or what places I saw on the way, or to how many

Turks I sold rides. Sometimes I thought I was on the Argo, beating up the Euxine, which lurched like the camel, for there's not a sea the passenger e'er pukes in, turns up more dangerous breakers than the Euxine, and sometimes I thought I had escaped from it and was hiding in the woods from Medea and longing never to have to board the Argo again. I remembered how Euripides had made Medea's nurse complain,

> " Oh how I wish that an embargo
> Had kept in port the good ship Argo . . .
> But now I fear this trip will be a
> Damned business for my Miss Medea, etc., etc."

And then I thought I was not from the Argo at all, but an emperor of Trebizond escaping from the Turks and from Mahomet the Conqueror, and I would kick the camel with my heels to make it run.

It seemed to me that I passed wonderful Roman and Greek buildings, aqueducts, temples, theatres and arches, and sometimes whole cities, either in ruin or as fresh as new, and dazzling in white marble and paint, and sometimes they were Byzantine or Seljuk, or even Hittite, but the Hittite ones must have been built up by the potion, because there never is so much Hittite showing above the ground, it has to be dug and delved for and never looks fresh, but I hurried by what I thought were Hittite buildings, for fear there should be Hittite characters about, for no one can like Hittites, they are full of gloom and menace and too long ago, like Assyrians.

So I cannot tell what I actually did see and pass. There were mountains and rocky heights and steep roads up and down, and great flat stretches, and woods and open spaces, and villages with wooden houses and women working on patches of dry land and among scrawny vines, and sometimes I stopped in cafés to rest and eat and drink, and every one was kind and helped me and gave me more than I could spare the money to pay for, and I grew fond of Turks. Once on a mountain side I came to a hut by itself, and I went into it and lay down, with the camel tied to a hook by the door, and I fell asleep or into a coma, and was woken by someone speaking, and it was the shepherd whose hut it was, but he did not mind my lying on his floor, he fed me with yoghourt and coffee and offered me some rice pilav, but I was not hungry that day, so he sat down and ate it himself, and I saw that it was his supper, and that he would have given it to me because he saw I felt ill, and because of this I almost cried, on account of Turks being so kind. I thought about aunt Dot and Father Hugh, and I hoped that Russians were being as kind to them, and I thought that Russian shepherds and their wives would be, but not the police, and it was most likely the police they would have to be a good deal with.

After that day I began to improve, and could do more riding, and was able to take more notice of what I passed through, and it seemed to me that these rocky Turkey mountains and great plateaus became less strange and out of this world and less like mountains and plains of the moon, and when at last I rode into Kayseri, I felt able to go and see the site of Roman Caesarea, a mile off, which was not much to see, as well as to look intelligently at Seljuk Kayseri inside its Justinian walls, and at the bustling modern streets with bazaars and cafés and restaurants, where at last I ate a good meal.

But I did not pay for this meal, on account of having met David in the square, where he was parking a car. We both said hallo, and he looked surprised to see the camel. He asked after the rest of my party, and I told him, and he laughed a good deal, because I suppose it seems rather funny, people's travel-companions suddenly disappearing into Russia and leaving one their camel to look after. Then he stopped laughing, and said in the voice one uses when a friend has been killed by a shark, " You heard about poor Charles ? "

I said I had.

"It was pretty awful," David said. "I mean, it's not the sort of thing one expects to happen, actually. It gave me a ghastly shock when I heard. I was in Antioch at the time. Of course I flew at once to Antalya—that was where it happened— to see after things and take charge of his possessions till his father came out. My God, Laurie, it was pretty bad, meeting his father. Poor, poor old chap. I wish we hadn't fallen out. But I'm trying to forget all that. We did quite a lot of work together on the book before we parted, you know; I mean, we planned it; I doubt if Charles got anything to speak of down on paper, though I did."

I said, " Charles did too. I found part of it in a drawer at the Yessilyurt—quite a long chunk. It was so good, I took it all about Trebizond with me."

I was looking at David's face, which is what is called an interesting thoughtful kind of face, and, though it had become so brown with sun that it was hard to detect, I saw it turn red.

" What was it about? " he asked.

I told him. " Trebizond, mainly. Then he went on to the country behind it, but I haven't read all that yet."

" Oh," said David; and added after a moment, " Do you know, I think it must have been by me, the bit you found. It was typed, I suppose."

" No, it was written, in Charles's hand, with a lot of corrections and things. It was by Charles. It was his style, too."

" What did you do with it? "

" I was going to send it to his people, but I haven't yet."

" Have you got it with you? If you have, I might put it with Charles's other papers and notes that I have. It ought to go into our book. It may be a copy of something I wrote; from what you say, I think it probably was."

David was looking at me to see how this went. But he knew that it would not seem likely to me that Charles should have copied out in handwriting, with a lot of alterations and

163

corrections, something which David had made up about Trebizond.

"No," I said. "Charles made it up. It's the way he writes. And I think I had better send it to his people, they might like it. If it is a copy of something by you, you must have the original, so you won't want it."

"But it may be Charles's own, as you think it is. In that case, I ought to have it for our book, with his other papers."

"You said he scarcely got anything down, so there can't be many other papers."

David looked more and more bothered.

"The less he wrote, the more important it is to have anything he did write, if he really wrote this, which I can't be sure of till I see it. Have you got it with you?"

"You don't need it," I said, "because a lot of it was in the *Sunday Times* the other week. I expect you have that. If not I can give you mine."

"Oh that," said David. "You saw that."

"Yes."

I was getting sorry for David, his position was so awkward, so I changed the subject.

"Is that your car?"

"It's Reggie Carson's, actually. He went home on leave from Izmir, and let me use it while he's away. He's disqualified for driving in England for a year; he did something silly and got nabbed. I find it pretty useful. I thought of going to see the Cappadocian caves tomorrow, and then on to Konya. Would you care to come?"

"Well, I wish I could, but I'm pushing on to Iskenderon as quickly as I can make it. I'm meeting someone in a yacht that may come in any day now. But I don't see that I can get there on the camel in much less than four days, and I can't afford the train fare."

"Cleaned out? I cashed a cheque on Reggie before he left. Look here, shall I drive you down to-morrow? You could leave

164

the camel here and pick it up later on. Or have it brought after you by a camel driver; there are plenty about. We could arrange that easily, if you like. I suppose you can come by some cash when you meet your yacht."

" I hope so."

" Well, let's do that. If we start early, we can make Iskenderon by the evening. Look, let's dine here; it's not a bad place."

So we went in to the restaurant and dined, and we had the food which I had envied the man in the phrase book when I was in Trebizond. I was growing fond of David, and felt glad that he had come into my life, to be so helpful and kind and pay for my dinner and drive me to Iskenderon and arrange with a camel driver to see to the camel and pay for my night's lodging, which I saw he was going to do.

Over dinner we talked, and I did my best to relax his nerves, as he seemed rather tense. I told him about aunt Dot and Father Chantry-Pigg vanishing, and aunt Dot's note, and we speculated about what they were doing now, spying or fishing or converting Caucasians, or sitting behind bars answering questions, or digging for salt. And I told him about the Trebizond sorcerer and his potion, and about my Turkey sickness, and the kind Turks who had been good to me, and about the interesting antiquities I thought I had seen on the road, and he told me that I could not have seen most of those things, the way I had come, and that I had probably been a little delirious.

" I wonder you got here at all," he said, " having fever and riding all that way on that camel in this heat."

I thought that perhaps he wished that I had not got here at all. Presently he said, " Whose yacht is it you're meeting, by the way?" and I told him which press lord the yacht belonged to. I could see he was uneasy that it was a press lord's yacht, and that he did not care for me to hob-nob just now with the press, or with the passengers on this yacht. He said after a minute or two, " Look, Laurie. Will you do me a favour and not mention to any one anything about my book—mine and

Charles's, I mean? I don't want it publicised at present, if you don't mind."

"Just as you say."

"Well, don't forget, will you. There's a reason."

"Yes."

"I mean, the book arrangements are still fluid, and in more or less of a muddle," he went on, in case I thought there was some other reason. "And I'd rather premature news of it didn't get about. The position's rather tricky, you see."

I thought tricky was quite a good word myself.

"I mean," he went on, "when there are two collaborators, and one of them suddenly dies. I have to straighten it out, I mean. One wants very much to be fair to Charles; though he hadn't yet contributed much, he had his part all planned; and in the circumstances one's inclined to lean over backwards to give him more than his strict due, if you see what I mean."

I said nothing; I watched him flounder.

"As a matter of fact, it would help me a good deal if you would hand me over that manuscript you have, and let me check up on it."

He kept throwing away his cigarettes half smoked and taking new ones, in an uneasy kind of way.

"You see," he said, "I really am supposed to be taking charge of Charles's papers. I told his father I would."

"Well," I said, "I'll look it up. I'm not sure exactly where I put it."

I was by way now of being kind, and soothing the poor chap. I did not want to torment him, only to keep him on a string a little longer, so that he might do kind acts for me.

He went on doing these. He ordered more wine for me, and a liqueur with our coffee, and told me all about the Cappadocian cave dwellings, and I told him about St. Basil, who had done so much for Caesarea in the third century and practically rebuilt it, and who, with Origen and Clement and St. John Chrysostom, is my favourite Christian Father, the prayers and liturgies they composed being so admirable and full of dignity and light and *sophia*, and the further the Church got from them the less light and *sophia* and dignity it seemed to get, falling into things such as sentimentalism and exaggeration and puritanism and pietism and the Reformation and the Counter Reformation and revivalism and Lourdes and Lisieux and reliquaries and pictures of the Sacred Heart in convent parlours and Salvationism and evangelical hymns, and many more such barriers to religion, which daunt those not brought up to them and keep them out, like fundamentalism and hell fire. And I told David, who did not care, but listened to oblige me, what wrong turns the Christian Church had taken after the first, making it so difficult for us all, and David, who knew the whole business to be non-sense anyhow, gave me more wine, which encouraged me to go on telling him about these Church matters about which he could not have cared less, and the more I talked the more I grew sure that what was keeping me from the Church was not my own sins but those of the Church. If Father Chantry-Pigg had been there, he would have looked severe and told me otherwise, but he was not there and aunt Dot was not there, and I had the Church to myself, and could tell an atheist about it and he had to listen because of wanting to appease me.

When I had explained to David about the Church for some time, I felt sleepy and full of wine, and said that now we would go and find a camel driver who would take charge of my camel and bring it after me to Iskenderon. So we asked the manager of the hotel in which we were going to sleep where was a camel driver, and he sent a porter out with us to find one and he was a well known camel man and trustworthy, and was setting out for Iskenderon next morning early, with other camels, so I gave the camel into his charge and he told me the address in Iskenderon to call for it in three or four days, and I told him it must not be excited, as it was a little mad, and must not have affairs with the other camels, but must just be kept trotting quietly along, unloaded, because it needed a rest after all it had been through lately. Then I patted it and bade it good-bye for the present, feeling delighted that I should be spending to-morrow bowling along in a car, with someone else driving, and me sitting back looking at the interesting country, and the road would climb up towards the Cilician Gates and through them, and so down to the plains and to the Gulf of Iskenderon, and by then it would be evening, and we should drive round the head of the Gulf to Alexandretta on its southern shore, and moored off Alexandretta would lie the press lord's yacht, twinkling with lights in the smooth dark sea, and Vere would have left a message for me at the Mediterranean Palace Hotel, and we should meet either that evening or next day, that is, if the yacht was already there. This would be all so much better than sitting on the camel for three or four days while it lurched along tiring my legs and back, that I grew fonder and fonder of David, and felt almost inclined to give him Charles's manuscript at once, for even if I did this he would still go on with his acts of kindness in order that I should not tell people what I knew. However, I decided to wait for a little while, till we had done the drive to Iskenderon, he buying food and drinks for me all day, and stopping when I wanted to look at anything, though usually one has little power over the driver, who is very loath to stop, whether for lunch or to look at anything, he feels impelled to drive on and on, and I feel the same when I am driving.

The day went by as agreeably as I had planned. No one could have been nicer than David was to me, and he knew a lot of archæology, so we stopped and looked at Seljuk archæology and Hittite archæology and Roman archæology, and we stopped for lunch and for drinks and for coffee, and spent quite a long time seeing Tarsus, where we were so hot that we had a bathe in the Cydnus, in spite of its having formerly been so cold that bathing in it had almost killed Alexander during a campaign, and, apparently, quite killed Frederick Barbarossa, and it seems rather surprising that this emperor should have been given to bathing, but I have a theory that all our ancestors bathed, and that we have invented the theory that they did not. Anyhow, the Cydnus was not too cold for David and me, and after it we thought about Cleopatra sailing up it to Tarsus to meet Antony and about the ancient famous university of Tarsus, and about St. Paul, of whom I told David, for he did not know much about this missionary before, and he pretended to be much interested, and said he might read St. Paul's letters sometime, as I told him they were full of interest. I remembered that Father Chantry-Pigg had said that his father the Dean, who was so interested in St. Paul and had been writing his life till death ended this task, had visited Tarsus and spent a long time in it, sorting out all the Pauline remains and looking into what had been the university curriculum at that time, and, as he had been an imaginative dean, he reconstructed it, and all the university buildings, and made a plan of them for his book, and a list of the subjects studied. Archæologists ought always to have the help of people like Dean Chantry-Pigg, because they imagine and reconstruct so well, or anyhow so freely, though I felt that David might scorn his reconstructions. While I told him about St. Paul, I felt that a little perseverance on my part might easily persuade him to enter the Church, whose doors he never darkened but for architecture, weddings and funerals, and I thought aunt Dot would have said I ought to go on with this good work while he was so malleable, but I did not, owing to thinking he would not make a good churchman, but would become immediately lapsed like me.

So we drove to the Alexandretta Gulf after dark, and round to Iskenderon, and the Gulf pushed deeply into the shore and lay shut in it like a dark, shining river, spangled with lights from ships and boats and from the shore. A battleship lay in the bay, all lit up, and it looked British. Nearer in shore there was a yacht, and this was lit up too, and we could read its name, and it was called Argo, and this was the yacht of the press lord who was Vere's friend, and there would be a message waiting for me at the Mediterranean Palace about when we could meet. David said we would both stop there that night, and he meant that he would not desert me until I had met my yacht friends and acquired money.

But what I saw when we entered this hotel was Vere standing at the reception desk and giving a note to the reception clerk, and so we met, and then nothing else seemed to matter.

At eleven o'clock Vere returned in the launch, with some other yacht passengers, to the Argo, and I went too, to meet the press lord and his other guests. But before that I said good night to David and thanked him very much for his kindness to me, and gave him Charles's manuscript, which he had certainly earned. I told him I should not speak about it to any one, which he probably did not believe, and he was right, for here I am writing all about it, but anyhow such matters never remain secret for long, owing to tittle tattle and people being so little trustworthy and so quick to think the worst and not having mostly read what St. Paul wrote about charity and St. James about bridling the tongue, which is full of deadly poison and is set on fire of hell. So all was guessed or suspected presently about David and Charles and the book, without my help. I did not feel it was any business of mine, and I thought, live and let live, David can do as he likes about all this, it is between him and his conscience and he must find his own way through it and I shall not tell tales.

16

I CASHED English bank cheques on three kind Argonauts, including Vere, so now I had plenty of Turkish liras again, enough to be able to push on south on the camel into Syria and Jordan when the Argo sailed away, which would be in three days. Till then Vere and I enjoyed the pleasures of the charming pretty Frenchified town curving round the gulf, set with palm trees and very gay. We drove to Antioch in a dolmuç, along a road that began as a wild steep mountain zig-zag and ended by prosily ambling through flat cultivated fields, till there was Antioch, Antakya, a Turkish town of tiled houses on the slope of a hill. Golden Antioch, Seleucid and Roman Antioch, was a remote ghost brooding high above us on the hill where the citadel had stood and the great walls climbed about it; we drove up to it, and British archæologists were busy digging up mosaic pavements. We drove down again to Antakya, saw the tiny early church in its rock cave on the rocky hill side, and drove out to the groves of Daphne, once the haunt of votaries of pleasure from Greece and Rome, very licentious, and a perpetual festival of vice, so Vere and I went to see it, but it must have been better once, when all the temples and shrines and orgies were there. Now there were cascades and stone steps and a steep hill with woods going down to a valley, and terraces with people sitting playing tric-trac and drinking drinks that were mostly soft, and it was not so much more licentious than other laid-out landscapes with woods and steps and cascades, and there did not seem very much for the votaries of pleasure to do there, except that votaries of pleasure seem to create their pleasures round them wherever they go. But Vere and I thought that all those waterfalls, and the shade of the trees, made the place rather dank and like Cintra or Scotland, so we did not spend long in Daphne, but drove back to Antioch and explored the medieval Turkish quarter, where there is much more pleasure in the crooked winding streets and deep arches and little tiled mosques, and donkeys and camels hitched to rings in the open squares which had once been caravan halts, and trees growing about, and carpenters and potters and goldsmiths and coppersmiths all working away in tiny shops in their trade streets. Here we bought Roman and Byzantine coins, which we gave to each other, then we dined in a garden restaurant under tree lamps, with the Antakya radio also in the trees and blaring down at us, then we went to the Turizm Hotel for the night. When we walked in the streets boys howled at us and shook their fists, and a German archæologist whom we met in the hotel said that Antakyans did not care about the British, they only liked Germans, and this was an old tradition because of the Dardanelles attack, but we thought it was just rude boys being spiteful to foreigners, and we did not really care, because we were so glad to be together, and we each understood what the other said, and we laughed at one another's jokes, and love was our fortress and our peace, and being together shut out everything else and closed down conscience and the moral sense. We used to wonder how long we should live in this doped oblivion if we had been married, and I supposed that the every-day life which married people live together after a time blunts romance, but we did not think we should mind that, if we had all the other things, even the tedious things, to do together, and could plan our holidays and argue about the maps and the routes and one would read aloud from a guide book while the other drove and we would be very fair about equal turns of driving and equal shares of everything, and I suppose we should like our children, and marriage would still be our fortress and our peace, just as love was now when we could be together but could be a sadness and a torment when apart.

Anyhow love lit up Antioch for us like fairy lamps, and it was awful when it was time for us to return to Iskenderon because the Argo was off to Cyprus. We drove in to Iskenderon an hour before it sailed, and said good-bye on the quay where the launch went from. After it had gone, and was dashing away for the Argo in a splurge of foam, I went off to the camel stables and found that the driver had brought in my camel from Kayseri, and it seemed well and fresh, and I decided to start for Aleppo and Syria next day, when I had got my Syrian visa, which I had forgotten to do in London.

That evening David and I dined together at the Mediterranean Palace. He was much easier in his mind now that he had Charles's manuscript, but still had a few anxieties and was a little self-conscious. He asked me how my book was getting on, now that I was doing it alone. I said it was not getting on, and I had never really meant to write a book alone, only to contribute bits, and of course pictures, to aunt Dot's. Then he said what about contributing pictures and bits to his instead, and I could see that he missed Charles, and would like to have me involved in his book, partly to keep me quiet about it. But I said I was still expecting aunt Dot back from Russia, and must keep any contributions I wrote for her book, and I could see that David thought that this was unfortunate, my being still involved in a rival book. He said, " Oh well, let it go," and offered to cash a small cheque for me if I still wanted money. But I told him I could get on all right now, and he saw that I was drifting away from him and that all he could do was to trust in God.

Next morning I went to the Syrian Consulate, which was open every day between 11.30 and 12, and filled in the visa form. The consul looked at what I had written, and at my passport, suspiciously, as if he did not care for either.

He said, " Have you ever been in Israel? "

I said, " *Israel?* Good gracious no. Why on earth should I want to go *there*, of all places? "

"It is," he said, "I who am asking the questions. Have you been to Israel?"

"I've told you once. No."

He looked through my passport, turning the pages with covetous inquisitiveness, as if he suspected them of obscenity.

"Profession," he then said, very loudly and angrily. "Why you have not written it here? You have written 'Independent.'"

"Yes. I couldn't think what else to put."

"*Independent*, you have written."

"Yes," I agreed. The conversation seemed rather repetitive.

"You know what means *independent*?"

"Yes, I think I do. It means no one pays me regularly for working."

"Independent," he said, turning the word over on his tongue in some disgust. "That means spy."

"No," I said. "Not in English. Spies aren't independent, they get wages."

"You are not here in England." He sounded as angry as people usually do when they make this remark. "In the East independent is spy. I do not give you visa."

Too proud to plead, I rose to go.

"Just as you please. No doubt I can get one elsewhere."

"You cannot get a visa anywhere, for you do not get your passport back. I keep it."

"No. I keep it. It is mine."

"I keep it," he said, and threw it into a drawer, which seemed full to the brim of purloined passports.

As he seemed to be in the stronger position, I left him, saying coldly, "I go to the British consul."

"You may tell him that I keep your passport, since you are a spy, and spoke insolently to me, and wish to visit Israel."

I went to the British Consulate. The consul said, "It is quite difficult to get out of the Syrian Consulate with your passport. The consul likes to collect them. I will ring him up, and you will hear. Get me the Syrian Consulate."

174

Someone got him this. The conversation they had seemed more or less one sided. Presently the consul hung up, and said, " He says you can't have it at present, he must make some enquiries about you. Have you a second passport?"

" Yes."

" Endorsed merely Israel, no doubt. *That* won't get you far, unless you fly direct there, and then you won't get out of it except into the sea."

" No," I said, " I won't fly," and I felt rather grand that he should think I had as much money as that. " Actually, I am on a camel."

" Then you'll have to stay here till the Syrian consul has finished his enquiries. You may get your passport back. I will do what I can, but he is an obstinate man. . . . *Are* you a spy, by the way?"

" Unfortunately, no."

" And are you independent?"

" Just now, unfortunately, yes."

" Well, that seems about all we can do for you. Look in another day and have a chat. Good morning."

I went out.

I spent three days in Iskenderon, and got to know it pretty well. It was very hot and humid; in the mornings and evenings there was a mist, but all day it was bright and clear, and the sunsets were red as if a great smoky fire burned over the sea to the west. The horse-shoe bay curved round, decorated with palm trees all along the front, and battleships lay in the bay, lit up all night. The bright little streets looked rather French, and there was still some French spoken in the shops. No one stared at foreigners, for they had been trained to this strange sight for years. From 9 a.m. on till evening men played games in cafés along the front. Boys bathed on the shore, and I walked a mile up the coast and bathed too. I got to know an agent of Shell Company and his wife, who were very kind to me. I should not have minded spending some time in Alexandretta, it was so gay and amiable. The girls were friendly and we chatted in French on the front. Dr. Halide had said that the Alexandretta women and girls were bird-witted, and perhaps they are, I don't particularly mind. When they asked me what I did, and whether I was married, I said I was a celibate missionary, which impressed them, so then I told them about the Church of England, of which they had not heard till then, though they knew about Roman Catholics. Dr. Halide said that Moslems would make better Anglicans than they would Roman Catholics. This may be so, but we did not make any, so we cannot know. But we did not talk much about religion in Alexandretta, and the girls were quite western and emancipated, and Atatürk would have liked them.

Every morning I called at the British Consulate for news of my passport, but it seemed the Syrian consul still had it. On the fourth morning, however, I was told that this consul was now ready to give it back to me, and would even grant me a visa, so I supposed that his enquiries had discovered nothing but good about me. When I got there, his affairs must have been going much better, for he did not scowl, but smiled and shook my hand and handed me my passport as if he were giving me a diploma or a cheque, and said he hoped I would enjoy my visit to beautiful Syria. There was Aleppo, he said, and Palmyra, and Baalbek, and Homs and Damascus and Saida, and many magnificent Syrian castles, such as Crac, and he talked on like a tourist leaflet, and quite forgot about how I was an independent spy. So we parted in kindness and pleasure, and I went off and loaded up the camel and we trotted away along the Aleppo road.

As I now had plenty of liras, and was not in a hurry, I enjoyed my weeks of camel travel in the Levant very much. I ambled along, sitting back comfortably on the soft saddle, while the camel tossed its head and its white ostrich plumes waved, and it pawed the ground and sometimes cried " Ha ha " like a war horse, and sometimes it would canter along roaring, either from excitement, pleasure, annoyance or love, and I never discovered which it was. I felt like one of the seventeenth century travellers who trekked across the Levant with so much zest, and that I and the camel were part of the gorgeous pageant of the East. I remembered how Evliya Efendi of Istanbul had written, " Forming a design of travelling over the whole earth, I entreated God to give me health for my body and faith for my soul," though he had also said " according to the tradition of the Prophet, a journey is a fragment of hell," which of course it can also be. But not when one has money for food and drink and a bed, and a camel to ride on, and travels the caravan routes across Syria, and sees Aleppo and Tortosa and Ruad and Byblos and Beyrout and the mountain garden coast of Lebanon, and Baalbek and Palmyra and Sidon and Tyre and Damascus and Amman, and Jerash emerging in Corinthian splendour from its rocky hill, and half a dozen Crusader castles, and deserts and mountains and valleys, and at last, after many weeks, one is in Judaea and Palestine, and this country is where my Murray's Guide, which is a century old, says beware of the inhabitants, who are Bedawins (and they sound dangerous when spelt like that), and behind many a rock, says Murray, you catch sight of the gleam of a matchlock or a tufted spear, and the country can only be traversed safely with an escort of this same type of person, and the Fellahin, who cultivated the soil, were nearly as bad, and all this tends to show that foreign travel is much tamer than once it was. But it is equally hot, and I went down a thousand feet beneath the sea to Jericho as if it was a descent into the fiery pit of hell. It was too hot for any one to be excavating; I went over the Ummayad palace they had been digging up, but this, though it had been a fine palace once, was too hot too, and the Ummayad kings had used it only in winter, and I saw that they were right. As for Canaanite Jericho, that city of palms and balsams and stately buildings whose walls had been too ill-built to stand up to trumpet blasts, and as for the Jericho which Antony gave to Cleopatra, and the Roman Jericho which

Herod built up and beautified, I saw little of any of them, and thought I had better come back in about twenty years, when the excavators had made more of them, for dug-up bits and pieces had palled on me by now, and I wanted buildings that stood up. So I rode through modern Jericho, which Murray had called a filthy and miserable village, and its few inhabitants both poor and profligate, having retained the vices of Sodom, but modern Jericho now has a smart, respectable appearance, not at all like that, though of course appearances are deceptive, and I hurried through it to the Dead Sea, and soon I found myself seated on this sea, clasping my hands round my knees and swaying to and fro as if I was in a rocking-chair or in the Droitwich baths, and gazing up at the mountains of Moab, while the camel dabbled its paws in the tiny waves that sizzled on the shore. Afterwards I had a Coca-Cola in the little Lido café and bathed in the Jordan to cool myself and wash off the stickiness, and I sluiced the camel, and it drank till it was full of water, and then, in the cool of the evening, I rode on to Jerusalem.

17

WHERE AUNT DOT stayed in Jerusalem was in St. George's hostel, which was in the cloisters of the Anglican cathedral, so I went straight there and rode into the close and asked for a room. They had one, and they let me tie up the camel in the garden, where it immediately knelt down and went to sleep. I went into the hostel, and the first person I saw in it was my mother, whom I had last seen five years back in the Adriatic, when aunt Dot and I were trying to walk through the sea to Dalmatia, which we had to give up not because the sea was too deep, but because we had not got our passports on us, and my mother passed by in a motor launch with her protector, and stopped to talk to us, and gave us a lift back to the Italian shore. We were always pleased to meet one another, in a calm, unexcited way, and we were pleased now. She and her protector were staying with friends in Jerusalem, and had come to St. George's hostel to dine with Stewart Perowne, and to look at some objects (Corinthian) that he had lately dug up and planted in his little garden. The protector was quite rich, so I was glad to think that my financial worries would be solved.

My mother was (indeed, is) rather large and plump; as she is also handsome, she faintly suggests a buxom goddess, who has perhaps been hatched from a good-sized swan's egg inspired by Zeus. She must have looked very well in the old days as a vicar's wife, carrying her children about in gardening baskets.

She said, "Why, it's Laurie. My dear sweet child. But I thought you were in Turkey. Has there been any news of Dot? The English papers think she and that Father Pigg are busy spying."

She had read about aunt Dot's disappearance in the papers, and had not, she said, been at all surprised, as Dot was always up to something. She herself was a more lethargic type, and, but for the natural energy and activity of her protector, would have been inclined to stay in one place, or drift about the world very slowly. By nature prolific, she had presented me with several half-brothers and sisters, by now good-sized and undergoing education. I told her there had been no news of aunt Dot, but that I had the camel.

"Well, darling," she said, "the sooner you get rid of it the better. They are very treacherous. I hope you are going to settle down here now for some time and have a rest. I can give you money to fly home when you want to go. Or to Cyprus, with Howard and I."

My mother is not common, but she has never been able to grasp grammar, or why it is wrong to talk about flying to Cyprus with I. I remember as a child my father disputing this point with her, but she could never understand, and went on saying it. She did not say "flying with I", but if any one else was flying too, she thought that this put the first person singular into the nominative case, and that this was a rule of grammar, and not really odder than many other rules, for she had not got a grammatical mind.

I said that, now I was so near it, I thought I had better go across into Israel before going home, as I would like to see the Sea of Galilee and Nazareth and the Palestine coast from Acre down to Askalon. She agreed that this was very beautiful.

"But you must avoid Telaviv; it's a quite dreadful town. And all those little kibbutzes are tiresome." (My mother never liked hard, or indeed any other, work.) "You'll enjoy Galilee. The bathing is delicious. And of course all those associations it has. Do you still go to church, darling?"

"Sometimes. Not very much."

"You should. Your father would have liked you to go. You'll have to see Jerusalem, of course. These nice Cathedral clergymen are so good at explaining it. We must drive out to Bethlehem one day; it's charming. What a shame for Dot to miss everything, she would enjoy it so. So would that old priest, of course. But really, trying to convert Turks—that was rather nonsense, wasn't it. We should all live and let live; it's much more sensible, as well as better manners. By the way, there's a young man staying here who knows you—David Langley. He has been writing articles about Turkey in one of the Sunday papers for some weeks; Stewart says they are quite good."

So at dinner I met David again. He gave me a haunted look when I walked in to dinner, but rallied and became very affable and even obsequious, offering me the peas and passing me the condiments and asking very nicely after the camel and my journey. He could scarcely hope that no one would mention to me his Sunday paper articles, though he kept it off as long as he could, and changed the subject with powerful modesty quite soon. My mother showed them to me after dinner, and I saw that they were straight out of Charles's manuscript, as the first one had been, and I thought that this would be a very useful secret for me always to have, and that it was convenient to have an assiduous apprehensive friend who would see that I lacked for nothing which he could supply. He said he would show me the walls and gates and streets next day, which he did, and he knew so much about them that I grew rather confused and wished he had known less, and was glad to drive to Bethlehem in the afternoon with my mother, who knew nothing, except about the shops where they made jewellery and mother-of-pearl crosses and olive wood Bibles and velvet jackets embroidered with gold. Whenever my mother was in Bethlehem she got some of these jackets or tunics, and gave them to her friends and relations. She had a notion that all the New Testament women had shopped there, and that on the Sabbath they had all put on these velvet coats, and walked out in them, and she pictured all the Marys, that is, the Blessed Virgin, and Mary of Bethany, and Mary Cleophas, and Mary Magdalene (so unjustly defamed by posterity on no evidence), as well as Martha, and old Anna, and the woman taken in adultery, and the woman with the ointment who was a sinner, and all the other women, walking out in these black velvet coats embroidered with gold thread, and over their heads they wore shawls of black hand-made lace. This was the kind of thing my mother liked to imagine in Bethlehem nineteen hundred years ago, and it really interested her much more than the Grotto of the Nativity and the church that Constantine had built over it. I liked the dark cavern glittering with silver lamps and gold and silver and tinsel ornaments and smoky incense fumes and tapestried walls, but this was not the kind of thing my mother liked, and I missed aunt Dot and Father Chantry-Pigg. Bethlehem was charming and moving and strange, and one does not mind either there or in Jerusalem whether the shrines are rightly identified or not, because the faith of millions of pilgrims down the centuries has given them a mystical kind of reality, and one does not much mind their having been vulgarized, for this had to happen, people being vulgar and liking gaudy uneducated things round them when they pray; and one does not mind the original sites and buildings having been destroyed long ago and others built on their ruins and destroyed in their turn, again and again and again, for this shows the tenacious hold they have had on men's imaginations; they were dead but they would not lie down. Many people are troubled by the quarrels and the wars and the rivalries that raged for centuries round the Holy Sepulchre, between different sets of Christians; my mother, for instance, thought all this was a dreadful pity and disgrace, and that the whole history of the Christian Church was pretty shocking, and she liked to think that this was partly why she had left the Vicarage and my father, but really it was not this at all, but that she had grown bored and met someone else and preferred to rove about the world with him. Of course from one point of view she was right about the Church, which grew so far, almost at once, from anything which can have been intended, and became so blood-stained and persecuting and cruel and war-like and made small and trivial things so important, and tried to exclude everything not done in a certain way and by certain people, and stamped out heresies with such cruelty and rage. And this failure of the Christian Church, of every branch of it in every country, is one of the saddest things that has happened in all the world. But it is what happens when a magnificent idea has to be worked out by human beings who do not understand much of it but interpret it in their own way and think they are guided by God, whom they have not yet grasped. And yet they had grasped something, so that the Church has always had great magnificence and much courage, and people have died for it in agony, which is supposed to balance all the other people who have had to die in agony because they did not accept it, and it has flowered up in learning and culture and beauty and art, to set against its darkness and incivility and obscurantism and barbarity and nonsense, and it has produced saints and martyrs and kindness and goodness, though these have also occurred freely outside it, and it is a wonderful and most extraordinary pageant of contradictions, and I, at least, want to be inside it, though it is foolishness to most of my friends.

But what one feels in Jerusalem, where it all began, is the awful sadness and frustration and tragedy, and the great hope and triumph that sprang from it and still spring, in spite of everything we can do to spoil them with our cruelty and mean stupidity, and all the dark unchristened deeds of christened men. Jerusalem is a cruel, haunted city, like all ancient cities; it stands out because it crucified Christ; and because it was Christ we remember it with horror, but it also crucified thousands of other people, and wherever Rome (or indeed any one else) ruled, these ghastly deaths and torturings were enjoyed by all, that is, by all except the victims and those who loved them, and it is these, the crucifixions and the flayings and the burnings and the tearing to pieces and the floggings and the blindings and the throwing to the wild beasts, all the horrors of great pain that people thought out and enjoyed, which make history a dark pit full of serpents and terror, and out of this pit we were all dug, our roots are deep in it, and still it goes on, though all the time gradually less. And out of this ghastliness of cruelty and pain in Jerusalem on what we call Good Friday there sprang this Church that we have, and it inherited all that cruelty, which went on fighting against the love and goodness which it had inherited too, and they are still fighting, but sometimes it seems a losing battle for the love and goodness, though they never quite go under and never can. And all this grief and sadness and failure and defeat make Jerusalem heartbreaking for Christians, and perhaps for Jews, who so often have been massacred there by Christians, though it is more beautiful than one imagines before one sees it, and full of interest in every street, and the hills stand round it brooding.

The Arabs stand round it too, refugees from Palestine and living in camps, and they are brooding also, and the United Nations and the Refugee committees feed and clothe them and try to distract their minds, but still they brood and hate, like a sullen army beleaguering a city, and are *sedentes in tenebris* because they cannot go home.

On the evening after I had seen the Church of the Holy Sepulchre, and was still feeling bemused by its complicated extraordinariness, which is like nothing else in this world, I sat in the cathedral cloisters, rather tired and a little drunk, and David came and sat down by me, and he was a little drunk too, and more than I was.

He said, " How did the Sepulchre church strike you? I mean, some people can't stand all that ornateness and tawdry glitter in the chapels, and some people are shocked at the squabblings between the different Churches over their different chapels—Latin and Greek and Syrian and Coptic and Abyssinian and Armenian and the rest, all fighting for position through the centuries and despising each other like hell. Lots of Christians are shocked at that. Were you?"

"No, I liked it. It's just church manners; I'm used to them. It's only lately that Churches have even begun to think of being at all eirenical. And I like the glitter, too. The Armenian chapel is the best, with all those coloured witch balls and jewels and baubles and silver and candles; it's like an Aladdin's cave. The Greek one is pretty fine, too; it has the most incense and the best mosaics, and what look like the most valuable candlesticks and chalice. The Franciscans seem rather drab."

"So you think churches should be flashy?"

"Well, I like them flashy myself. Either flashy, or nobly built and austere. There's no room for noble building in the Sepulchre church, so they must glitter and shine. Like that little San Roque church in Lisbon."

"Of course you *believe* in the Church, don't you; I keep forgetting that. Tell me, Laurie, do you really? Believe it, I mean? It seems so fantastic."

"It is fantastic. Why not? I like fantastic things. Believe it? What does believe mean? You don't know, I don't know. So I believe what I want. Anyhow, it's in the blood; I probably can't help it."

"As to that, it's in all our bloods. But we don't all believe it. It's very odd, you'll admit. A Church that started up out of a Jewish sect in Palestine nearly two thousand years ago, spread by Jewish missionaries, catching on in the east and west, expanding into this extraordinary business with a hierarchy and elaborate doctrines and worship, growing into something entirely unlike what its founders can have dreamed of at first, claiming to be in communion with God, who was this young Jew in Palestine . . . Well, I ask you."

I said, "It's no good your asking me anything. I haven't got the answers. Go and ask the Bishop. Actually, I'm pretty sleepy. But you've left out most of it. You should read some of the liturgies and missals. Especially the Greek. Sophia, divine wisdom, *O Sapientia, fortiter sauviterque disponens omnia, veni ad docendum nos.* And light. *O Oriens, splendor lucis aeternae et sol justitiae, veni et illumina sedentes in tenebris et umbra mortis.* The light of the spirit, the light that has lighted every man who came into the world. What I mean is, it wasn't *only* what happened in Palestine two thousand years ago, it wasn't just local and temporal and personal, it's the other kingdom, it's the courts of God, get into them however you can and stay in them if you can, only one can't. But don't worry me about the Jewish Church in Palestine, or the doings of the Christian Church ever since; it's mostly irrelevant to what matters."

David remembered then that he was appeasing me. He said, " Don't mind me. You believers may be right, for all I know. All I say is, it's damned odd. You can't deny that it's pretty damned odd."

I agreed that it was pretty damned odd, and I had never tried to say it wasn't.

"Well," said David, still appeasing me. " I'll get us some drinks," and he went inside to get these, and I sat on in the cloister, hearing the cicadas chirp hoarsely in the garden and seeing the moon rise up among enormous stars, and agreeing that the Church was pretty damned odd, and I had really had quite enough drinks, for presently I dropped to sleep, and all those gaudy jewelled chapels shimmered through my dreams, and the cicadas sawing away in the warm scented garden became hoarse chanting among drifts of incense, and nothing seemed odd any more.

Then, between sleeping and waking, there rose before me a vision of Trebizond: not Trebizond as I had seen it, but the Trebizond of the world's dreams, of my own dreams, shining towers and domes shimmering on a far horizon, yet close at hand, luminously enspelled in the most fantastic unreality, yet the only reality, a walled and gated city, magic and mystical, standing beyond my reach yet I had to be inside, an alien wanderer yet at home, held in the magical enchantment; and at

its heart, at the secret heart of the city and the legend and the
glory in which I was caught and held, there was some pattern
that I could not unravel, some hard core that I could not make
my own, and, seeing the pattern and the hard core enshrined
within the walls, I turned back from the city and stood outside
it, expelled in mortal grief.

I was woken by my mother coming out and saying, " My
dearest child, the mosquitoes, you'll be eaten up."

18

I SPENT a week more in Jerusalem, and after that I was going to cross the Great Divide from whose bourne no traveller returns except with immense cunning and difficulty, and make my way to Haifa to get a ship to Istanbul. In Istanbul I would visit the British Embassy and find out if they had any news, and if there was anything that could be done, and I would also see Halide. I could not book my sailing till I crossed over to the Israel side, and I did not know when a ship that took camels would sail. Meanwhile I went on exploring Jerusalem and the country round it, often driving about with my mother. We drove one afternoon to what she called " the house of those nice Bethany people ", and she made it sound like paying a social call in the country. She liked to picture those two good sisters and their brother; Martha, so busy and bustling and hospitable, doing all the work, Mary, whom I always thought rather selfish, choosing the better part and sitting listening, and then getting praised for it, which never seemed to me fair, when listening must have been so much more pleasant and interesting than helping in the kitchen; and Lazarus somewhere in the olive garden seeing to the trees and goats, and Christ arriving for supper, and talking so that Mary could not tear herself away, even for a moment. I wondered what he had been saying that evening. Always when I read the Gospels I wonder what was really said, how far the evangelists had got it right, and how much they left out, writing it down long after, and some of the things they forgot and left out might have been very important, and some of the things they put in they perhaps got wrong, for some sound unlikely for him to have said. And that is a vexation about the Gospels, you cannot be sure what was said, unless you are a fundamentalist and must believe every word, or have an infallible Church. Anglicans have less certainty but more scope, and can use their imaginations more. My father, however, used to say that we must not pick and choose and invent, for where would that end? We had to take it or leave it, my father would say, and Father Chantry-Pigg said the same, but that is where the clergy make a mistake, for there is no need to be so drastic, and few things are ever put down quite right, even at the time.

We went to Bethany, in the cool of one evening, but still the burning heat of the day lay about in patches on the white dusty road and on the little hill where Bethany stood, a tumble-down Arab village among olive trees, and the house of the nice Bethany family was pointed out to us at once, and it did not look very old. My mother looked at it kindly, and as if she was wondering if she ought to leave a card. She would not visit the tomb of Lazarus with me, as she did not care for tombs; I told her it was not likely to have been a tomb, but still she did not visit it.

Next day my mother and her protector Howard, whom I quite liked, flew off to Cyprus, for they lived like birds, winging about the world with the greatest of ease. I missed my mother, but she left me very comfortably off, and I had no more money worries, but could pay for my ship to Istanbul, and my ship from there to London, and all my living expenses and the camel's as well.

I crossed over into Israel one morning with the camel, among great difficulties and a great fuss about my papers and a long lecture from the Arab customs officer about the wickedness of Israel, and of Britain for encouraging it. He had fierce black eyes that flashed while he spoke of these things, and he told me what a terrible crime it had all been, and I agreed that it had been a terrible crime, and he begged me not to forget what a crime it had been, and still was, when I was in Israel, which really belonged to the Arabs. So I said I would not forget that, and at last he let me go across, and the camel and I paced over no man's land into the Jerusalem of the Children of Israel. This made me feel very strange, and as if I had died, for I could send no communication back to the Jerusalem I had left, I was a cut-off soul, I might have passed from earth to the halls of Zion, except that they were not golden, or jubilant with song, and seemed to have no milk and honey or social joys, though no doubt the Children of Israel find it full of these things.

I went to a travel agent and got a passage to Istanbul on a cargo ship that sailed for Haifa in ten days, so I had these days in which to see Israel, which is a very beautiful country indeed. I went to Acre, and spent a night in an inn that looked as if the Crusaders might have spent their last night in it before fleeing from the Holy Land to Cyprus in 1291, and I bathed in a blue and green sea outside the citadel. I went to Nazareth, which was full of tourists and touting guides and fake holy places, and I went on to the Sea of Galilee, and this was so beautiful that I stayed by it for several days, stumbling about the ruins of old Tiberias and going out with the fishermen in their boats while they cast their nets, fishing alone from the shore, sleeping in a small Franciscan guest-house above the lake, with a balcony from which I could every morning watch the sun rise over the wild brown and mauve mountains on the Syrian shore. The days were very hot. I rode the camel up the shore, to Magdala and the ruins of Capernaum, and the little bays beyond, where I swam in buoyant blue water. Every place along the Genesaret shore was in the Gospels; Magdala, and the ruined Capernaum synagogue, and the sermon on the mount, and the feeding of the five thousand on the opposite shore, and the rowing on the lake, and the drafts of fishes, and the healings, and the floutings of Pharisees and sabbatarians, and the vision in the dawn to Peter and the rest as they fished, and the calling of the disciples in turn to leave their work and follow. St. Matthew, people think, sat at the receipt of customs on the quay of Capernaum, taking the dues from those who landed there. When he arose and followed, did he have time to hand over his job to someone else, or did he just take up his cash-box and go, so that for a time people landed and departed without paying anything? There is nothing at the customs now but the black basalt quay stones lying about, and the little waves of the Sea of Galilee lapping among reeds.

In all these places that I go through, I thought, he once was, he once taught and talked, and drew people after him like a magnet, as he is now drawing me. And I thought that if David had been with me and had asked me again what he had asked me in the cloister of St. George's Cathedral, I would have answered him rather differently, for by the sea of Galilee Christianity seemed local and temporal and personal after all, though it included Hagia Sophia and all the humanities and Oriens, *sol justitiae*, that has lighted every man who has come into the world.

I would have liked to spend a long time in Galilee, fishing and rowing and swimming and riding about the hills and trying to paint the changing colours of the water and of the mountains across it on the Syrian shore, and everywhere coming on fragments of Rome and of Greece. But I had to leave it, and I did not think I should come back, it was too subversive, it filled me with notions and feelings that were dangerous to my life. I did not want Vere to come there, though Vere had not my brand of flimsy and broken-backed but incurable religion, of which I have always been ashamed, so it might work out all right.

I rode away from Galilee early on a still, hot morning, on the road that went through Cana and Nazareth to the coast. I tried to see Château Pèlerin, which is one of the best Crusader castles, but the Israel marines were in occupation there, doing whatever foolish things marines do when they manœuvre, and this manœuving, whether it is by marines or armies or navies or aeroplanes, spoils so much land and sea and sky and historic sites and beauty in every country that it does not really seem worth while, and governments should rid their minds of this foe complex which leads to so much trouble, but, if they must manœuvre, they should manœuvre in dull, ugly places, not in Lulworth Cove or on

Dorset downs or in charming villages which they raze to the ground or in Crusader castles which jut out into the Mediterranean with the waves washing at their feet.

I rode on to Dor, which was the Roman Mantura, and St. Jerome says it was a mighty city once, but now no more, and not even an Arab village, but just a desolate reef-bound harbour and bay and a few ruined houses, though no doubt when it is all excavated the little that is left of mighty Mantura can be made to stand up again. As it was, there was nothing to do in Dor except bathe among the reefs and in the breaking sea beyond. Caesarea, farther down the coast, was a far more magnificent ruin, and Herod's splendid theatres and hippodrome and marble temple and palace and towers and harbour walls with great columns thrust through them were being excavated and looked very grand, and when Pontius Pilate lived in the palace he must have been very happy, for Caesarea is one of the harbour cities in which one would have liked to live, and it had been the capital of Palestine, and though there was nothing in it with a roof on I spent the night there in a digging with a large-size female statue they had dug out, rather than go on to horrible Telaviv. When the sun rose I rode the camel into the sea and made it kneel down in the waves and splashed its head to wash it and make it more sane, for, though better, it still was a little mental, and then I rode on to Telaviv for breakfast. This Telaviv is a very frightful town, which I will not describe, for I looked at it as little as I could and then dashed south to Askalon in a bus to see the Philistines, and the orchards and the shallots and the melons and the ruins curving round the bay, and to find any buried treasure that Lady Hester might have overlooked. This Philistine city was full of the Children of Israel come from Telaviv to bathe in the breakers. These Israelites were very kind and pleasant and encouraging to foreign visitors, hoping that we should think highly of the State of Israel and not so highly of the Arabs, about whose faults they told us quite a lot, and, as the Arabs had told us quite a lot about the faults of Israel, we felt that we knew just how very faulty both these nations were, and also the British, about whose faults they both told us, but the Children of Israel, because they had got what they wanted, told us of these more politely. In Telaviv they kept asking me if they could direct me anywhere, but I could not think of anywhere, except out of Telaviv, as nothing in Telaviv seemed as if one could want to go to it, though this was not a thing I liked to tell them.

When I passed the tourist office, a bus stood outside it labelled Caesarea, and it was full of American and British tourists, and a guide stood outside it touting, calling out to the people who went by " Come and see a big Roman pleasure city two thousand years old, with theatres, circus, hippodrome, palaces. . . ." When people passing heard of anything so gay, so much better than Telaviv, they stopped and asked how much to go there, for the Americans thought it sounded like Coney Island, and the British thought of Brighton. The guide told them how much, and some of them got in the bus, looking as if they were off to a great treat. I suppose, they said, we can eat there, there are sure to be good cafés in a city like that. And then, they said, we will go to the circus. That will make a nice day. The guide tried to make me come too, but I told him it was a place I already knew. He said, " Very fine, yes? " and I said, " Yes, very fine," and the people in the bus were pleased to hear me say this. What they said when they saw it, I did not ever learn, for I left Telaviv and rode off up the coast again to Haifa, which I reached in two days. When I asked the way to the harbour, several boys came with me and the camel to show me the way and find my ship for me, which they did with great·skill and ease, and I saw that Jews were more intelligent and progressive than Arabs and would get further, but which race ought to have had Palestine, or how they ought to have shared it out, is not a thing to be decided by visitors.

So I sailed away from the Holy Land, and got to Istanbul in the evening.

19

I DINED that night with Halide. We talked about aunt Dot and Father Chantry-Pigg, who were now, it seemed, news in three continents, on account of being spies. The continents were Europe, America, and Asia Minor.

"They have been seen," said Halide. "Everywhere in Russia they have been seen. In the Caucasus, in Tiflis, in Siberia, in Stalingrad, in Moscow, in the Crimea. They have been seen in cafés with your Burgess and Maclean."

"What were they doing?" I asked, hoping that they had been having a good time.

"How should I know?" said Halide, who was not hoping this at all. "Drinking vodka, playing tric-trac, talking, telling secrets, spying. Then too, Father Pigg has been seen in churches, hob-nobbing with priests."

"It sounds as if they were pretty free."

"But again, they have been seen also in Siberia."

"What were they doing there?"

"Some one said Father Pigg was performing miracles with his relics, curing people of their diseases."

I thought this sounded real, because who would know about the relics unless he had been seen using them?

"They get about, then," I said.

Halide shrugged her shoulders.

"Oh yes, they get about, if half what is said is the case."

"Who are the people who say they have seen them?"

"Spies. Russian spies coming over here, and our spies who come back from there. They tell one another. They tell your Embassy. They even tell me. Or rather, the people they have told tell me. But the trouble with spies is that they are liars. It is their métier, it is how they live. So it does not do to believe what they say, but always some may be true. Your Embassy in Moscow has heard no news of them, only these *on dits*. The London papers work it up, and send reporters to Istanbul to write stories about them. If they discovered you were here, they would besiege your hotel, as they besiege me."

"It would be no use. I have nothing to tell them."

"They don't need that. They would send to London articles about how you have talked to them and what you have said. No, not what you have said, but what they invent that you have said. They have no truth, they are as great liars as the spies. They would, too, tell tales of the camel, what it does, how it pines for Dot, about its love-life and its little ones."

"It has no little ones, that I know of."

"Oh, what does that matter? There would be little ones in the reporters' stories. And there would be a Romance in your life."

"Well, there is."

"Yes, and you would read it in the papers, with names. Romance! All they mean by romance is some commonplace tale of love. What do they know of the romance of the deserts and the mountains and the sea, the great Turkey cities buried in sands that we dig out piece by piece, the roaming of nations across wild lands to build grand civilizations . . ."

"And palaces," I added, for romance excites me, "and harems and eunuchs and fountains playing in the courts, and peacocks spreading their tails in the sun, and paved roads running down to the port where the ships go in and out with purple sails, laden with cargoes of nuts and Circassian slaves, and camel caravans coming up from Arabia, jingling their bells through Petra and Palmyra and Baalbek, heading for Byzantium and the Bosphorus, and the walls of Acre standing in the green sea, and the Sea of Galilee in the dawn, and Jerash standing with its carved colonnades in the mountains, and Tenebrae in the darkness of some great church, and Mass among tall candles, and . . ."

"Yes, yes," Halide broke in, "but we cannot now tell all the tale of Romance, it is too long. We are agreed you and I and Dot, and all our friends, what is Romance. But these newspaper gossips, they do not understand all that, they do not read poetry or look at beauty, they only know Love. Yes, some wretched girl who acts in films or competes in beauty contests, so that she has become perhaps Miss Istanbul, or even Miss Turkey, or Miss America, she is asked, what is her Romance, and she, I dare say, tells those who ask her of the Bosphorus and the Golden Horn and the great march of the New Turkey, but they do not listen, they write that her Romance is some man of the films whom she will, for a short time, marry. Love, marriage, what are they?"

We both brooded over this. I wondered how Halide's affair with the Moslem man was going, and what would come in the end of my own affair to which I was hurrying back. Love, marriage, what are they indeed?

Since we did not know, we did not discuss them further.

Halide added, "The newspapers have even made a romance for Dot and Father Chantry-Pigg. True they are middle-aged and elderly; that matters nothing when there is Love. Are they spies, have they been kidnapped, or do they elope, that is what the journalists wonder."

"When I get home," I said, "I will perhaps write a piece myself, about how they just wanted to see Russia."

I went to my hotel and to bed. Next morning I called at the British Embassy. I thought they were rather cold about aunt Dot and Father Chantry-Pigg, and it seemed to me that they had adopted the spy theory, and of course they may have been quite right, but I said, if they were spying for Russia, it would not be in Russia that they would be, but hanging round Harwell or the Foreign Office, and if they were spying in Russia it would be for us. But the Embassy, I could see, thought that it was in their past that they might have been spying for Russia, and that they had now perhaps gone there (for how without Soviet connivance could they have crossed the frontier?), because they thought their activities had been discovered. The Embassy man asked me if aunt Dot had ever belonged to the Party, or had been a fellow traveller. I said this was most unlikely, for aunt Dot had always been a liberal, and had not voted in elections lately because no liberal had stood, though no doubt the Embassy man was thinking that probably no communist had stood either.

" She is a very keen Anglican," I said, " she goes to church a lot."

The Embassy man said, " Actually, that is a not uncommon cover. As to that, her companion, Mr. Chantry-Pigg, is, of course, a priest, and that is a better cover still."

I said, had not this cover been rather damaged by the Dean of Canterbury, but he said it was still used sometimes. Then he said that, according to the accounts that had come over, very likely unreliable, aunt Dot and Mr. Chantry-Pigg were doing a good deal of hob-nobbing with the Soviet police.

I said, " My aunt hob-nobs with every one. Father Chantry-Pigg is probably trying to convert the police to the Church of England. Or, it may be entirely the police who are doing the hob-nobbing, which is usually the way round, it is in any country. I have heard that they are also in Siberia."

The Embassy man nodded, as if he had heard that too, and sighed a little.

" So entirely unreliable, all this news. Spies are trained, and so very successfully, never to tell the truth, whatever it may cost them to refuse. In this case, it costs them nothing; indeed, they receive payment for lies. Well, we will let you know if we hear any firm news; please leave us your address in England."

There seemed no point in staying on in Istanbul, and I left it next day by sea, with the camel in the hold. I had a small ape too, which I bought from a Greek sailor, on the quay side;

it was a nice little ape, and I thought I would try to teach it to play chess, like the ape I had seen in my dream of the Byzantine court at Trebizond when the Greek enchanter had given me the elixir, for it is a fact that apes have learned chess, and particularly in the East. I thought I would also try to teach it to drive my car, and I supposed that the most difficult thing for it to learn would be to know when the petrol was running out. I kept it with me on the voyage, and played chess with it and it was quite quick at picking it up, but always made the same moves that I had just made, and I wondered if this was the way the Byzantine apes had played too.

The voyage was erratic, and took some time, but at last we arrived at Tilbury and disembarked. I had to leave the camel and the ape in quarantine, which was a good thing, as I did not want them in my flat. I thought that later I would put the camel in the Zoo till aunt Dot came home, and perhaps the ape too, for I did not really want that either.

20

COMING HOME after some months abroad is very neurotic. The letters that have not been forwarded lie in a great mountain, and one feels that one will never climb it. A great many can be thrown away unopened, such as all the ones called on the envelope " Free Bulgaria ", which is a magazine that has been arriving in my flat for several years, and, as I have never opened the envelopes, I never have discovered whether the magazine is about some Bulgarians who have come to Britain to be free, as the Free French used to do, or if it is about the Bulgarians in Bulgaria who believe they are free, which is a very common belief, and I suppose I never shall know this as I shall never have time to open one of them.

But most of the letters are bills. Some of these say that the gas and the electricity and the telephone will very soon be cut off if the bills for them are not paid, and higher up on the pile there lie more letters on these subjects, saying that this has now occurred, and that the gas, electricity and telephone are now quite gone, and it will cost a very great deal of money to put them back. The rent for the flat was also overdue, and the land-lord's letters had gone on getting stiffer and colder ever since midsummer day, and I half expected to find bailiffs and their daughters sitting about playing canasta and smoking my cigarettes and drinking my gin, or perhaps asleep in my bed, for I had now missed Lady Day and Midsummer Day and Michaelmas without sending my landlord a line. It is a pity how we spoil these feast days by paying rent and bills on them, or else by feeling that we ought to, whereas on Lady Day we should be eating lamb and mint sauce and listening in vain for cuckoos, and on Midsummer Day eating strawberries and cream in gardens or punts, and on Michaelmas Day eating goose and sage and apple sauce, instead of which we are scribbling away in our cheque books and getting ruined.

I saw that I would soon be ruined now, what with the rent and the bills and putting back, at great expense, the telephone and the electricity and the gas, and generally resuming life once more. The worst thing is income tax, and this is a thing that no one can face alone, so I send all the letters which look as if they were about this subject straight on unopened to the accountant who does my income tax returns, for if I open these letters I become neurotic and cannot face life. I do not care that publicans should write to me, or I to them, for they have had always a very bad name, and though we know that they have been sometimes justified in the sight of heaven, that is only if they repent, and the publicans who write to me have not yet repented. Certainly Christ ate and drank with them, but that is one of the many ways in which I do not try to follow him, so I send on their letters unopened, and do not even say " God be merciful to him, a sinner ".

Sometimes I think I should like a secretary, who would open all my letters and answer them, so that I need never see them, but actually to have a secretary about would make one more neurotic still, and it is better to push on, desperate and alone.

Presently I had a martini to pull myself together, and then went out to a kiosk and telephoned to Vere, and on account of the martini and talking to Vere, I stopped feeling neurotic and felt instead happy and at peace and as if nothing mattered but that we should be together in an hour. And then I thought how odd it was, all that love and joy and peace that flooded over me when I thought about Vere, and how it all came from what was a deep meanness in our lives, for that is what adultery is, a meanness and a stealing, a taking away from some one what should be theirs, a great selfishness, and surrounded and guarded by lies lest it should be found out. And out of this

200

meanness and this selfishness and this lying flow love and joy and peace, beyond anything that can be imagined. And this makes a discord in the mind, the happiness and the guilt and the remorse pulling in opposite ways so that the mind and soul are torn in two, and if it goes on for years and years the discord becomes permanent, so that it will never stop, and even if one goes on living after death, as some people think, there will still be this deep discord that nothing can heal, because of the great meanness and selfishness that caused such a deep joy. And there is no way out of this dilemma that I know.

During the next few days I read a lot in the papers about aunt Dot and Father Chantry-Pigg. It seemed that they were spies, probably long known as such by the Foreign Office and M.I., neither of which departments would consent to reveal to an eager and anxious public what they knew. The people of this country had a right to know; they were deeply concerned and worried by the affair, and less, it seemed, by what aunt Dot and Father Chantry-Pigg might be revealing on the other side of the Curtain than by who was protecting them on this side, for it was apparent that some one was, and probably this was because of their hyphenated names and their ties. Later on, when I had, at great cost, had my telephone replaced, I was several times rung up about these ties, and I explained that Father Chantry-Pigg never wore ties, on account of his collar being round, and that I did not remember that aunt Dot wore ties much, though I had seen her in ties in old school and college hockey groups, but I did not actually know of what colour or pattern they had been. I was asked also about their names, Chantry-Pigg and ffoulkes-Corbett, and why these names had hyphens. I said that I supposed that marriage and property arrangements in some past period of their family histories had occasioned this, and it did not indicate duplicity or double-mindedness, or any desire for an alias. One of them said, " Funny, those two little fs," and his voice sounded as if he thought the two little fs stood for fanatical foes, or fleeing fellow-travellers, or something of that kind. I said I did not think it was so terribly funny, and anyhow ffoulkes-Corbett was not my aunt's original name but that of her husband.

"Dead, would he be?" said the reporter, hoping that aunt Dot's husband was less dead than cuckolded, or a *mari complaisant*.

I said he would.

"From natural causes, no doubt," said the reporter, still hoping, and before I thought I had answered, "No, he shot himself, ages ago."

The reporter said, "Ah", as if he had expected no less and did not blame aunt Dot's husband at all for his rash act. Had he known that before his fatal shot the Reverend Reginald ffoulkes-Corbett had attempted his wife's life also, this reporter still would not have blamed him. Before I got round to explaining that my uncle by marriage had taken his life because of advancing cannibals, he had changed the subject from this clergyman and asked if there was any question of a Romance between aunt Dot and her companion.

"An autumn Romance," he suggested tentatively. "Was there a question of that?"

"No question at all."

"Ah," he said. "I thought as much."

Leaving this topic, as if he had got what he wanted about it, he enquired whether the Reverend Chantry-Pigg was protected by the Archbishop of Canterbury. I said I did not know about this, but I thought that archbishops certainly ought to protect their clergy, within limits, so I hoped that this was the case, and that the Archbishop was protecting him, so far as was possible, from the Soviet police.

Then this reporter rang off, first saying that he knew I would not have minded being bothered, and would realise that the people of England were very anxious and concerned about this matter of espionage. I said I believed that the people of England could not care less what information was passed to any one, but that they did enjoy a good spy melodrama, there were few news items they enjoyed more. He said, "You're dead right," and rang off.

Next day I read the piece in a newspaper which was headed, "Vanished priest is under Canterbury protection", and the writer seemed to have rather a poor opinion of Canterbury, such as used to be expressed in the seventeenth century by puritans and papists, when the puritans wrote, "Look about you for the protector and prime mover of them that creep among us spinning plots against this state of England and spying out the land for foreign princes, and you will see Canterbury in his rochet, rowing out from his palace of Lambeth," and the papists wrote, "Canterbury himself is our prime foe," and these two Canterburies were Laud.

Half-way down this article there was another heading, which was "Autumn Romance", and it said that it had been revealed to this paper that there was no question but that there was a romance between Mrs. ffoulkes-Corbett and the Rev. Chantry-Pigg.

I rang up the paper and said that there seemed to be some mistake here, as I had said the opposite to this, and would they please withdraw it. The girl I spoke to, who was perhaps only the telephonist, said she would pass up my message. Nothing, however, happened about it, so I wrote the paper a letter, pretty firm and stiff, but it did not seem to get into print, so I saw that they would stick to their autumn romance. They did, however, print a letter from the Archbishop's chalpain, as no doubt letters from archbishops' chaplains have to be printed; it said that the Archbishop had failed to understand the statement about how he was protecting Father Hugh Chantry-Pigg, and would the paper be good enough to explain it. Under this letter there was a little piece by the editor saying that this item had been given to the paper by me, for I had said that I hoped the Archbishop was extending his protection, so far as was possible, to this clergyman. After that the chaplain wrote and asked me about it, and I saw that I had said the wrong thing, and I tried to

explain it away, by saying that it had merely been wishful thinking and I did not really think that the Archbishop had any
opportunity of protecting any one in Russia, though the Dean
might possibly be able to do so if he tried.

After this, I was asked to write an article myself about the
whole affair, in a Sunday paper. As I needed the money, which
seemed quite a lot, and also thought it was time that the readers
of this paper had something true to read on this subject, I said
I would. They said there was no need to sign it if I preferred
not, and I thought I would prefer not. So I wrote an article
about how my aunt and Father Chantry-Pigg, who were
travelling together to do mission work among Turks, had gone
across the Russian frontier to fish in a very nice lake there was
and to see the Caucasus and some Armenian churches, and I
feared that they might have got into trouble with the Soviet
police.

This article did not actually come out quite as I expected,
owing to not being signed, so that it could be altered a good
deal in the newspaper office without my being asked, and they
put in a lot of mystery, and referred to the suicide of aunt Dot's
husband the Rev. ffoulkes-Corbett, and mentioned again the
autumnal Romance, and referred to their having been reported
to have been seen in chat with Burgess and Maclean in Moscow.
So it really seemed in many ways a quite different article from
the one I had written, and I decided that I would not write any
more unsigned articles. Vere said it was an idiotic thing to do,
and I saw that Vere was right, though the money came in useful
for paying some of the bills, and later even the publican got
some of it, which vexed me a good deal, but my accountant
thought I had better pay him something on account, to keep
him quieter. I thought, if David were to turn up from Turkey
now, I might borrow some money from him, because his
articles were still coming out in that paper, which would make
him still anxious that I should be his friend. And soon after this
I met David at a party. It was a good party, but I got there

rather late, owing to having come on from another party, for the autumn party season had by now well set in. When I came in some one said to me, you've missed something, and it seemed that David had thrown a glassful of hock cup, full of fruit and vegetables, into some one's face, because of something this man had said to him that he did not like. I thought it seemed rather early in the night for people to be throwing wine about, but I am used to such things occurring either just before I get to a party or just after I have left it, or, if anything happens while I am there, it happens in another room from the one I am in.

When I spoke to David I asked him why he had thrown his hock with fruit and vegetables at this man, and David said the man had been damned offensive to him. I asked him what the man had said, but David did not seem quite clear as to this, or perhaps he was being evasive, for David is a rather reserved man.

" Actually," he said, " I don't like him."

I thought that if David were to go round a party throwing his hock cup at every one he did not like, he wouldn't himself get enough to drink to reach the wine-throwing stage at all.

David, who had really quite reached this stage by now, said, " It's an extraordinary thing about Turkey. People who go there are always insulted and slandered. The same with the Levant, and Cyprus. Look at Hester Stanhope and Wilfrid Scawen Blunt and those Wortley-Montagus and T. E. Lawrence and all those. One can't write a book or an article without some one being offensive. One's friends are so damned malicious. One travels all over the place and no one one meets out there is malicious at all. . . ."

I asked, " Where? Who isn't malicious? How do you mean?"

David said, " Oh well," and took another glass of hock cup.

" And then," he went on, " one comes back to London, and it all starts, people being damned offensive about one, and other people repeating it. I suppose *you've* been saying things."

"No," I said. "I haven't mentioned you actually. Or not much. I've not been offensive."

But I could see that David thought I probably had, and I edged away from him, because he now had his new glass of fruit salad and hock.

He called after me, "I thought you wrote a damned offensive article about your aunt and that priest."

"Who says I wrote it?"

"Every one. It was obviously yours."

"As a matter of fact, not. I supplied the facts, about how they got into Russia and why, and they filled in the surround in the office. They say I can't get an apology, because it wasn't signed."

"I must say, you're more of a mutt than I thought. After all, you've been writing some time now. I don't know why you don't know the facts of life."

Then he saw that he had insulted me, and remembered that this was a silly thing to do in the circumstances, so he asked me to lunch with him next day, and I went round talking to other people, who of course all wanted to know about aunt Dot and what was behind it. As they were mostly intelligent people, they didn't attach any importance to what the Sunday paper had made of my article, all they wanted to know was how much I had got for it. Some of them believed in the spying, others not. Some of them thought aunt Dot and Father Chantry-Pigg were spying for us, not for Russia, and that this was why the Foreign Office would say nothing.

"With the strong church views that it seems they had," some one said (he said "had", as if they had died, and a lot of people tended to do this), "it seems pretty unlikely they would be commies. Unless, of course, the church business was a blind."

I said, "They aren't commies. They are extremely anti. Father Chantry-Pigg will scarcely say the word." In fact, I thought, he would never have called those minions of the devil by that pet name. Aunt Dot would, but she was more kind and genial.

" So one supposed. Then do you feel they may be spying for us ? "

" It certainly wasn't what they went there to do. They may be doing it now, I suppose. I mean, they may be going to report what they are seeing there when they get back."

" Well, we all do that when we get back from places. The point is, is the Foreign Office in touch with them, and paying them ? "

I wished I could think so, it was a happy notion. But I said, " I doubt if the Foreign Office has a clue where they are."

" Then what on earth are they living on, all this time ? "

Some one said, " Probably on the Soviet government, in Soviet prisons, if . . ." He didn't add, " if they are living at all," but this was what we all thought.

So it was a depressing kind of conversation, and I was glad to talk to an agent of the Shell Company of Turkey (British) who had been very kind to us in Istanbul, and to Stewart Perowne and Mrs. Antonius, who told me some Jordan gossip and talked about my mother.

I left the party before one, and at 1.15 an art critic punched the director of an art gallery on the head, or it may have been the other way round, so I missed both the incidents that occurred at this party, as I always do.

21

TIME WENT ON. I felt pretty unsettled and sad, but I worked a little on the Turkey book that aunt Dot and I had planned, for I had aunt Dot's note-books as well as my own, and I thought she might like me to get it into some kind of shape, as well as the illustrations that I had roughly sketched. I tried to describe the missionary attempts, and how aunt Dot hoped that the Turkish women might take up with the Church of England and become more liberated and advanced, and how this had not, in fact, much occurred. But I wrote more of my own part of the book, about the Black Sea and Trebizond, and our journey into Armenia, the towns and the lakes and the churches and the people and the fish, and the final vanishing of aunt Dot and Father Chantry-Pigg over the frontier, and it seemed to me that this made an interesting story. I put about our expedition to Troy, too, and the Gallipoli graves. I described how Charles and I had swum the Hellespont and been nearly drowned by being carried out to sea by the tide, as Byron and Mr. Ekenside had been. I got very worked up writing this, and it seemed to me that it had actually happened, and I felt the cold green water slapping at my mouth as I struggled with the tide. I was very relieved that it turned in time to carry us in to the Sestos shore after an hour or two. As poor Charles was dead, I did not have to ask his leave to put in all this, and anyhow I thought he would have liked it. I thought of making aunt Dot swim with us, as she certainly would have done if we had gone, but then I thought no, aunt Dot was truthful, it was part of her religion, and when she came back and read it she would be vexed with me.

I did not want to vex aunt Dot. I did things to please her; sometimes I went to see the camel in its quarantine, and petted it and fed it roots, and I thought it seemed to know me, and looked at me with spiteful memories in its insane eyes and stamped with its paws. The quarantine keepers told me they were watching it carefully, and giving it small jobs to do, dragging lawn mowers and things about and carrying workmen and their tools from place to place, as physical labour was better for its mind than standing about chewing and brooding all the time. When its quarantine was over, I meant to leave it at the Zoo, until aunt Dot's return, where it would have healthy companionship and take children for rides.

The clergy of Father Chantry-Pigg's church kept ringing me up in case there should be any news. What was in their minds was that the time would probably come eventually for a Requiem Mass. I wondered if, later on, when hope dwindled, they would perhaps have a conditional one, but I saw that this would be awkward. They prayed for him often, and so did aunt Dot's church pray for her, but always as prisoners and captives and those in distress of mind, body or estate, not that they might have rest eternal and perpetual light, which would have been premature, though actually rest and light would have been nice for them to have, wherever they now were, and it was terrible to think that instead what they were now having might be labour and darkness.

When I got time, I was thinking a good deal about religion just now. I would go to High Mass in some church or other, and the Christian Church would build itself up before me and round me, with its structure of liturgical words and music which was like fine architecture being reared up into the sky, while the priests moved to and fro before the altar in their glittering coloured robes and crosses, and the rows of tall candles lifted their flames like yellow tulips, and the incense flowed about us. Here was the structure, I would think, in which the kingdom was enshrined, or whose doors opened on the kingdom, and sometimes the doors would swing ajar, and there the kingdom was, clear and terrible and bright, and no Church is able for it, or can do more than grope. Churches are wonderful and beautiful, and they are vehicles for religion, but no Church can have more than a very little of the truth. It must be odd to believe, as some people do, that one's Church has all the truth and no errors, for how could this possibly be? Nothing in the world, for instance, could be as true as the Roman Catholic Church thinks it is, and as some Anglicans and Calvinists and Moslems think their Churches are, having the faith once for all delivered to the saints. I suppose this must be comfortable and reassuring. But most of us know that nothing is as true as all that, and that no faith can be delivered once for all without change, for new things are being discovered all the time, and old things dropped, like the whole Bible being true, and we have to grope our way through a mist that keeps being lit by shafts of light, so that exploration tends to be patchy, and we can never sit back and say, we have the Truth, this is it, for discovering the truth, if it ever is discovered, means a long journey through a difficult jungle, with clearings every now and then, and paths that have to be hacked out as one walks, and dark lanterns swinging from the trees, and these lanterns are the light that has lighted every man, which can only come through the dark lanterns of our minds. Ficino and the Florentine Academy used to light lamps before the bust of Plato, and were called heretics because they wanted the light of Greek learning let into the Church, and Erasmus and Colet and More were called heretics because they too wanted that light of Greek learning, and to correct the mistakes in the Vulgate by it, and the Cambridge Platonists were called Latitude men, for wanting the same kind of thing, and all these people knew that if we stop trying to get fresh light into the Church, the Church will become dark and shut up. Yet human beings are so strange and mixed that though More was for humanism and fresh light in the Church, he was also for burning people for heresy, and said of one who had been burnt for erroneous opinions about the date of the Judgment, "Never was a knave better worth burning," and looking at it all round, churchmen and the Church have greatly advanced in humanity since then.

Most of my friends are not Christians, but I have some who are Anglicans or Roman Catholics, and some who belong to no Church but are interested in Churches and in the history of religion and like to discuss such things, even when they do not know much about them, so sometimes the question turns up among us. Vere said one day, did any clergymen believe all of the Thirty Nine Articles, which they have to read aloud when they are inducted into a church, and, if no one believed them, why were they not abolished? And, as they are really German and Lutheran, and taken from the Augsburg and Württemberg Confessions four hundred years ago, what are they doing in the Anglican Prayer Book at all, since many of them say the exact opposite to what most Anglicans believe, and this goes for the clergy as well as the laity. So we sent for a Prayer Book, though it was difficult to get hold of one, because the people we were spending the week-end with did not go in for Prayer Books, but in the end the cook had one, so we read the Articles aloud, to see which of them we should have been able to say if we had been clergymen being inducted, and had had the ordinary Anglican beliefs. As I was the only practising Anglican, though I did not practise much, the others asked me to say which I should have had to leave out or alter, and it came to quite a lot. There was all that about the Fall, and man being far gone from original righteousness, whereas I suppose most people think that man was never very righteous, but has crept slowly up to a greater righteousness than any he had when he was neanderthal or otherwise primitive, though he has not yet got at all far. So all that about the fall of Adam, though it is an interesting story, probably does not mean anything to most Christians now, except as a symbol. But a Roman Catholic who was there said it was still believed, though allegorically, by his Church, which of course does not drop so many things and leave them behind, because it believes more in the faith once delivered, and, though it adds a good many things to this, it does not take them away, but is very tenacious. Of course the other Churches too are tenacious, though less so, and theology seems the only science which does not keep adapting its views and its manuals to new knowledge as it turns up, as history does, and geography, and medicine, and anthropology, and archæology, and most people think this is a pity, and part of the reason why Christianity is less believed than once it was. But others, such as Roman Catholics, think the Church should stand firm and change nothing. The Anglican Church compromises, and discards things little by little, leaving them behind casually and quietly, as if it had never really had them, but it has not yet succeeded in mislaying those of the Articles which are not now held, and this is perhaps because they are all numbered; anyhow some of them annoy a lot of people, and particularly the clergy, who have to repeat them every time they get a new church, and the churchwardens have to go into the vestry and sign something which records that the new incumbent has done this.

The Article about the fall from righteousness was really St. Augustine's fault. St. Paul got the idea from somewhere, no one seems quite to know where, but it was not from Genesis, which does not mention that Adam and Eve were ever righteous, and in point of fact they were not, and it was not from the Gospels, as Christ made no reference at all to the affair. Augustine took it up and nailed it on to the Church, as he did Predestination and Election, which come in Article 17, but only very neutrally, and not as Augustine would have wished, for, though the first half of the Article says how nice this doctrine of election is for the elect, and how much it elevates and improves them, it does not recommend it to the reprobate, because for curious and carnal persons to have continually before their eyes the sentence of God's Predestination is a most dangerous downfall, whereby the Devil doth thrust them down either into desperation or into wretchedness of most unclean living, no less perilous than desperation. So, though this doctrine makes the good better, it makes the bad worse, and, as there are always more of the bad than of the good, it does not break even, but does more harm than good, and on the whole Article 17 does not seem to advise it. This Article ends very sensibly, saying that we must all follow the will of God in our doings, and washing its hands of election and reprobation, which the translators must have seen looked pretty silly in English and in print, so there is really not much harm in Article 17, though it does not seem to mean anything in particular, and any one except Calvinists would feel rather foolish saying it; as Sir Thomas Browne said, that terrible term Predestination hath troubled so many weak heads to conceive, and the wisest to explain. But St. Augustine, being so intellectual and dominating, managed to put it across in a large way, and got the better of Pelagius, who was right, but much less intellectual and dominating, not being Carthaginian but only Welsh, and later Aquinas, who was intellectual and dominating too, took it up and spread it about, and Duns Scotus, who was Semi-Pelagian, never had so much influence as he did, so that, owing to all this, Predestination, in spite of being the sort of idea really only suitable for lunatics (who have often had it, and it has made them worse, like poor Cowper), took a firm hold on the Christian religion, and was always waiting like a wild jungle animal to spring on this or that schoolman or divine and drive them mad. It sprang powerfully on Zwingli and on Calvin. Erasmus and Colet and More hated it, and if they had been allowed to go on with their reforming of the Church, and if this reforming had not instead fallen into the hands of Augustinians, it would have been quite a different reformation, and very much better, and both Protestants and Catholics would have a better Church now, one they had reformed between them. But the Augustinians were got down in the end, and the Arminians and the Pelagians, or perhaps they are Semi-Pelagians, now have it all their own way, and it is the Predestinators not the Pelagians who, as it says in the 9th Article, do vainly talk.

"But there are plenty *of* them," said the Roman Catholic, who meets them on account of going to Scotland and sometimes Wales for fishing purposes. "They are by no means an extinct species. They flourish on Celtic mountains, like wild goats."

"But not now in my Church or yours," I said. "So we ought not to keep that article about them, because articles about dissenters ought not to be bound up with the Church of England Prayer Book. Nor the one saying that the Athanasian Creed can be proved by Scripture. My aunt Dot, who is the most devout Anglican, always sits down when they say the Athanasian Creed, because of hell fire and without doubt perishing everlastingly on account of not thus thinking of the Trinity."

The Roman Catholic, who was a very thoughtful, truthful man, considered for a moment, then said that he could thus think, and every one applauded him, in the way we applaud Roman Catholics, because they can thus think about so many things, and it is a great feat.

I said, "So can aunt Dot," in order to keep up the Anglican end, but I did not actually know whether aunt Dot could or not.

"Well," said one of our hosts, who is not a religious man, "these Churches are really the most extraordinary contraptions. Where did they *get* it all from? I mean, the way they've built it all up, tier on tier, pinnacle on pinnacle, without any apparent relation to its base? Of course it's a wonderful artifact, and very magnificent, but what's it all *about*?"

The Roman Catholic and I started to explain the relation of the edifice to its base, which always does need some explaining. After all, I said, the Christian Church is the tabernacle and shrine of a God, as the pre-Christian temples had been shrines of gods, and these tabernacles and shrines have always been as elaborate and imposing and highly organized as their builders could make them, and have had hierarchies of priests and prophets and rulers to preside and to mediate with the gods. Look at Delphi, I said, and the Temple of Artemis at Ephesus, and the Temple of Solomon at Jerusalem. People don't want to worship God in a barn with no liturgy and no rites, unless they are Quakers. So of course the Christian Church, once it had got out of the catacombs, grew and grew till it towered like a Christmas tree, hung with glittering things and shining lights, because it is the shrine of a God, and all its walls and doors and roofs were carved and sculptured and painted and mosaicked, because human beings are artists, and like to build their shrines like that. That is partly what draws people to the shrine; then, once in it, they discover what it is all about. But of course if you like, I said, you can have it penny plain and no nonsense, as the predestinating Calvinists in the Celtic mountains do. Their rites are probably more like what the apostles did.

" They have such ghastly hymns," the Roman Catholic said. " The words, I mean. I saw one of their hymn books once."

I said, " All churches have a lot of ghastly hymns. Mine has, yours has. Most people have ghastly taste, and always have written bad religious verses and painted bad religious pictures, and had tiresome thoughts about religion. That doesn't interfere with the structure. Nor does the nonsense people talk about it. Nor does all the quarrelling and the wickedness, and the frightful damned things the Church has done since it got power to do them. Human beings have always done frightful damned things. But they are improving, and so is the Church. It's working its way through."

" Well, through to what exactly? I mean, to what more than all the well-meaning people outside it are working their way to?"

I said, " Oh, it's so obvious," but I thought they had better work it out for themselves, as I couldn't begin on it.

The Roman Catholic thought it was time he took a hand, so he said that the point about the Church was that it was a supernatural body, not man-made. He looked polite and reserved, and we could see that he was referring to his own Church, which he knew was the only Catholic part of the Christian Church, and he was remembering that no other Church has priests or orders or sacraments or Mass or could rate as supernatural in any at all high-grade way. I did not start to argue about this, as I did not want to vex him or tire myself or bore the others, and the Pope had said once for all that Anglicans do not have orders, so for him it could not be an open question, and it vexed him to know that Anglicans even thought they had such things, which were quite above their station. I once heard an argument between him and aunt Dot on this matter, and it lasted quite a long time, though both are by nature eirenical, but they did not get anywhere, though they each thought they had won. Aunt Dot ended by saying that even if we had no altars and no Blessed Sacrament on them, it would be only polite of outsiders to bow to where we thought we had them, especially at requiem and nuptial Masses, also to join in the Creed and the Lord's Prayer at christenings instead of shutting the mouth tight as if afraid of infection, which looked so unchristian and stuck up.

"I suppose," said aunt Dot, "you would walk into a mosque with your shoes on," which was not really fair, as Roman Catholics do take off their hats in Anglican churches, and even, I think, in dissenting ones.

"And I suppose *you*," said the Roman Catholic, "would, if you had been an early Christian, have offered a pinch of incense to Diana, out of politeness to the pagans."

So they left the subject and played croquet, which is a very good game for people who are annoyed with one another, giving many opportunities for venting rancour.

Anyhow, I did not take up the question of the Anglican Church with this papist now, but while he was talking I thought how the Church was meant to be a shrine of the decencies, of friendship, integrity, love, of the poetry of conduct, of the flickering, guttering candles of conscience. And, above all this, it seems to be playing some tremendous symphony; the music drifts singing about the arches and vaults, only faintly and partly apprehended by us, the ignorant armies that clash by night in perpetual assault and rout, defeated by the very nature of their unending war, for ever on the run, for ever returning to the charge, then on the run again, like the surging of the waves of the sea.

Then I thought, the Church is like a great empire on its way out, that holds its subjects by poetic force, its fantastic beauty heightened by insecurity; one sees it at times like a Desiderio fantasy of pinnacles and towers, luminous with unearthly light, rocking on their foundations as if about to crash ruining in decadence and disaster into the dark sea that steals up, already lapping and whispering at the marble quays. Yet, though for ever reeling, the towers do not fall: they seem held in some strong enchantment, some luminous spell, fixed for ever in the imagination, the gleaming, infrangible, so improbable as to be all but impossible, walled kingdom of the infrangible God.

Such to me, I thought, is the Christian Church. The fact that at present I cannot find my way into it does not lessen, but rather heightens, its spell; a magic castle, it changes down the ages its protean form, but on its battlements the *splendor lucis aeternae* inextinguishably down all the ages lies.

When I had done thinking all this, and the Roman Catholic had done his piece about his Church, we all felt that we had had the Church, and we passed on to the affairs of the people we knew, who were, as usual, behaving in a great number of strange ways. Some of them had lately returned from Turkey or the Levant, as I had, and some had been there last year or the year before that and had had time to get on with their travel books, which were now cheeping and chipping at the shell, almost ready to hatch out. There was a little friction because some of the ones about the same part of Turkey, or the same bit of the Levant, seemed likely to hatch round about the same week or

217

month, and authors do not like this, though it may be a good thing, as it shows they are in the fashion; you get a Cilician season, or an Ionian season, or a month when the books about Istanbul or the Lebanon or the Dead Sea hatch out, and they have a modish air, like fashions in clothes, but still it annoys authors, though reviewers rather like it, as they can get several books, or anyhow two, into one article, and make invidious comparisons between them, which pleases one author but vexes another, or several others. "Mr. So and So's is the best of this Cilician batch," they will say; or "It is a far cry from Mr. Flatfoot's rather pedestrian description of the Syrian scene to the fireworks of Mr. Pyrotechnic," and they find it is easier to utter this far cry than merely to plod with Mr. Flatfoot about the Syrian sands of which they know so little themselves.

So there is always some intriguing and arrangement and protesting between authors and their various publishers in the matter of publication dates, but it is not always successful. The only safe thing for travel writers to do would be to invent some remote piece of some remote country, very inaccessible and expensive, and people it with Bedouins of the forbidding, old-world breed, and with various discouraging animals, and travel all about it alone and write one of those questionable travelogues like Plato's on Atlantis, and Sir John Mandeville's, and some of the bits in Marco Polo, and others about the Polar regions and darkest Africa, and many more. Then there would be nothing else on the same subject till at least a year later, when people had got round to thinking they had gone there themselves. Some reviewers would think this at once, and would write learned criticisms and corrections and say how nostalgic for this fascinating country, which they had seen from the air during the war, Mr. ———'s vivid account made them feel. Others might review it more sceptically, as the Greeks used to review the travelogues of Pytheas, that great Marseilles liar (which were actually much more accurate than they thought), but at least it would be the only book on that bit of country and there would be no rivals.

This Sunday evening conversation then took an unfortunate turn, for David's articles, of which one had appeared in the paper that morning, were mentioned. How had David, some one said, come to write so well, never having done so before? It must have been Charles's influence, and indeed he had taken to writing very like Charles, almost as if poor Charles's spirit had passed into him after Charles had been devoured by the shark.

"You saw something of him in Turkey, Laurie, didn't you?" some one said, and I said, "Yes, quite a bit. I saw Charles too."

"Both telling you the story of their quarrel, no doubt. What was Charles's?"

"Oh, it's too difficult. I was half asleep in a café garden in Çanak, and didn't follow. You know what they both are— were. *All* their rows were complicated."

"All rows are. Well, did you ask David why he had taken to writing like Charles?"

"No. I knew. Charles's spirit had passed into him. He had all Charles's papers, and he thought, why shouldn't he use them?" I had been drinking rather too much, and spoke under the influence.

"Use them? Oh, as a model, you mean. Well, he certainly did. But what's he going to do with Charles's own stuff, if he has it?"

"My dear Tim," said Vere, "it's obvious every Sunday morning what he's doing with it."

I had not told Vere, but of course every one thought I had, and I saw the light dawn.

I was sorry then, and tried to put the light out.

"I suppose he admires Charles's writing, and is rather aping it. It's quite natural, because David hasn't actually got much of a style of his own. Now look, for heaven's sake don't put it about that I said that, I mean what Vere said. It's entirely untrue."

" But that's what David threw his hock cup at Henry for saying at the Hamiltons' party, wasn't it ? "

" I don't know. It happened before I got there. I never knew what it was in aid of, and I think David was too tight to know either. No one ever seems to know for certain why any one has thrown his drink about, it always sounds idiotic when they try to tell."

" Well," said the Roman Catholic, " I heard that was why. It seems pretty reasonable. But, if David is really passing off Charles's work as his, and is going to use it in his book too, there ought to be a first-class row. I mean, Charles's family or friends ought to take it up and queer the pitch. What about you, Laurie ? "

" Certainly not. I know nothing, and it's no business of mine."

" Would you think he still has Charles's originals, or has taken copies of the lot by now ? "

" I've no idea. And I think we'd better forget it. It's really no business of ours."

" Well, it's bound to get about. All of us here will dine out on it, for one thing."

" I shan't."

" I didn't know you felt so loyal to David. I thought it was Charles you knew well. What's David offered you ? "

I did not like this conversation. I had betrayed David, broken my promise, and I was remembering all the meals he had given me on my journey to Iskenderon, and the drive in his car and the archæology he had told me about, and the money he had advanced, and how earnestly he had bribed me, and how he had perhaps trusted me, though more probably not, and how now he would be talked against and despised, and might get into trouble with Charles's family and with his publishers, only after all nothing could be proved, it would be his word against their suspicions, and I should say nothing, so as time passed he would live it down. But I wondered what the reviewers would say about his book when it came out, I thought he would very likely ask me to review it, if ever he trusted me again. For my part, I decided to go out of London for the present and stay at aunt Dot's, which she always let me do when she was away if I wanted to. There I could get on with my own book, and I thought I would fetch my ape, which would soon be out of quarantine, and go on teaching it chess and driving, and start it on croquet, which it might be quite clever at. All this would distract my mind from my own worries and problems, I thought.

We finished talking about Charles and David, and started the game of adapting well-known lines of poetry or prose to suit our acquaintances and guessing who was meant, such as " Lobsters I loved, and after lobsters, sex," and the evening ended cheerfully. The night went well too, as Vere and I spent it together.

22

SOON AFTER this I collected my ape from its quarantine and went down to aunt Dot's house near Abingdon with it, and with my sister Meg, who was a Roman Catholic, owing to having married one, and had so many children that sometimes she had to get right away from family life to relax. Meg and I had always been friends, and we were both fond of aunt Dot, and we both were allowed to stay in her house when we felt like it, with the elderly servant called Emily who looked after it. We sometimes had friends there for week-ends, and often Vere drove over from Oxford and spent a night, and, as Meg and I were together, Emily was not shocked at this.

I was determined to educate the ape, and to find out how high it could climb up the path of civilization, and how near to a man or woman it could get. It would, I thought, shed some light on human progress from the ape stage. Meg had a notion that it could not develop a soul, as she held that this was a solely human privilege, and in fact her Church teaches this. But she could never explain to me precisely what a soul was, and where the line comes that divides a soul from the kind of consciousness and psyche that animals have. I am not sure what my own Church teaches on this matter, and it may be the same, but I do not take much notice, and, my Church being more elastic, it is probably open to fresh light. Anyhow, I was interested to see how far my Stamboul ape would get. Its chess was only moderate, because, as I said earlier, it copies all my moves. I wondered how much it understood of the moves and their consequences, but it would take my pieces as I took its pieces, and remove them from the board. It really seemed more at home with draughts, and also played a quite good snakes and ladders, but was furious when it came to a snake and had to go back. When it was angry, and particularly at croquet, a game which engendered in it as much fury as it does in other beings, it set up a great gibbering and chattering, and whenever it could it cheated. As I was trying to start it in moral sense, I spoke to it very sharply about this, and put on its collar and chain as a punishment, but I was not sure if it fully understood. As a partner it was very good; we would play together against Meg with her two balls, and it had a very precise aim and powerful force; all I had to do was to indicate what ball it was to make for, and it would hit it from any distance and send it to the other end of the lawn. Sometimes we played tennis, and at this it was better still, it had a very fine overhand service and a tremendous volley from the back line, and when it hit me on the head with the ball it was because it had tried to. It was an excitable player, dancing about and somersaulting in triumph when it had sent an untakable return, throwing its racket at the net when it had missed a ball, and pelting its opponent with balls with the strength with which its ancestors had no doubt flung coconuts at their enemies in their native jungles. A little more training in etiquette and sportsmanship, and it would easily qualify for Wimbledon. I saw no reason why there should not be an apes' four and singles, which would bring in a wonderful gate.

Meg was against my putting an L on my car and teaching the ape to drive, but to my mind driving was a crucial test of brain, and I persevered. At first I only took it along the private road through the field, where it did no harm when it ran off on to the grass. It grasped the wheel very strongly and firmly in its hands, after watching me do it for some time, and turned it right or left as I directed with my arms, and when it began to turn the wrong way, I held the wheel and turned it myself, which vexed it rather, as it was very vain, and it would shove me away with its elbow and finish the turning itself. Changing gears was a little harder, and I am not sure if it ever quite understood the principle underlying this, but then I am not sure if I do myself. It soon grasped that it must press down the clutch with its foot whenever it moved the gear lever, but when to move this, and in which direction, and why, troubled it a good deal, and for some time I had to manipulate it, covering its hands with mine. Then I stopped doing this, and merely said " Change down," or " Change up," jerking my arm down and up as I said it, and in time it mastered not only the straight ups and downs, but the first to second (my car only had three fortunately) which had an elbow to it. It seemed to me definitely quicker at every branch of the driving art than most human learners, owing to being such a good mimic and not trying to work it out with its brain. But it seemed to have difficulty in connecting the low position of the petrol indicator needle with the stoppage of the car, or either with my getting out and pouring stuff from a can into the hole at the back, though I always made it get out too and watch me. I did not know how soon it would be up to opening the boot and getting a petrol tin out and pouring it into the tank for itself, or to stopping at a public petrol pump for it. In any case I did not see how it was likely to get any that way, as it would not be able to say how much it wanted, or to pay for it, so I decided that it must not go driving alone when the tank was low.

It had a tendency to speed, pressing on the accelerator with all its might, and also continuously on the horn, which it enjoyed greatly. I forbade it to do this except when something was in the road in front of it, but I was never sure that it understood about this, though it listened attentively to me and I could see it was trying to follow, by the way it frowned and ground its teeth. I showed it how, when I was at the wheel, I hooted, but only slightly, when anything was in the way, but not at other times, and I hoped it took this in, but it had a great tendency to exaggeration and overdoing, and I saw that it would be a hooting driver. The postman and the newspaper boy on their bicycles, who used the field path, were rather alarmed by its style of driving, and the people in the village began to talk, but I assured them that everything was under control. One day it got alone into the car, which was aunt Dot's small Morris and was standing in the drive with the engine key in, and it started it up and drove off alone through the gate on to the field path, where it put on a tremendous speed and rushed along with the horn blaring after the gardener, who was pushing a wheelbarrow full of leaves for burning. The gardener barely had time to leap aside on to the grass edge, leaving the barrow, and the Morris crashed right into it and broke it up and bent a wing. The gardener was very angry about this, and so was I. Meg and I came back from a walk to find a scene of rage going on, the gardener shaking a stick at the ape, the ape blaring the horn and gibbering at the gardener, who did not dare to get very near it.

The gardener told me and Meg that the ape had no right to be on the road; Meg rather agreed, but I explained that the road was a private one and I said I would pay for the barrow. The gardener said, "Mrs. ffoulkes-Corbett won't be best pleased about her car, nohow," and I was not best pleased either, as the insurance did not cover accidents caused by L drivers driving alone, and I should have to pay.

I was very much vexed with the ape, and told it so in no uncertain manner. The gardener said he would know what to do to it if it was his, and looked at his stick, but I did not approve of corporal punishment and would not thrash it. Instead, I spoke to it very sharply, and chained it up for the rest of the day and gave it the dullest kind of food, and did not take it out driving for two days, and then did all the driving myself, which always vexed it. It seemed ashamed of itself, and I thought it was increasing in conscience and sense of sin. I was teaching it a little religion (Anglican), which Meg thought was wrong, her Church being rather narrow about animals, and she would not have allowed it to go with her to her church, but I took it, on the lead, to mine, where it behaved quite well, sitting and standing and kneeling when I did, and it was a great interest to the congregation and choir at Mass, but the vicar did not care for it, he thought it distracted people's attention and was not really reverent. It always rather enjoyed being an object of interest, as it was vain and exhibitionist, but how much it knew about where it was, I did not know. I liked the way it fell on its knees at the right place in the creed, seeing other people do it and not waiting to be pulled. When the congregation made the responses and joined in the service, it joined too, softly chattering. I taught it to genuflect as I did when we went in to our seats. Soon I saw that it was crossing itself too, and I was not quite sure that it ought to be doing this, it seemed going rather far, but it liked it, and did it again and again, even when no one else did, its tendency to excess and showing off coming out as usual, and the vicar and the churchwardens did not much like this. It was certainly a very devout Anglo-Catholic, though I fancied that it might be also something of an Anglo-Agnostic. During the sermon it leant against me and fell asleep, snoring a little, because it was rather old-fashioned, and possibly something of an anti-clerical too. I thought it was a very fine convert from the Moslem religion, to which I suppose it had nominally belonged before. But I suspected that if any one took it to a Billy Graham meeting, it would follow the crowd up and decide for conversion in a rather impulsive and shallow way, and I remembered the parrot in the seventeenth century play which was converted to Calvinism by a serving-woman.

> Yesterday I went
> To see a lady that has a parrot; my woman converted the fowl,
> And now it can speak naught but Knox's words;
> So there's a parrot lost.

I should not have cared to see that happen to my ape, so I

decided that it should stick to Anglican churches, eschewing both Knox and the Romans, and it seemed to take very kindly to this, becoming almost foolishly extreme, and I thought Father Chantry-Pigg would be pleased with it. Besides religion and driving and games, I trained it to help in the garden, weeding and mowing and planting, and it seemed to be developing some social and civic sense, much more rapidly than our ancestors did, for I suppose we live in more rapid times. As it seems that one of the first things done in primitive life is drawing and painting pictures on walls, I took it to the garage and painted pictures of men and women and animals on the white-washed walls below the church gargoyles. Then I gave a brush to the ape (whose name was Suliman, the Turk who sold it to me had said, and it sometimes answered to it, but I thought I really should give it a more Christian name, now that it had become so High Church), and let it try for itself. It was very pleased, and chattered to itself as it painted, and made bold sweeps with the brush, dipping it in the tin of red paint as it had seen me do, and its painting was not at all bad for a beginner, and it must be true that one of the most primitive activities is making pictures, as one sees if an infant over nine months old gets hold of a pencil or brush. Our ancestors used to paint bisons a great deal, owing to hunting these animals, and I watched to see if Suliman painted anything like the wheelbarrow which he had hunted and caught, but I could not identify one of these; of course he was pretty smudgy at first, so some of his pictures may have been wheelbarrows. I could see he was going to be a painter of the abstract type, and rather surrealist in style, and when he did what he seemed to mean for an animal or human being he usually put both the eyes on the same side of the profile, which small children and surrealists also tend to do. I rather like this myself, as it is nice to know what both a person's eyes look like, and also one can see people with an eye on each side all about, without having them also in pictures. Still, I thought Suliman ought to try and be a little representational too, and hoped that this would come with time.

Meanwhile I was teaching him the alphabet, writing the letters in large black capitals on a large sheet of paper, and pointing to each in turn with a stick, telling him what it was. Then I would say the letter and make him point to it with his stick, and he picked this up very quickly. I got a copy of *Reading Without Tears*, with which Meg and I had been taught to read when we were about four years old, and which is a very good book, because once it gets past how the cat lay on the mat, its stories are most exciting. There is a very good one about wolves, which entered a woodcutter's cottage one day, ravening, when only a little girl and her infant brother were at home, and the little girl shut up her brother in a grandfather clock but was herself eaten up, and when the parents came home there were only blood and bones on the floor and the little boy shut up in the clock, and Meg and I used to like this story very much. But I did not know if Suliman would ever get as far as that, or beyond the alphabet, or would ever even really quite grasp about the cat on the mat; it was difficult to tell, because he could not so far use human language, and if he ever learnt to do this he might only be able to say things like, " Brother, thy tail hangs down behind." I tried to teach him to say words after me, but he did not make much of it, and I thought he might be of a species which was no good at any languages but its own, and, as to that, I did not think that I could ever learn his.

But what he really was picking up was morality. He was learning not to throw things at people when he was vexed, not to steal, not to cheat at games, to do what he was told, anyhow sometimes, and to help in the house and garden and do little errands and chores like peeling potatoes. He would ride Emily's bicycle to the village, with a label tied to the handlebars saying what shop he was bound for and what he was to buy there, and people would stop him and read the message and take him to the shop and put the things into his basket and send him back.

He became more and more obliging, though sometimes, like any one else, he had bad moods and sulked. Meg thought it could not be in his nature to attain to true religion and virtue, as his ancient and ignoble blood had crept through scoundrels ever since the Flood; but I did not see that we had any evidence of this, as we had not known his ancestors, and anyhow, since our species had climbed upwards, why not his? There seemed no reason why the light of conscience should not influence the minor apes through our missionary efforts, as it has always influenced dogs. I told Meg that one cannot draw these rigid lines between human beings and the other animals, it must always be a question of degree, where minds exist at all. Still, I sometimes wondered, and thought that perhaps it was true that human souls are specially privileged in this matter and the other creatures definitely under-privileged.

Music, on the other hand, Suliman really seemed to take in. We tried him with different types of it, and he seemed on the whole to have rather a vulgar ear. Trained on Turkish radio music, he took very kindly to crooning, also to jazz, which made him leap about and dance. Romantic and saccharine melody went well with him too, and gay tunes and jigs, and, for some reason, he had a taste for opera, particularly for Verdi; at the drinking song in *La Traviata* he would prance round the room waving his arms and giving little cries of joy. More serious music he cared less for; Beethoven seemed rather outside his range, and most modern music affected him disagreeably, making him grind his teeth together and scowl. Mozart he liked, and indeed Mozart is every one's tea, pleasing to high-brows, middlebrows and lowbrows alike, though they probably all get different kinds of pleasure from him. I thought Mozart was good for Suliman, and might elevate his taste and mind, so I played him a lot of records. I should like to have taught him the piano, but was not very good at this instrument myself.

When not instructing this ape or seeing my friends, I tried to get on with the Turkey book, arranging aunt Dot's notes and my own and writing it all up to look like a book. Doing this reminded me all the time of aunt Dot and made me pretty sad, as the weeks and months went by and there was no news. All Hallows came on, then All Souls, and it seemed to me that aunt Dot and Father Chantry-Pigg had almost qualified for commemoration as souls who had passed out of our ken; but still I believed they would be back.

23

I WAS quite right. On the fifth of November, in the middle of
the swishing and bangs of rockets exploded by the junior no-
popery parliament-lovers of Oxfordshire, while I was telling
Meg that I saw no reason why gunpowder treason and plot
should ever be forgot, and she was telling me that " plot " was
right, but that it had of course, as every one now knew, been a
protestant plot, and Suliman, excited by the riot in the blazing
skies, leaped and somersaulted in the garden, we turned on the
nine o'clock news. After a good deal that did not matter at all,
it said, " News has been received from the British Embassy in
Moscow of Mrs. ffoulkes-Corbett and the Reverend Hugh
Chantry-Pigg who disappeared over the Turkish frontier into
Russia last July, and have not since been heard of. They called
at the Embassy a few days ago, requesting repatriation. They
have since then been staying under Embassy supervision, while
enquiries were made with respect to their activities in the Soviet
Union. They will be escorted to this country next week by
boat from Leningrad. It is understood that a serious view is not
taken of their activities, but that they will remain under observation for a time after reaching this country. Both are said to be
in good health and spirits."

I think I had not known till then how dark my fears had been
that I should never see aunt Dot again. Joy overtook me like
a flood, the rockets banging and cascading in the sky for poor
Guy became celestial explosions of delight. I need not have
been afraid for aunt Dot; once again she had revealed her quality
of resilient and invulnerable immortality, which had enabled
her in the past to surmount a thousand hazards, escaping from

perils of water, perils of mountains, perils of brigands, cannibals, mercy-killings, haarems, crocodiles, lions, camels, and now Russia, from which she was due to emerge in good health and spirits, no doubt having enjoyed herself very much. And Father Chantry-Pigg, less resilient and adaptable, but protected by the mantle of her invulnerability, had also suffered no harm. About aunt Dot I felt that attired with stars she would for ever sit, triumphing over Death, and Chance, and thee O Time.

And next morning I got a letter, sent in the Embassy bag, and dated a few days earlier. It said,

" My dearest Laurie,

I expect you will be surprised to get this and will be wondering what we have been doing all these months and why I didn't write before. Well, actually I did, but I gather that my letters never reached England, and it seems that letters from people like us are closely vetted by the police and usually filed away as dossiers, the Russian police being, of course, so very inquisitive. I hope you didn't worry. This letter is going by the Bag, and I won't say anything in it, it would take too long if I began, but we have had a most interesting time on the whole. I will only say now that we have reached the Embassy, after a good deal of trouble, and are being sent home by boat from Leningrad under escort, and should be with you in about a week. Please tell Emily. If you can meet the boat, which is called *Molotov*, at Tilbury, it would be very nice and a great help with the mare."

" The *mare*? " said Meg. " What mare is that? "

" Just a mare she's picked up, I suppose. Aunt Dot often comes back with some animal. I wonder if I'd better bring the camel from the Zoo. It hates horses."

Meg said that what with the camel and the ape and now this mare, aunt Dot's house was becoming a Zoo itself.

"And it's not as if she really *liked* animals."

"No. She just finds them useful. Probably this mare she's got is a very rapid Caucasian, and can speed about with a droshky at about thirty miles an hour."

"Should you think she's bringing a droshky too?"

"Quite likely. Or she can get one here. I dare say she's been rushing about the steppes like mad. I wonder how she got the mare. Perhaps it was a reward for her services. Do you think she told them no end of things about this country and our way of life?"

"That wouldn't be much use to them."

"Well, nothing is much use actually that people tell foreign countries about their own country. Except in war time. But governments seem to like to be told things, and they pay for it. I remember aunt Dot saying in Armenia that she would like that job. So she just went over and got it."

"What would you think Father Chantry-Pigg told them?"

"About the Church, I expect. Religious life in Britain, the Church of England, how it differs from theirs, education, schools, and all that. Probably aunt Dot was more interesting. I wonder what ' under escort ' means."

Meg said they would probably be put straight into jug, perhaps the Tower, and kept there.

So I met the *Molotov* at Tilbury, and coming down the gangway were aunt Dot, plump and pink and gay, and Father Chantry-Pigg, still lean and ascetic and pale, but with a firm, confident look, and neither of them looked like traitors. But it seemed true that they were under escort, who were two quiet men walking beside them and keeping off the Press, which was there in strength. This escort conducted my aunt and the priest to the customs and then to a waiting room, a small secretive place, where I was allowed to see them. It seemed that they would be conducted to London by the escort, and detained there for questioning.

"It won't take long," aunt Dot cheerfully told me. "We

have done nothing wrong. When we meet properly, I'll tell you all about everything."

"What about the mare?" I said.

"In quarantine," said aunt Dot. "When she gets out, I shall take her down to Troutlands and mate her. Then when she foals I shall mix her milk with a wild donkey's, and that will make koumiss. Most refreshing and invigorating. Father Hugh and I have been thriving on it. But there may be trouble with the camel; you know how they can't bear horses, nor horses them. How is it, by the way? And did you ride it all about the Levant?"

"It's in the Zoo just now, giving rides to children. Mentally, it seems rather better."

"Well, it mustn't meet the mare, so it had better stay there for the present."

Then the escort took them away to a car for London. Father Chantry-Pigg said as they went out, "I don't know why we are being treated in this extraordinary manner."

I saw his point, but after all people are usually treated in some extraordinary manner when they return from Russia, on account of being usually thought to have behaved there in some extraordinary way, for Russia is so odd a country that it is difficult to believe that people going there and staying there some time have not been odd there too. Actually, aunt Dot and Father Chantry-Pigg were rather odd anywhere abroad, and had been, probably, less odd in Russia, which is full of British and other people behaving most oddly, than they were elsewhere.

They remained in custody for three weeks, during which time their Russian activities were investigated, and they were questioned closely about the information they had given to the Soviet Government. The thing that most told against them was their having said, when accosted by the police near the frontier, that they had come to seek political asylum from the capitalist west. Aunt Dot said she had had to put it like that, to avoid being turned out or incarcerated as spies. She had also told them that she was an acquaintance of Mr. Maclean and Mr. Burgess, and that Father Chantry-Pigg, a very progressive Church of England dignitary, knew the Dean of Canterbury. Father Chantry-Pigg, knowing little Russian, had not followed all this talk, but thought he had better leave it to aunt Dot. His own main object in Russia, which was to look into the state of religion, he kept in the background, mentioning only such creditable and improbable desires as to study Soviet drama and literature, the prison system, education, and the birthplaces of Dostoievsky, Tolstoy and Chekov. Aunt Dot had said she was particularly anxious to learn all she could about the position of women, which compared so favourably with that of their sisters in the provincial parts of Turkey. Approving all this flattering curiosity, and looking forward to a flow of information about the capitalist way of life in Britain, the visitors had been treated kindly, taken on conducted tours, and invited to communicate all they knew. Aunt Dot told me later the kind of way it had gone. Some of it had been rather difficult on account of the interpreter's acquaintance with the English language not being very close, so that a good deal of what was said was no doubt slightly deformed in transit. They were questioned about British democracy: were they under the impression that this existed? Aunt Dot, who had strong views on this matter, said certainly not; the public were not consulted in most emergencies, there was no referendum, and, having voted members of Parliament into power, we had to accept their very disputable decisions. Not democracy, said aunt Dot, but bureaucracy. And presided over by monarchy, they suggested to her, but to this she demurred; monarchy had no say in any governmental matter, it was kept for social purposes, and to please a monarchically minded nation. Father Chantry-Pigg, asked about democracy, said, on the other hand, that he feared there was only too much of this, and made remarks about King Demos that aunt Dot had thought not fully understood by their questioners. Asked about education, both Britons thought we had, by and large, singularly little of this. " The rich go to one kind of school, the poor to another, is it not so?" and they agreed that this was, on the whole, so. The Russians knew about English schools for the workers, for *Nicholas Nickleby* was one of the standard books on the subject, and was widely studied.

" Ancient history," said aunt Dot. " You might as well read *Oliver Twist* for information about modern Public Assistance, or *Newgate Visited* for prison life. There are no schools like that to-day. The children of the workers go first to primary schools, then either to modern or grammar schools. Modern schools seem to have a bad name, for some reason, and grammar schools a good one. They are both attended mainly by the children of the workers. The *bourgeoisie* usually send their children to other schools, paid for by themselves."

" Capitalist schools," said the interrogators, and aunt Dot admitted that this was so.

They asked Father Chantry-Pigg about British religious life. All too little of that, he told them, and the people all too little doped by this opium. The topic of Mr. Billy Graham came up; were his activities well regarded in Britain? The Russians obviously considered Mr. Graham an important purveyor of opium, and would never on any account allow him in Russia. Father Chantry-Pigg spoke of this missioner in a manner they thought very proper, and they began to think his investigations into Soviet religion would do no harm to the Soviet republics.

Anyhow, after a time they decided to allow these two fugitives from British capitalism to travel about, under supervision, and see how things were in a Socialist state, and pass on their message about the iniquities of the capitalist world to the Soviet people. It seemed that they had collected quite a number of capitalist fugitives from various countries who were doing this, and, when not doing this, were telling the Soviet Government all kinds of things about their native lands.

" My dear, the things we told them!" aunt Dot said afterwards to me. " Such nonsensical things, and we made them sound so important. It all goes to show what I have always said, that *anything* does as information to a foreign government, and that none of it really matters a bit, and that espionage is the most over-paid profession in the world. I must say I did enjoy it. And Father Hugh was marvellous. He told them how little power the Church had, and how its odd behaviour in South India was discrediting it and driving many people to the Roman obedience, and what a mistake it all was, South India, I mean, and the Roman obedience, he spoke very strongly against both, but one could see that they couldn't really take in about South India, though they quite understood about Rome, because of course they dislike it too. Father Hugh had to undertake not to try to missionise people, and naturally he was closely watched, but he did quite quietly cure a policeman's wife in Tiflis of bad lumbago with a relic of St. Jane Frances de Chantal, because it was on her day, and the policeman was so pleased that he didn't report it, but two days later had his own duodenal cured by a relic of St. Philip Benizi on *his* day. Russians always believe in miracles, of course; I dare say they thought the relics were bits of a coat Lenin had worn, you know how Leninolatrous they are, though it's really no sillier than our basilikolatry, and I'm sure bits of the queen's dress would be most useful to doctors. Anyhow Russians seem the perfect subjects for such things, being natural mystics. It must be rather like the country parts of Turkey, which have taken so little notice of poor Atatürk, it's wonderful how people go on in their old ways of thought long after they have been revolutionised and reformed; it's so discouraging for reformers, the way reformations often don't seem to do more than scratch the surface, so that the mass of the people stay just as they were. Of course Father Hugh couldn't say Mass, or preach, or baptise; but his cures made a great impression, and more and more people came to him for them. And he was allowed to see a lot of churches, and talk to a lot of priests. We had a wonderful tour in Armenia; we were in Erivan for the consecration of the new Catholics; the church was packed out. But they say they all are, all the year round. And you know how magnificent the country is. I got some nice fishing. We didn't want to leave Armenia and the Caucasus a bit, but we were dragged off to Moscow and set down to work —interviews at police headquarters with solemn men who wrote down all we told them and always wanted to know more; my dear, we were pumped dry. Those note-books of theirs must be full of the most extraordinary nonsense. When we weren't giving information we were conducted round all the tedious things I hate—hospitals and welfare clinics and institutions and schools and administration departments, and railway stations and labour exchanges and whatever; *what* dull things governments are proud of. But of course we had to see them, and admire them. We had to see football matches, too, Britain being beaten off the field by the Dynamos. They thought that would please us; they told us it always pleased the fugitives from Britain to see British teams beaten, so we had to look delighted, but really, you know, it's quite annoying. Even Donald Maclean and Guy Burgess told us it still vexes them; yes, we saw quite a bit of them, they were rather cagey, and very smug and respectable, and it wasn't at all clear just what they were doing, but they were interested in English news—all the gossip, I mean, particularly the gossip about themselves, but we scarcely liked to tell them all that. Then we were taken on a visit to Leningrad to see the same kind of tiresome things there, and of course Father Hugh would keep calling it St. Petersburg, which didn't go at all well; I had to keep on explaining how old-fashioned and dated he always was. Then after a time we both wanted badly to get home, but, as we were never allowed near the Embassy or any other English except the spies, we didn't see how it was to be managed, we were followed and watched all the time. But one evening we were taken to the theatre to see a new play about collective farms, and there was such a crowd in the street coming out that our policeman lost us for a minute, and right in front of the theatre stood a British Embassy car with two young men in it, so we opened the door and got straight in, and I said, 'Look, we're British, can you take us to the Embassy, we've just escaped from the men who were watching us, and we want asylum' (you know, that's a very useful phrase, it gets you anywhere), so off they drove and landed us at the Embassy, and gave us asylum there for the night, in fact they took us prisoner, and were pretty chilly, because of course they had heard about us and how we were informing. In the morning we were interviewed and questioned and treated more coldly than ever, but finally we were bundled on to a train with steamer tickets to London, watched all the way by Embassy police lest we should seek asylum again from the ship's captain. My dear, we got so tired of being *watched* all these months, it's such a blessed feeling now not to be."

I said, "I dare say you *are* being watched, only more tactfully than before. I should think your telephone is certainly tapped."

Aunt Dot agreed that this was probably the case: she did not seem to mind.

"I have been thinking what I can say on it to interest them. I feel I do owe them that, after all I said to interest the Russians. You've no idea how easy it is to interest foreigners, it takes no effort whatever, only a little mild invention. But now what I want, after these months of excitement, is a little quiet home life. When I get my mare out of quarantine, I must start training her in English ways. She isn't used to lanes and roads, only to steppes and mountains. Do you think I ought to have the camel here, and let them get used to each other? But I suppose they would both bite and kick. Animals have such bad tempers. Actually, the mare and the camel are both a little mad. Halide says so many animals are, not at all only bulls. They are mental from birth, she says, and every so often go quite round the bend. And of course the way they are brought up makes them worse; most come from broken homes; their fathers take no notice of them as a rule, and we often take them from their mothers too young, and treat them most oddly, and of course they feel deprived and frustrated and their minds and tempers and nerves give way, not that their minds and tempers are ever strong at the best, they're so neurotic."

I told her how Suliman's mind and temper had been improved by religion and moral teaching, but she did not think this would do much for the camel or the mare, who were less assimilative.

" How very nice," she added, " it will be to go to church again. That is one thing that travel teaches one—there is really *no* other service so good as our own High Mass. I keep telling the B.B.C. Religious Department that if they televised it every Sunday they would make *hundreds* of converts, but they don't take much notice, though they often televise the Roman one, which most viewers don't understand because it's Latin, you know how unlettered they are, while all the time and every Sunday in half our London churches we have this superb service, with everything people like, beautiful singing, clouds of incense, priests in fine vestments moving about in the most impressive way, the action of the Mass, a magnificent liturgy, and all in English but for the Kyrie and a few oddments, so it really can be followed. Father Hugh thinks it would have a tremendous effect on simple, inexperienced people like tele-viewers; he thinks they would say, ' I must join the Church, if that's what its services are like.' Mind you, I wouldn't let *him* take part, he'd put in far too much Latin and worry people. For all he says he isn't, he's a bit of an ultramontane, in practice though not in theory, and we can't have *that* in the Church of England, we must stay dyed-in-the-wool Anglican. I don't say the B.B.C. doesn't try to be fair, it does provide an equal number of communion services from all the chief denominations, but look at the *type* of Anglican service they usually have, whether it's sound or television—oh very dignified, cathedral and what not, or some simple middle-of-the-road church, nice of course, but dull not showy, not the kind that impresses and excites and converts. So that the majority think we haven't got High Mass at all, and that they must go to Rome for it. What they mostly get on sound radio is an Anglican monkish office set to music with a sermon thrown in, or else prayers and hymns from some Nonconformist chapel, which I've nothing against if nonconformists like them, it's their affair, but I do complain of the choice of Anglican churches, because that's *our* affair, and I shall go on complaining. If you ask me, it's a popish plot to reclaim England for Rome."

I felt sure that aunt Dot would go on complaining. I did not share her anxiety, because I am less bigoted about the Church of England, and anyhow I do not listen to radio services and am not a televiewer, and I am not really a missionary either, as aunt Dot is, so I do not care what other people listen to or view. Though I personally think Anglicanism is the most attractive branch of the Christian Church, its prayers being dignified and beautiful and in fine English, and not abject or sentimentally pious, or hearty and pally and common, or in Latin, and having a theology which is subject to new light and development, and a Mass mainly from pre-Reformation rites, and Church ornament and much of its architecture on the whole, though by no means always, in good taste—though I like all this, and could never belong to any other Church (indeed, I only with difficulty, and in part, belong to this one), I see no reason to press it on other people, who may prefer, as they obviously do, to be Roman Catholics or dissenters or agnostics, and seem to get on all right as they are, in fact often much better than I do. So I live and let live, but that is not what aunt Dot does at all, she is a true missionary, and has it in her blood, and I have too, but with me it has not taken so well.

Next day aunt Dot had a letter from Halide. She wrote a little guardedly, as if she was not quite sure just how far aunt Dot had gone in espionage, but was grudgingly willing to give her the benefit of the doubt. She had married her Moslem man

241

after all, and had reverted to Islam, and not only because of her marriage, for,

"I have come to see," she wrote, "that we emancipated Turkish women, if we are to lead our poor countrywomen into freedom, must do this from within. What is the use that I speak to them in villages and tell them I belong to the Church of England? What is that to them, when they belong to the Church of Turkey? What is the use to tell them, as many do, that we, the educated women, have no religious faith at all, when this is to the simple men and women the great sin against Allah? No, we must speak to them as Moslems, we must tell them that our religion and theirs allows these things that they think they may not do, and this way we shall wake them to ambition and to progress, and make their men ashamed to keep them down. There is now a band of educated truly Moslem women, who will go into the backward villages and teach them along these lines. So, my dear Dot, do not come with your Church of England missions, nor Father Pigg, for that is not the way. I can assure you that I am very happy, and determined to atone for my Anglican error and infidelity by serving my country and my faith as best I may. Perhaps you and I may meet again one day, though now it is rather soon that I con- done that strange Russian expedition, and what you may have told them about Turkey how can I know? I can only hope that, if the great war breaks out between our enemy and us, they will not find themselves assisted by anything which you and Imam Pigg have told them, but more probably they knew it all before, and could find their way from Trua to Eski-Stamboul better than you. All the same, you should not have gone to Russia, I cannot condone that. But I send you my affection, and the faithful well wishes of a friend. Also to Laurie, and I hope the camel grows better now that it leads a quieter life.

Your friend,

Halide Yorum"

I wondered if Halide's Moslem man could, by chance, be that Mr. Yorum to whom I had so often asked the staff of the Yessilhurt Oteli at Trebizond to telephone, and who had at last arrived there, and with whom I had, until he got tired of me, enjoyed more than one drink. Anyhow, the relations between Halide and my family seemed for the time being closed, and I was sorry, so was aunt Dot.

"Turks," she said, "won't condone, they won't co-exist. And that old-fashioned religion they have will get their women nowhere. I think Halide has made a great mistake. I am disappointed in her. But I shall ask her later to come and stay, so that we can thrash things out, and I can tell her about Russia. She can go to mosque in Oxford, on the camel, to remind her of home. But for the moment I shall leave the camel in the Zoo, and concentrate on training the mare."

I asked if I could leave Suliman at Troutlands when I was in my flat. I told her how useful he was helping in the garden, sweeping up leaves, pulling up weeds (though here he was a little indiscriminate) and bicycling to the village on errands. Aunt Dot said all right, so long as he didn't get too violent at croquet or paint on the walls without leave or bother Emily in the kitchen or insist on driving the car. She would not, however, take him to church, she thought this a little on the irreverent side, and the vicar and the churchwardens did not care for it either, so Suliman had better be a blue-domer.

I said I did not care, so long as he did not take to chapel, which I did not think would suit him. Aunt Dot said that no one from Troutlands had ever done that, so far as she knew. Anyhow Suliman was a born ritualist, and if he was ever to stray from the Anglican Church, it would be into a Roman one, and there they would not let him in.

So aunt Dot settled down to home life again, and got very busy with her Turkey book. I showed her the parts I had done since we parted, and she thought I ought to have put in more about the Black Sea women as compared with the Arab ones in

Syria and Jordan and the women of Israel, but I told her that this was her job, and she could now put in the women of Russia as well.

"And a very fine lot they are," said aunt Dot. "If Halide knew them, she would *like* them. Idiotically patriotic, of course, but then so is she. Smug, too; they think they are doing things no women have ever done before, and when I told them what our own women do, and did in the war, I am certain the interpreter didn't translate it properly, because they only looked smugger than ever, and quite sorry for me. Of course I can speak a little Russian, but not their kind, and when they looked as if they understood me, the interpreter always chipped in. What I am going specially to enjoy now is walking about the villages talking to every one, and not being followed and watched. You know how absurd I have always thought it to boast about the free world, slaves as we all are, but we certainly do have *some* freedoms they don't."

I said, "On the contrary, you will be followed and watched all the time by the local police force and relays of reporters, all hoping that you will get talking to one of your contacts. You and Father Hugh will now always be under observation. Probably I am considered smeared too."

Aunt Dot said, "Fiddle-de-dee!" and she is the only person I know who utters this cry. (I have known her also to exclaim "Tilly vally!" but this is only when she is a good deal annoyed.) She added, "Anyhow, they'll soon get tired of it."

24

So LIFE ran on again, and it was very pleasant. Through the winter I worked at the book and the illustrations, partly in my flat and partly with aunt Dot. We thought the book was shaping pretty well, and we both rather liked my pictures; particularly aunt Dot liked the ones of the shawled women trudging along behind the men riding, or cowering against the wall hiding their faces, but I preferred those I had done in Trebizond, of the Comnenus palace ruins standing among the little Turkish gardens and hovels in the sunshine, of the slopes of Boz Tepe striped with all the colours of the evening light, of Hagia Sophia with its sculptured west portal, of the fishing boats on the beach, and of the palace as I had seen it after I had drunk the enchanter's potion and fallen half asleep—I had painted the throne-room and the emperor on his throne, the mosaicked floor and the gold-starred ceiling and the painted walls, the crowd of Byzantine courtiers and priests and jugglers, and in one corner the man playing chess with the ape, and the ape I drew from Suliman. I liked that picture, and so did aunt Dot. I told her about the enchanter and his potion, and she said she was not at all surprised, as of course there had always been enchanters in Trebizond. I wished I could meet him again, as I would have liked to get some more of the potion, and I thought I would return one day to Trebizond and look him up, and lay in a good stock of the stuff.

By Easter, my part of the book was finished, and Vere and I went off for a fortnight to Venice, driving in my car. I left aunt Dot cantering about Oxfordshire on her Caucasian mare, which she had got into good training, so that it no longer bolted like a cannon ball when it met cars, leaping over hedges and galloping for miles, as if pursued by wolves over boundless steppes, bucking and kicking its heels up as if it hoped that aunt Dot would be thrown upside down and would ride on in that position singing, like the Cossacks. Now that it was more British mannered, aunt Dot liked riding it very much; she said it saved a lot of time, taking her about much quicker than the camel did.

I told aunt Dot we were going to Venice.

" Spoilt," she replied, as she combed the mare's long beige mane.

This was her reaction to most European cities and seaboards. According to her, Rome was spoilt, the Campagna was spoilt, Venice, Florence, the bay of Naples, Capri, Sicily, the whole Italian and French rivieras, most of France and Spain, the best things in Portugal, almost all Britain.

" *I* remember it," she would say, if one proposed to visit any city or shore, " forty years ago. Now it's spoilt. If you want somewhere that isn't spoilt yet, you have to go east. Greece, Jugoslavia, Turkey, the islands—they're on the way there, but still attractive. Cyprus is being ruined by us—all those dreadful barracks and pre-fabs round Famagusta, and the hotels on the Troödos, besides what the Cypriots have built round Paphos and all over the place. Rhodes is better. And the smaller islands are still good, though now we have friends living on most of them and running over to call on each other by boat. I never had a more sociable time than staying with Paddy and Joan on Hydra, but I like that. Of course you can't *really* spoil Venice, because it can't be built on to. But I remember it when there was nothing on the canals but gondolas, none of those horrid steamers and vaporetti. Oh well, go to Venice, you and Vere don't remember the old days. All you people under forty miss a lot of memories. But I dare say you have as good a time. You know I don't approve, but you can send me some picture postcards."

Aunt Dot had a morbid appetite for these, and what must have been about the largest collection in private hands in the world. I must say picture postcards are nothing like in the same class that once they were, when artists went about Europe painting impressionist views and had them printed on postcards and sold everywhere, and you do not get anything like that now, in fact in the smaller places you are lucky if you find any postcards at all. As aunt Dot would say, the industry is practically spoilt.

All this about the world being spoilt makes me see it in a kind of green corruption, like over-ripe cheese, glistening in morbid colours and smelling of decay as it moulders to pieces. Of course this is not really what is happening physically, as the spoiling is by raw brashness and ugly drab newness, a kind of rash, spreading and crowding everywhere. I would rather have the greenish putrescence. Vulgar buildings, vulgar music, vulgar pictures, vulgar newspapers, vulgar taste, all raw and brash and ugly, but underneath is the putrescence and the soft-ness and the falling apart like rotten cheese, in which we are the greedy mites, eating away at it all with enjoying relish.

We set off on Easter Day, and made the Dijon-Mt. Cenis run down France (and France after all is not spoilt except its sea-side), and across Lombardy. We had a night at Verona, and saw *Romeo and Juliet*, an artificial play to which a ruined Roman theatre does no good, and got to Venice on Thursday. We were met by the gondola of the friend who had lent us his palazzo floor, and the Grand Canal was in festa with music and flags, and when we passed the Piazza it was bannered and glorious for Easter, and a band was playing Verdi. Our gondola took us on to the Rio della Pietà, where was our palazzo, just behind the Schiavoni Riva, and from its balconies we looked west up the Canal to the Salute shining like a great pearl against the sunset.

It was the best week we had ever had, and there will not be another. I mean by best that it was full of fun and gaiety and beauty and glamour, all the things that Venice can give, and all the things that we could give each other. Vere had wit and brains and prestige; in ten years I had not got used to all that brilliance and delightfulness, nor to the fact of our love. When we were together, peace flowed about us like music, and fun sprang up between us like a shining fountain. We had the gayest week: like Florimel and Olinda in *Secret Love*, " there were never two so cut out for one another; we both love Singing, Dancing, Treats, and Musick . . . we sit and talk, and wrangle, and are friends; when we are together we never hold our tongues; and then we have always a noise of fiddles at our heels, he hunts me as Merrily as the Hounds does the Hare; and either this is Love, or I know it not."

When Venice was the setting for all this, it was like (but of course with important omissions) paradise, where

> *. . . they live in such delight,*
> *Such pleasure and such play,*
> *As that to them a thousand years*
> *Doth seem as yesterday.*

> *Thy turrets and thy pinnacles*
> *With carbuncles do shine;*
> *Thy very streets are paved with gold,*
> *Surpassing clear and fine.*

Even the gardens and the gallant walks and the sweet and pleasant flowers seemed true that Easter, with massed blossoms on the stalls in every *calle*, smelling stronger and much sweeter than the canals, and strewing the pavements so that our feet crushed them as we passed.

> *There's nectar and ambrosia made,*
> *There's musk and civet sweet;*
> *There's many a fair and dainty drug*
> *Is trodden under feet.*

248

while

Quite through the streets with silver sound
The flood of life doth flow,
Upon whose banks on every side
The wood of life doth grow.

Or, if not woods, carved stone and rust-red brick, and marble steps at which the green water lapped. And look about, and there are marble angels in plenty, and Our Lady singing Magnificat, and St. Ambrose and St. Austin, and old Simeon and Zachary, and Magdalene who hath left her moan (or sometimes not), and all the saints one could wish. Not that I wanted to be reminded of this aspect of Paradise that week; the other aspects were enough.

Vere was apt to lead a sportive life of pleasure and palaces, yachts and private planes, villas in France and castles in Italy, being invited to these amenities by friends, and this week in Venice we led this palazzo life, and were asked to parties at other palazzi, by Italian, French and English friends, some of whom were my friends too, but most were Vere's. It made for great *luxe*; the one who had lent us this palazzo had left his servants in it—a cook and a gondolier—so we gondoled everywhere and ate well, though as to that we usually ate other people's meals in the other palazzi. We sat late in the Piazza and listened to music, or we gondoled up the Canal and watched fountains of fireworks playing, on account of there being a fiesta every night. By day we rambled about the *calli*, looked at pictures and churches and fountains and bridges, all the usual lovely Venice things, took a vaporetto out to some haunted lagoon island with a derelict church, bathed from the Lido, which was not, in April, a mob, and then back to the Piazza to meet some one or other for drinks.

Fortunately that hymn has got it wrong. It should be

> *. . . they live in such delight,*
> *Such pleasure and such play,*
> *As that to them one happy week*
> *Doth seem a thousand years.*

This seems always to be the case, when the happiness is eventful and full of getting about, which is why, when one has been travelling abroad for a month it seems more like three months, and when one gets back one's friends have scarcely noticed that one is gone, and say, " You're back very soon," which does not seem to oneself to be at all the case. Anyhow, this Venice week, and the days we spent driving there and back, seemed like all summer compressed into a fortnight, and, looking back, it still seems that.

25

WE DROVE from Folkestone in time to join in the great Sunday evening crawl into London. It was so different in France and Italy that after a time we began getting cross. We had meant to be up in time to dine quietly before we parted, and we felt that this would ease the parting a little. But it began to seem that we should not reach London in time for this, or for anything else. Every one had had the idea of starting for home early, so as to miss the crawl, but, since every one had had the idea, no one missed the crawl. People got peevish, they began hooting and cutting in, and I got peevish too, so I took a euphoria pill, which makes you feel as if you would get there in the end. After we were in London the buses all seemed to be rushing on against the lights for about ten seconds after they had gone red. This trick of buses, and of a lot of other drivers, but buses are the worst and the most alarming, has always made me full of rage, it is the height of meanness, stealing their turn from those with the right to cross, it is like pedestrians crossing against the lights and stealing the turn of cars which have been waiting for their chance, but this in England is not actually a legal crime, only caddish, whereas for traffic it is a legal crime as well. The taxi drivers say that when they do it they are run in if seen by the police, but that the buses usually get off, as if a driver is prosecuted the other drivers come out on strike, but this may be only the anti-police malice of taxi drivers.

When Vere was driving, I kept saying, "Push off the moment they go green. Don't let those cads get away with it," but Vere said, "Better let them get away with it and stay alive." When I took over, I was feeling like an avenging policeman, furious for the cause of legality, buoyed up by my euphorian pill, and all set to show the cads they couldn't get away with it. But they kept at it, and usually I could do nothing about it but hoot, as I was not the front car. Presently I was, and as the lights changed I saw a bus dashing up to crash the red, and I was full of rage and shouted, " Look at the *lights*," and started off the moment they were green. I heard Vere say, " Famous last words," and that was the last thing I ever heard Vere say. The crash as the bus charged the car and hit it broadside on and smashed us was all I knew for quite a time. When I came to, everything was a mess and a crowd, and I was lying in the mess with some one sponging blood from my face. I tried to turn my head and look for Vere, and saw a figure lying in blankets close by, quite still, and the head was at an odd angle. I think I was only partly conscious, because all I said was, " that murdering bus crashed the lights," and went off again.

They kept me in hospital a fortnight, with sprains and cuts and concussion and shock, then aunt Dot drove me down to Troutlands. The bus driver was tried for manslaughter, as so many witnesses had seen him pass the lights, but he was acquitted on the grounds of this being such common form, and only got six months for dangerous driving. He had, after all, driven no more dangerously than buses and many other vehicles drive every day, only this time he had killed some one. I do not think he was even disqualified. No one blamed me, except myself. Only I knew about that surge of rage that had sent me off, the second the lights were with me, to stop the path of that rushing monster, whose driver had thought that no one would dare to oppose him. The rage, the euphoria, the famous last words; only I knew that I and that driver had murdered Vere between us, he in selfish unscrupulousness, I in reckless anger.

I had plenty of time to think about it; no doubt my whole life. It seemed impossible to think about anything else. I don't think I talked much to aunt Dot, who nursed me back to health with the most exquisite kindness and patience. But I do not think she had ever loved any one as I had loved Vere, and nor had she killed her lover.

There were other aspects. I had come between Vere and his wife for ten years; he had given me his love, mental and physical, and I had taken it; to that extent, I was a thief. His wife knew it, but we had never spoken of it; indeed, I barely knew her. We had none of us wanted divorce, because of the children; I liked it better as it was, love and no ties. I suppose I had ruined the wife's life, because she had adored him. Vere always said that he was fonder of her because of me; men are given to saying this. But really she bored him; if she had not bored him, he would not have fallen in love with me. If I had refused to be his lover he would no doubt, sooner or later, have found someone else. But I did not refuse, or only for a short time at the beginning, and so we had ten years of it, and each year was better than the one before, love and joy gradually drowning remorse, till in the end it scarcely struggled for life. And now the joy was killed, and there seemed no reason why my life too should not run down and stop, now that its mainspring was broken. When a companionship like ours suddenly ends, it is to lose a limb, or the faculty of sight; one is, quite simply, cut off from life and scattered adrift, lacking the coherence and the integration of love. Life, I supposed, would proceed; I should see my friends, go abroad, go on with my work, such as it was, but the sentient, enjoying principle which had kept it all ticking, had been destroyed.

I could not, all the time, believe what had happened. I would forget; and then I would remember, and say to myself, " Vere is killed. We shan't see one another again, ever," and it would seem a thing too monstrous to be true. John Davies of Hereford's dirge for his friend Mr. Thomas Morley kept beating in my ears like waves on a beach—

253

Death has deprived me of my dearest friend.
My dearest friend is dead and laid in grave.
In grave he rests until the world shall end,
The world shall end, as end all things must have;
All things must have an end that Nature wrought. ...
Death has deprived me of my dearest friend . . .

And so on, *ad infinitum.* In fact, I became sunk in morbid misery. If the object of pleasure be totally lost, a passion arises in the mind which is called grief. Burke: and he did not overstate.

Aunt Dot, I know, hoped that I should make my peace with the Church, now that the way was open. She spoke of it once, but with a warning note.

" I think, my dear," she said, " the Church used once to be an opiate to you, like that Trebizond enchanter's potion; a kind of euphoric drug. You dramatized it and yourself, you felt carried along in something æsthetically exciting and beautiful and romantic; you were a dilettante, escapist Anglican. I know you read Clement of Alexandria: do you remember where he says, ' We may not be taken up and transported to our journey's end, but must travel thither on foot, traversing the whole distance of the narrow way.' One mustn't lose sight of the hard core, which is, do this, do that, love your friends and like your neighbours, be just, be extravagantly generous, be honest, be tolerant, have courage, have compassion, use your wits and your imagination, understand the world you live in and be on terms with it, don't dramatize and dream and escape. Anyhow, that seems to me to be the pattern, so far as we can make it out here. So come in again with your eyes open, when you feel you can."

But I did not feel that I could. Even the desire for it was killed. I was debarred from it less by guilt, and by what seemed to me the cheap meanness of creeping back now that the way was clear, than by revulsion from something which would divide me further from Vere. It had always tried to divide us; at the beginning, it had nearly succeeded. To turn to it now would be a gesture against the past that we had shared, and in whose bonds I was still held. " Your church obsession," Vere had called it. " Well, some people have it. So long as you don't let it interfere with our lives . . ."

I had not let it do that, and now I did not want to, for a stronger obsession had won. I could not argue against the gentle mockery of that mutilated figure whom I had loved and killed. I had to be on the same side as Vere, now and for always, and in any future there might be for us.

Not that I believed now, as once I had, in any such future. Father Hugh had once said to me on the Black Sea that if one went on refusing to hear and obey one's conscience for long enough, it became stultified, and died; one stopped believing in right and wrong and in God, and all that side of life became blurred in fog: one would not even want it any more. I had got to that stage now; I wanted nothing of it, for even to think of it hurt.

Some one once said that hell would be, and now is, living without God and with evil, and being unable to get used to it. Having to do without God, without love, in utter loneliness and fear, knowing that God is leaving us alone for ever; we have driven ourselves out, we have lost God and gained hell. I live now in two hells, for I have lost God and live also without love, or without the love I want, and I cannot get used to that either. Though people say that in the end one does. To the other, perhaps never.

However this may be, I have now to make myself a life in which neither has a place. I shall go about, do my work, seek amusements, meet my friends, life will amble on, and no doubt in time I shall find it agreeable again. One is, after all, very adaptable; one has to be. One finds diversions; these, indeed, confront one at every turn, the world being so full of natural beauties and enchanting artifacts, of adventures and jokes and excitements and romance and remedies for grief. It is simply that a dimension has been taken out of my life, leaving it flat, not rich and rounded and alive any more, but hollow and thin and unreal, like a ghost that roves whispering about its old haunts, looking always for something that is not there.

The passing years will, no doubt, pacify this ghost in time. And, when the years have all passed, there will gape the uncomfortable and unpredictable dark void of death, and into this I shall at last fall headlong, down and down and down, and the prospect of that fall, that uprooting, that rending apart of body and spirit, that taking off into so black an unknown, drowns me in mortal fear and mortal grief. After all, life, for all its agonies of despair and loss and guilt, is exciting and beautiful, amusing and artful and endearing, full of liking, and of love, at times a poem and a high adventure, at times noble and at times very gay; and whatever (if anything) is to come after it, we shall not have this life again.

Still the towers of Trebizond, the fabled city, shimmer on a far horizon, gated and walled and held in a luminous enchantment. It seems that for me, and however much I must stand outside them, this must for ever be. But at the city's heart lie the pattern and the hard core, and these I can never make my own: they are too far outside my range. The pattern should perhaps be easier, the core less hard.

This, indeed, seems the eternal dilemma.